BREAKING NEVERLAND

A RETELLING OF PETER PAN, PART II

CLASSICAL KINGDOMS COLLECTION
BOOK NINE

BRITTANY FICHTER

To Tim & Audrey
In the spirit of happily ever afters, I want to thank you for raising my Prince Charming. Your son is a good man, a good father, and my best friend, and I'm so grateful that you brought such a son into the world.

WANT MORE FROM YOUR FAIRY TALES?

Sign up for a free no-spam newsletter and free short stories, exclusive secret chapters, and sneak peeks at books before they're published . . . all for free.

Details at the end of this book.

CHAPTER I
LOOKING UP

Wendy frowned down at the map of Ashland for what felt like the hundredth time that day. A week had passed since the incident with Jay, and she was still no closer to making a decision. In theory, working on an apple orchard in east Ashland sounded lovely. But when she looked at the distance between her parents' home and the royal orchards...

"Wendy, look!"

Wendy was pulled from her dark musings at the sound of her name, and she looked up to see Curly holding out his sticky green and blue fingers to point at his leaf. Wendy rubbed her strained eyes then stood and went to his side.

"Oh, Curly," she said, putting her hands on the little boy's shoulders. "It's absolutely wonderful." Then she paused, trying to make out what the little blobs of paint might be. "Tell me about it, would you?"

"This is Neverland," he said proudly, dipping his hand in more paint, red this time, and smearing it all over the green. "This is back when it was pretty."

"What do you mean? Neverland is pretty."

"If it were in the Old World, it would be," Nibs scoffed. He was

1

painting his own leaf several feet away. "But not the way it was before."

Wendy looked around and sighed. With Peter gone nearly all week, trying to fix the island, she'd hoped teaching the boys to paint might give them an outlet for all their pent-up feelings and frustrations. At Wendy's request, Moon Flower, one of the few fae who tolerated Wendy and the boys, had lent them jars of the paint made from the clay in Color Canyon. And instead of paper, the boys used large palm leaves from the trees by the beach. They also lacked brushes, so Wendy simply had them use their hands. So far, the boys seemed to be enjoying it immensely. But no matter how much fun they had in this or that activity, a feeling of dread always seemed to settle over the boys. Even little Slightly had been out of sorts.

As the boys focused again on their painting, Wendy returned to the flat rock where she'd laid out her maps. They weren't fancy, and some of the countries had probably been cheated of some land here and there, but Wendy had studied enough geography at home to know where the general boundaries lay. And that was all she needed to make her decision.

She hoped.

A distant rumbling rolled down the mountain and through the trees, and the ground began to shake. Such a quake would have alarmed Wendy when she first arrived at Neverland, seven weeks ago, but Wendy and the boys were so used to the earth tremors that she didn't even have to shout directions anymore. She merely snatched up her maps and rose into the air, along with the boys.

Tremors were commonplace enough now that the boys hardly ever commented on them. Two or three a day weren't even considered abnormal. But this one was long and unusually violent.

Jay, the man the fae had blamed for much of Neverland's

crumbling, was gone, and the paradise was still falling apart at the seams. No wonder Peter was such a nervous wreck these days.

When it was finally over, the boys' shoulders all drooped.

"Peter won't be back tonight," Pop said, going back to where his leaf had fallen on the ground and picking it up slowly. Sand was stuck to the paint. The other boys mumbled in agreement. Nibs threw his leaf painting in the air and let it fall to the ground.

They were probably right, but Wendy wasn't about to have them spend the whole evening pouting. So instead, she clapped her hands and did her best to smile.

"All right, that's enough painting now. Go wash your hands and then bring in your leaves. We'll hang them from the ceiling to look at as we go to sleep."

This seemed to brighten their spirits a little, and the younger boys went to do as they were told. But John stopped and whispered, "How long do you think this place will hold?"

Wendy sighed. "I think Peter's trying to figure that out for himself."

John frowned. "Do you think it's time to go back to Mother and Father?"

She gave her brother a sad smile and held up her maps, which she'd collected from the ground. "As soon as I know where I'm going, we will."

"This is really what you want, then?" He studied her.

No.

"I think the more precise answer would be, it's what I'm content with." She forced a smile. "We have no other choice. Now, go help Michael before he splashes the twins, and everyone fights and gets dirty."

Supper was a somber affair as well, no matter how many questions Wendy asked or how much she teased. Eventually, she had but one thing left to try.

"I was going to tell you all a new story tonight," she said

slowly, looking at the boys sitting in their hammocks around her. "But I'm going to need your help." A few heads rose off their pillows, and Wendy smiled. "That's more like it. But before we begin to tell the story, you must all come sit near me."

As usual, John and Nibs, being the eldest boys, scoffed at the idea of acting out a story. The younger boys, however, cheered and jumped out of bed. Soon, they were seated in a circle, as even Nibs and John had been cajoled into joining them.

"What's our new story about, Wendy?" Michael asked. "Is it about Peter?"

Wendy reached over and tapped his nose. "Not this time."

The boys gasped.

"But you always tell stories about Peter," Tootles said.

"Peter will be in it." Wendy tilted her head. "But tonight, we're going to tell the story of Neverland itself. Now, who wants to be the moon?" The boys excitedly raised their hands and began to talk all at once, and Wendy laughed. *Thank you*, she prayed silently to the Maker. If she had to leave them, she wished to make them smile just a few more times.

While Wendy's knowledge of Neverland's history was basic, she knew enough. After much arguing and several fights, the twins were assigned to be the moon and sun, and Slightly was the naughty little breeze that blew wherever he pleased. Michael was the crocodile, which Wendy hoped never to meet again after her first night in Neverland, and Curly was the water, splashing everything on the beach. Even Nibs and John were talked into being the star and one of the fae. And by the time the story was done, the boys were chattering again about all the new characters they wanted to be tomorrow.

"Your stories are like magic!" Curly cried as he leaped into his bed. "I don't ever want them to end!"

Wendy's eyes pricked and self-loathing burned in her belly as she tucked them in and kissed them on their soft little cheeks.

Tomorrow. Each tomorrow was borrowed, one day closer to the decision she still hadn't made.

It was too late to wonder whether or not she might remain a piece of the golden wheatfield landscape at home. Her parents weren't going to yield in their plans for her, and neither was she. Going home was not an option anymore.

So where did that leave her?

Seven weeks ago, it had left her with the perfection of Neverland. The promise of escape from the unhappy betrothal her parents had arranged with the town's local magistrate couldn't have been more welcome. And beyond mere escape, she'd lived the last two months in a world of wonder and adventure. Flying with her brothers and Peter's Lost Boys, sitting atop a crystal rainbow, and making food appear at a whim, all while time stood still, had been like something out of a storybook. And, of course, there was Peter Pan himself.

But then Captain Jay, Peter's best childhood friend all grown up, had returned to Neverland against the rules and asked Peter to do the impossible. And soon after their arrival, the island had begun to quake and crack daily. The flowers and trees no longer grew thick and healthy. There was just as much brown foliage as green. Fruit trees which had produced more than the boys could ever eat—which was a lot—no longer brought forth plump, juicy fruit. When they did provide food, it was on par with the fruit Wendy saw in the Old World, slightly misshapen and possibly munched on by crawly things.

To make things worse, before he left, Jay, in a desperate attempt to change Peter's mind, had kidnapped Tiger Lily, the fae leader, and held her hostage. Desperate to keep Wendy and Tiger Lily safe, Peter had broken Neverland's second sacred rule. There were only two.

No growing up.

No shedding of blood.

Breaking the rules, Peter had warned Wendy, would bring the destruction of Neverland itself, breaking the power the fantastical land had been built upon. The fallen star that upheld the hidden world of Neverland could not continue in its timelessness if people grew up or blood was shed. For all that change would force time to move again, and the frozen state of perfection would shatter. And now, sure enough, Neverland, for all its beauty and wonder, was falling to pieces, and would eventually cast Wendy out as well. She was on the cusp of womanhood. She knew it. The fae knew it. Jay had known it.

And Neverland knew it. The way Peter had looked at her on the beach as they were rescued by the fae after Jay's attack had made that clear. *I have to leave*, she chided herself silently. *I can't stay here.* As if sensing her thoughts, Nana gently pressed her soft head into Wendy's lap and looked up at her through large brown eyes.

"Don't worry," Wendy said softly, tracing the dog's ear. "Wherever I go, you'll come, too."

But no matter how long she put it off, eventually, the tomorrows would end. Wendy, John, Michael, and Nana would fly away. Then what would become of her darling Lost Boys?

Soon the only sounds were the wind above the treehouse and the slight creak of Wendy's chair as she rocked in front of the fire. She pulled out her maps once again but realized after only five minutes of staring at them that she was too tired to look at them anymore. She rolled them back up in frustration and stared at the fire. She was tired but didn't feel comfortable leaving the boys alone to go to bed until Peter returned. She wished he would return now, so, at the very least, she could sleep.

Peter was always late these days. He was always quiet, hardly even looking at her as he bid her a mumbled good night and immediately fell into his hammock. And then Wendy was left to wonder at the point of it all as she trudged back to her little rose cottage just outside the boys' tree.

The obvious answer was the boys. With every passing day, they became more a part of her heart. And with every day, she was positioned to break theirs more.

If only she could know where to go. Then perhaps this wouldn't all be so hard.

A scuffling sound came from the ceiling, and Wendy braced herself for what was coming. Or rather, what wouldn't come.

Sure enough, Tink slipped through first. She looked around and sent Wendy a satisfied smirk before shaking out her short, platinum curls. Then she flitted over and into the hole in the wall that led up to her room, which was in the branches, rather than down in the roots with the boys. She was followed immediately by Peter, who, as he always did of late, had deep, purple circles beneath his eyes and looked as though he was hardly awake enough to stand.

"Wendy," he said simply, the way he acknowledged her every night for the last week, and it cut her heart. How had it been that just a week ago, he'd all but confessed his love? And yet now, he seemed to feel it a burden to say anything more than her name?

"Peter," she responded in like. But as she stood to leave, she dropped one of her maps on the ground. She bent to pick it up, but another hand grabbed it as well. She looked up to find Peter only inches away. And for a moment, she wondered if he just might finish that kiss he'd nearly begun when he thought they were going to die in the water.

After a long moment of staring into her eyes, though, he shook his head slightly and stood before handing her the paper. "Have you chosen where to go?" he asked, keeping his eyes on the ground.

"I've narrowed it down to western Ashland near Kaylem, or Destin or Voksam." Wendy took the map back.

He nodded. Annoyed, Wendy moved to leave, but before she could get there, he grabbed her wrist and held her in place.

"Thank you," he said quietly, his green eyes on hers once more.

She blinked. "For what?"

He gave her a small, sad smile. "For being here." Then he took a deep breath and let it out slowly. "I know I've been distant lately. And I'm sorry. But it's going to get better." The corner of his mouth turned up in the ghost of the smile Wendy had grown to love. No. She couldn't let herself love that smile. Not now.

"How do you know that?" she asked.

"Because I talked to the star today." For the first time in a long time, Peter's eyes brightened. "She says that after that tremor today, Neverland is happier again. It was as though the island was releasing its angst. Jay is really gone this time, and she says we ought to try having a little fun."

Wendy gave him a wry smile. "The last time we tried having a little fun—"

"Wendy, the island is beginning to heal." His eyes seemed to spark with hope, and his grip on her hand tightened. He glanced at the necklace he'd given her, which she never took off. "Now that Jay's ship is gone for good, things are looking up."

Yes, Jay's ship was definitely gone. He'd promised her it would be after he'd come to his senses and apologized after his attack.

For some reason, this thought brought a different sadness over Wendy, one she didn't want to think about. So instead, she let it give way to her second strongest feeling, which was curiosity. She knew better, of course. If she was leaving, it was foolish to ask anything that might bring her closer to the one man she should be distancing herself from. Still...she wanted to know.

"You told me you and Jay were close," she said softly, glancing at the boys to make sure they were still sleeping. "Is that why you took so long to chase him out?"

Peter looked away from her, and for a moment, she wondered if he would even answer. Without lifting his head, he spoke.

"I had a brother." He gave a nearly inaudible, humorless chuckle. "I don't remember much about my life before the fae. But my brother, he was..." He swallowed. "He was like my shadow."

Wendy's throat was so tight it hurt. She looked back at her brothers' faces, peaceful in their slumber. "How old was he?"

"About a year younger." His jaw tightened. "I guess Jay reminded me of him. I'd taken in boys of all ages by the time he showed up. But none felt so much like my brother. Not that he was a replacement, of course. But..." Peter put his fist up to his mouth, then back down again. When he spoke again, his voice trembled. "I felt closer to my family with him than I had since they died."

"What happened to him?" Wendy asked, tears rolling down her face. "To your brother, I mean?"

Peter drew in a deep, shaky breath. "He died, too. Same day as my mother."

"So when Jay returned," Wendy said slowly, "it was like your brother was coming home."

Peter nodded at the ground.

"So many years you've spent trying to fill that hole," Wendy whispered. "So much pain. When does it end, Peter? How much longer will you suffer by losing those you love to time that isn't yours?"

Peter's green eyes seemed to burn as they met hers, and for one perfect moment, Wendy saw indecision. He looked as young as he claimed to be, his eyes hungering for what Wendy knew no time would buy. Finally, he swallowed.

"It's getting late." He smiled, but it didn't touch his eyes.

Wendy nodded, her chest tight and uncomfortable and her eyes stinging. She moved toward the entrance, but before she went through, Peter pulled her back once more.

"Now that Jay's gone," he said softly, "things will get better." He touched her necklace, the one he'd given her when she'd first arrived. The green stone seemed to glow against his hand. "Just give it time." He swallowed. "Please."

"Time is something we're running short on."

Peter kept his eyes on the necklace, the ghost of a smile at the corner of his mouth. "Then I intend to make the best of what I have."

CHAPTER 2
DAY

P eter had a hard time falling asleep after Wendy went back to her little house, and it wasn't for lack of exhaustion. In the week since Jay had left, he'd spent nearly every waking moment going over every inch of the island, fixing what he could and examining the rest. Not everything had been salvageable. Much of the wildlife had died, and some sort of beetle had begun to feed on several forests, particularly on the southern and eastern parts of the island where Peter spent the least of his time. He'd spent more hours than he could count imagining up the correct number of deer, lizards, rabbits, and other little animals that had died, and replenishing the missing flora and fauna.

But he'd spoken the truth to Wendy when he said things were getting better. As he removed the dead and dying plants and saved the animals that weren't too far gone, the island had once again begun to look like itself. It was by the grace of the Maker that they hadn't lost more, actually. New sprouts were poking their heads out of the ground, and buds were forming on trees that had been close to death. He'd created enough animals that the island was once again teeming with life.

If only he could bring about the same kind of healing to his relationship with Wendy.

After finally falling into a fitful sleep, Peter awakened with the dawn. At first, this made him groan. He wasn't ready for another day. But when he slipped outside just as the golden rays rose above the ocean and washed the island in their warmth, he felt a renewed sense of purpose. Even more importantly, he decided as he soaked it in, he felt hope.

Wendy was still planning to leave. And while he couldn't engage her the way he wished to deep down in his heart, he still had a little time to do all he could to get her to stay. There had to be a way. There was always a way. He smiled wanly to himself as he watched the sparkling waves glisten as they rolled in the distance. The fae didn't call him clever for nothing.

"Peter!"

Peter turned to see Pop staring at him. The boys spilled out of the trunk behind him, each looking just as surprised as the last.

"You're not gone yet?"

"What are you doing here?"

"Are you going to play today?"

"Today," Peter said, grinning at his boys and ruffling their hair, "we're going to be reckless."

The boys stared up at him with wide eyes and open mouths. Even Nibs and John looked shocked. Wendy came out of her little house and looked confused as well, and Peter winked at his boys.

"Today, we're going to have fun."

"Can we go to the slides, Peter?" Curly bounced up and down.

"Why not? First thing after breakfast!"

The boys let out a cheer, and Wendy watched them, an enigmatic expression on her face. The boys didn't give Peter time to study her, though, as they all grabbed onto his arms and shirt and trousers, trying to talk over one another all at once.

"You and Wendy *have* to go down the slides with us this time," Top piped. "Last time, you just sat and watched like boring people."

"Yeah." Pop tugged on his sleeve. "No going to work on the island today, either."

"I promise," Peter laughed as the boys dragged him back to the stump, "today is just for us."

They scarfed down breakfast so fast it nearly gave Peter a stomachache. Tink came down during the hullabaloo and threatened every single one of the boys for making such a racket, but as soon as she heard about their little expedition, she sat down and began to eat, too.

Peter had a hunch that the boys were terrified that he was going to change his mind. Not that he could blame them. Every attempt at fun recently had been either canceled or thwarted. Nothing, however, could stop his plans today, short of the island itself splitting into two. He had his boys to care for. And more importantly, he had the girl of his dreams to convince to stay.

His hunch about Tink made him watch her a little more carefully as they readied themselves to leave for the day. Well, actually, it was Wendy's hunch about Tink. The very idea that Tink wanted something more than their friendship, something more... mature? The more he considered it, the more unease he felt that Wendy must be right. But right here and now, he didn't have time for such foolishness. It would just have to be considered later.

He studied Wendy discreetly every chance he got. She'd brought those blasted maps with her again, and the way her brow furrowed when she examined them wasn't comforting. He'd have to get creative.

Soon they reached the rock slides, and the boys immediately launched themselves down into the mountain, their squeals echoing up and lingering behind them. As Peter had expected,

Wendy settled herself onto some of the large rocks nearby and prepared to look at her maps, as though this new session of study might reveal something that hadn't been there for the last week.

"Come on," Peter said, reaching down and taking her maps. "Today is for fun. You can look at those tomorrow."

"Give them back!" Wendy grabbed for the parchment, but Peter was already in the air. Wendy bolted up after him. Before she could snatch them back, Peter dove back down to the ground and stuffed them in a hole in a rock.

"You brat!" Wendy cried. But her eyes were laughing as she shook her head, which made Peter even bolder.

"I told you," he said, darting back to her and wrapping his arms around her, reveling in what it felt like to hold her close, "this is a fun day. You can go back to your maps tomorrow. But for now," he let his grin grow, "just have fun." Then he darted over to the slides, dragging Wendy along behind him. Nana followed at their heels, barking and growling up a storm until John hauled her back to watch from a distance.

"I've already gone down the slide!" Wendy protested, trying to hold her skirts away from the splashing of the water. "Remember? On the first night?" She let out a little cry as the cold water reached her dress.

"But that," Peter said, lowering himself into a sitting position with his back to the slide, his arm still wrapped around her waist as he pulled her down next to him, "was facing forward."

Wendy tried to turn around to look at him, her eyes wide. "Wait. What?"

Peter laughed as he used his legs to push them backward. Wendy screamed long and hard as they hurtled into the mountain. Water splashed their faces, the only light coming from the blue-purple phosphorous algae that hugged the tunnel ceiling above them. Peter, who had ridden down the slides countless times, knew exactly how to lean so they spun around at the biggest bends in their slippery path.

And it all paid off. Wendy clung to his arm as though she were going to die, and in the dark, Peter didn't even try to hide his smile or smother his laughter. When they got to the little pool at the bottom, he didn't give her time to catch her breath or get angry. Instead, he pulled them right into the second slide's path, and they were sucked back up the next slide the same way they'd gone down the first. If Peter had feared Wendy's wrath at all when he'd pulled her down with him, he knew he didn't have much to worry about by the time they reached the surface again. Wendy was soaked, but she was also laughing.

"What next?" Peter asked the boys when they were all too tired to go again. Wendy looked like she was nearly dry, her dress rumpled and her hair wild and beautiful. The days in the sun had given her skin a bronze kiss, and it was driving Peter a little crazy. She was leaning back against the rocks again, watching the boys and laughing at their antics. Just as Peter had hoped, the maps had stayed in the little hole he'd stuffed them in, and she hadn't even glanced their way once.

"I know! Let's coax the crocodile out of the marsh!" Michael cried.

Wendy, whose face had been the picture of content serenity, sat straight up. "Excuse me?"

"Oh, come on, Wendy," John said, rolling his eyes. "Tink lets us do it whenever we're with her!"

Wendy turned a hard gaze on Peter. "Is this true?"

He just shrugged and grinned. "See what happens when you're gone?"

Her eyes widened slightly, and she glanced back at the boys.

"The crocodile can't fly," Peter reminded her gently, holding his hand out. The look she gave him was not trusting, but she did let him pull her along behind the boys.

If Peter had harbored hope that teasing the crocodile would bring Wendy some sort of relaxation, he'd been dead wrong.

First of all, there was Nana, who barked so much and tried so hard to attack the crocodile that the Darling children had to tie her to a tree for her own sake. Then Pop, holding out a stick with a hunk of meat he'd imagined up, succeeded in getting the thing not only to come out of the tall grasses but to even come toward them. Rather than stopping with the meat on the stick, which Pop eventually dropped, however, the crocodile seemed to decide that Pop would be the more rewarding treat after all. The boys screamed, and Wendy made a poor attempt at thrusting Slightly into John's arms and running for Pop. But instead of yanking Pop away from the creature, she stumbled into him, and they both fell over just as the great reptile opened its enormous jaws.

Peter, who had been watching with great amusement, decided it was time to intervene if he ever hoped for her to forgive him. He dove down and snatched both Wendy and Pop away, Wendy screaming the whole way, and ordered the thing back to its home.

"That!" Wendy said, shaking herself off with as much dignity as she could muster, "was not fun."

"Usually, that doesn't happen," Peter assured her as he helped dust the beach sand off of Pop. "Hey," he turned to the little boy, "that was rather brilliant, though. I've never seen any of the boys think up meat just to lure him out."

"If you're trying to convince me it's a good, responsible game, then you're not doing yourself any favors," Wendy snapped as she reached up and gathered her mussed hair to pin it up again.

"Then how about I show you something I know you'll approve of?" He raised his eyebrows and took her by the shoulders. She glared up at him.

"If we're going to poke badgers with sticks—"

He laughed. "Nothing quite that exciting. Come on." He took

her hand and pulled her up into the air. "Time to visit the Memory Gems, boys."

"What are those?" he heard Michael ask John. But Peter just smiled and kept going. Deep inside, though, his heart was thundering. Wendy would love this next part. She'd probably be enthralled, actually. But this was one of his last stops, and if this didn't convince her to stay in Neverland, he wasn't sure what could.

Much to his delight, she gasped as they flew over the southern part of the island, and they were greeted by the reflections of many large purple amethysts from below. Their little group landed in the middle of a large clearing that was filled with gems the size of Michael.

"What is this?" Wendy whispered as the boys took off and scattered like bugs in the light.

Peter walked over to the nearest gemstone and leaned over to see its largest, flattest side. He gestured for her to stand beside him.

"Look here, right in the center," he said.

Wendy did as he said. "It's like a mirror."

"At first. But watch."

Wendy stared into her reflection for a few seconds more before letting out a little cry. Peter felt the wry bite of bittersweet emotion fill his mouth as he knelt down and joined her.

"Who is that?" she asked, pointing at the face of a young boy that played on the gem's flat surface. The child in the gem's reflection laughed and pointed at them before clapping his hands and staring. After a few seconds, it happened again. And again. And again. "How is it...he moving?" Wendy asked.

"These are the Memory Gems," Peter said, gesturing to the hundreds of gems surrounding them. Wendy's eyes widened as she took in all the different reflections of other faces in the other gems. The Lost Boys were all at their own gems and were doing various silly things in front of them. Even Nana, who had made herself comfortable at Wendy's feet, seemed confident, for the first time that day, that Wendy was in a place she was less likely to be killed.

"How do they work?" Wendy asked.

"Every Lost Boy gets one," he said, leading her to another clump of gems. Each gem had another face in it. Each reflection a point of peace and pain, pricking his heart like a needle, even though hundreds of years separated him from their owners. "I created them when I realized my first Lost Boy wanted to leave." He swallowed, his throat suddenly feeling tight. "I suppose I wanted a way to remember him." He'd just never expected so many to follow.

Wendy's face softened. "You miss them, don't you?"

He had to blink several times and clear his throat before he could answer. "Every day." Then he shook his head and took her hand. "Come here," he said, leading her to the nearest empty one. "Look inside."

Wendy peered into the reflection. Peter's heart swelled as her large, gentle eyes searched the center, looking, he knew, for another child.

"You won't find anyone in this one," he said softly.

She stopped searching and turned to look up at him, a golden curl slipping from her hairpins and falling gracefully in her face. "Why not?"

"Because," he said, "this one's yours."

Wendy stopped trying to study the gem and turned to look at him slowly. For an eternal moment, she simply stared into his eyes. Finally, she cleared her throat. "But I'm not lost."

He held her gaze. "Are you sure about that?"

She turned slowly away from him to gaze back into the gem. And the only thing Peter could do was pray that she was feeling the same questions inside that he'd felt his entire life. The questions that had led him to her.

"Peter!"

They turned to see Tink hovering several feet away. Her brow was creased, and she wrung her hands, as if not sure what to do with them.

"What is it?" Peter asked, pasting a smile onto his face.

"Um...the boys said they want to go to the beach."

Peter nodded and looked back at Wendy. She smiled and nodded, too, though he could see the questions lingering in her eyes. If only that uncertainty would stay.

Peter wasn't ready to move on, but at least the beach would be pleasant. Their little group walked the beach as the boys gathered shells, loudly shouting about who found the biggest one and then competing to see who could throw them the farthest. Between interruptions and having to break up fights, Wendy told him of her antics on the farm when she was little, and he told her stories about the boys. Tink bounced back and forth, walking strategically between Peter and Wendy and taking flight whenever an offending boy had thrown dirt too close to her or called her a name. Peter closed his eyes and breathed in deeply, letting the warm salty air fill his lungs, and the sounds of life fill his ears. The mermaids' songs echoing from their lagoon in the distance, the boys' chaos, and Wendy's laughter surrounded him like a blanket on a chilly night. Never had Neverland felt so perfect. Never had it felt so real.

Supper was a lively affair. The boys demanded that Peter make up the most outrageously decadent dinner ever seen on the island. When Peter turned to ask Wendy what she thought of the scheme, she looked doubtful, but she threw up her hands and said she didn't think anyone would listen to her anyway. Peter laughed and then concentrated on thinking up the most horrifying supper the boys had ever seen, which turned out to be nothing but vegetables, and their screams of horror only encouraged him to add more.

"All right," Wendy finally said, after Peter had eventually provided what the boys considered to be edible food, "it's time to clean up."

"Aw, Wendy!" Michael pouted. "Today's been perfect. Don't go messing it up like that."

"Now, Michael," Peter said, fixing the little boy with one of his best warning looks. "You never know what mischief will happen if you don't clean up in Neverland."

Michael frowned. "What mischief? We've not cleaned up before, and—"

But he didn't get to finish his sentence. A miniature whirlwind had formed in the middle of the room and swept him up. Screams went up from the boys as they were pulled into the vortex, too.

"Peter!" Wendy shrieked, "what's happening?"

"Peter, put me down this instant!" Tink shouted. "This is stupid!"

But Peter only laughed and grabbed the nearest boy, who happened to be little Slightly, and began to twirl him around within the whirlwind.

"My turn, Peter!" Tootles cried, and before long, all the younger boys were demanding to spin with Peter. After he'd gotten through them all, Slightly demanded another turn, but Peter told Nibs to take him.

"It's Wendy's turn," he said. Taking her waist in one hand and her hand in the other, he spun her within the windstorm. The warmth of her skin through her dress and the brightness of her eyes nearly overcame him.

She was so close, every bit as near as she'd been when they'd first danced at her friend's wedding all those weeks ago. Slowly, slowly, he pulled her closer. The desire for more raged within his chest as he drank in the hesitant curiosity in her eyes. Then suddenly, holding wasn't enough. He wanted to crush her against his chest and press his lips against hers.

"Wendy," he whispered. The words he'd left unsaid the day they'd nearly drowned in the ocean were there on the tip of his tongue, and the way her eyes widened, told him she knew it. But before he could finish, he felt a tap on his right shoulder. When he looked down to his right, there, flying beside them, was Tink.

"My turn," she said a little too brightly as she held her arms out.

She wanted him to hold her as he had Wendy. That was clear enough from the way she raised one hand higher than the other. But after the warning Wendy had given him on the beach, about how she'd believed Tink to be in love with him, Peter had begun to be more cautious in his dealings with his little friend. He hadn't been sure if Wendy was right or not. At least, not until now. But from the way Tink's eyes sparkled with hope as she continued holding her arms out to him, the answer was all too clear. And he hated himself for it and for what he had to do.

"Actually," he said, slowing the whirlwind until it was no more, and everyone fell gently to the ground, "I think it's about time for everyone to go to bed." He purposefully turned to herd the boys toward the washbasin Wendy had insisted he create for washing faces and hands. But he wasn't fast enough to miss the heartbreak on Tink's face as she seemed to understand exactly what he wasn't saying.

"Come on, boys," Wendy said, already washing Slightly's face. "It's been a busy day, and you're all going to sleep well tonight."

This brought a round of objections from the boys, half of whom were already yawning, and Peter was grateful. Anything to keep him from having to see just how far his little friend had actually fallen while he, in his apparent oblivion, had been unconsciously making promises he would never be able to keep.

Tink wasn't his only worry, however, as Wendy finally wiped

her hands on her apron and smiled up at him with tired eyes. Today had been...well, to borrow Wendy's term, nothing short of magical. But the maps were rolled up in her apron pocket once more, and he could already hear the goodbye before she even uttered the words.

Let her stay, he prayed as she sat in her rocking chair and began to tell the boys a bedtime story. *I don't know how. Just please let her stay.*

Wendy's story was unusually long, and by the time it was finished, most of the boys were already asleep, barring Nibs, John, and Curly. A few minutes later, the room was filled with quiet snores, and Wendy and Peter were finally able to breathe.

"Today was..." Wendy laughed a little. "Everything I ever dreamed of and more." Her blue eyes sparkled as they met his. "So, thank you."

He straightened his shoulders. "Did we exceed your expectations, now that you've had a proper day in Neverland?" He couldn't tremble or let his voice slip because then someone might see how truly afraid of losing her he had become.

She arched an eyebrow delicately. "If I didn't know better, I'd think you were trying to change my mind about staying."

If only she knew.

But what to say to that? Did he bare his heart and beg her to stay? Or would that frighten her away forever?

He reached out slowly and touched the green stone of the necklace he'd given her when she'd first come to Neverland, hoping desperately she would feel it for what it was. A kiss that, like the thimble she'd given him, would never be enough. But it was all he could do as they straddled the rules of one world with the desires of another.

"I know I tease that I won't know what to do with the boys after you leave," he finally choked out. "I do know, though, that they won't know what to do without you."

Wendy closed her eyes, and her jaw tensed. "Don't do this, Peter. Please."

"I wasn't finished." He took the green stone between his fingers and stepped closer so their faces were only inches apart. "The boys might not know what to do when you're gone, but neither will I."

Wendy opened her mouth, but her eyes then focused on something over his shoulder, and she stiffened slightly. He turned to follow her gaze.

Tink was standing just beneath the entrance to the tunnel that led to her bedroom. The potent, unadulterated emotions that were pinging across her face at a speed which could only belong to a fae, told him that she'd heard every word. Not only that, but her eyes were transfixed on the green stone that hung from Wendy's neck and was still pinched gently between Peter's fingers.

"We can talk in the morning after we've all had some sleep," Wendy said, taking a slow step back. "Good night, Peter. Tinkerbell." She nodded at both of them, then left, Nana at her side, as always. And with her, every bit of the color in Peter's world.

As soon as Wendy was gone, Tink huffed.

"Are you serious, Peter?"

Peter rolled his eyes. "About what?"

Not one to be easily distracted, Tink zipped over and hovered in front of him. Her short platinum hair seemed to stand more on end than usual, and her eyes blazed bright.

"I know what you meant when you touched her necklace like that. And don't pretend to be stupid and say you didn't. Because sure as darkness you've never given me a necklace, and furthermore, you've never *touched* anything you did give me."

"Tink," Peter said, rubbing his eyes, "I'm tired, and I really don't know what all this fuss is about. Wendy's had that necklace for weeks. Why are you so obsessed with it now?"

"Because," the little fae snapped, "I know that it's your way of showing affection. The kind of affection you're not supposed to have as a *boy*. And what's more, you're playing with fire—"

"Tink—"

"If you think that I'm the only set of eyes Tiger Lily has on you, you're dead wrong." She pulled herself up to her full height, which was adorable and pathetic at the same time. "I may not be human, but I'm also not blind." She took a step forward and put her hands on his arms. At the warmth of her touch, an uncomfortable heat set fire to the back of Peter's neck. How had he not seen this before? Or was it just blossoming now because Wendy was there to set off this terrible jealousy that seemed to have sprouted before his eyes?

"I'm telling you this because you're my friend," she continued. "If you let this world crumble, you had better be ready to accept the fallout. Because if you think Tiger Lily is going to let Wendy break Neverland, you've fooled everyone but me ." She moved closer. "Besides, if you let Neverland die, you won't even get to enjoy a life with Wendy or any other pathetic female for that matter. Is it worth it? Destroying everything we've worked for for a fleeting moment with a girl?" She paused. "You know what will happen to you if you don't stop this."

Peter tried to swallow, but a lump the size of an egg seemed stuck in his throat. Of course, he knew. He could feel it in his bones and blood. But that was something he really didn't want to talk about. Instead, he shook his head.

"I'm not worried about Tiger Lily. She can't hurt Wendy or the boys without breaking the laws herself," he choked out.

"That would push Neverland closer to extinction, and she knows it."

Tink leaned in so close he could smell the slightly sweet scent the fae carried with them. "Have you forgotten what we are when we're not frozen in time?"

Despite his reluctance, his mind raced back to the day he'd accepted the fae's offer, the day he'd bonded with the star. He'd told Wendy all of this, of course, and about how the fae had threatened to call the constable to have him locked up if he didn't do as they wished. What he hadn't told her about, though, were the fae's additional methods of persuasion. How, even now, he still suffered occasional nightmares of the night they'd spent *convincing* him to take the star.

Peter shivered, and Tink nodded. "I thought so." She let go of his arms and flitted back to the entrance to her tunnel. Then she paused at the door. "If you're not going to worry for yourself, then at least fear for them. If Neverland goes, Wendy and the boys might escape with your help, but so will we. And just think about how Tiger Lily would repay the person who destroyed the life she worked so hard to build for our people. Do you honestly think she would let the humans who ruined all that carry on with their happy little lives?"

No. Tiger Lily might consider herself some sort of benevolent patroness of Peter and his little posse, but he knew the fae well enough to know that Neverland wouldn't fall without retribution.

Tink opened the tunnel cover then paused. "I have to know, though."

Peter looked at her through bleary eyes. "What?"

Tink's face softened. "What was it," she asked softly, "that you didn't have here that you had to leave Neverland to find?"

Peter didn't answer, just watched her warily.

After a moment, she gave the slightest of sighs and nodded. "That's what I thought. Good night, Peter."

Peter sighed and left the tree to sit on one of the fallen logs in the clearing beside the treehouse. Good, it certainly wasn't. And night?

Most of his life had been spent in the night. Why was it so hard to find the day?

CHAPTER 3
CREATURE IN THE NIGHT

As Wendy walked back to her little rose-covered cottage under the big Neverland trees, she berated herself for feeling so foolishly giddy. She was leaving soon. So what use was it mooning over the boy-man that she was leaving behind? If anything, she ought to be drawing away, distancing herself. She'd worked hard to do so recently. Encouragement was the last thing he needed. It would only hurt both of them.

But the way he'd touched the green stone he'd given her and the longing in his eyes had felt so incredibly intimate. Even now, as she closed and locked the cottage door behind her, her heart beat fast, and her cheeks heated.

"Why do you keep him here?" she asked the Maker aloud as she changed out of her clothes into her nightdress and climbed into bed. "He feels trapped. Surely there has to be a way to free him."

There was, of course, no voice that echoed from the sky, or any other sort of obvious answer from the Maker. Not that she'd expected one. But for some reason, the silence made the night seem even colder and darker than usual. Wendy was gladder than ever that Nana had come with her to Neverland. The dog's breathing was soothing. Wendy draped one arm over the side of the bed so she could bury it in Nana's soft white and brown fur. Thanks to the day's exertions, she was exhausted. And yet, Wendy might not have been able to sleep at all, except for the warmth she found in her faithful friend that helped her drift slowly off to sleep.

But her mind seemed determined to torture her even there. She turned from side to side in what felt like an eternal coma. Oppressive darkness that wouldn't let her wake, nor would it grant her the peace of rest. Voices of the fae haunted her, Tiger Lily and Tink specifically. Over and over again, through tired eyes, she blinked up at the moonlight coming through her window, only to fall into the sleepless slumber once more.

Eventually, though, the voices fell silent, only to give way to the sounds of the night, frogs and crickets, which rang out louder and louder with each passing minute. She scrunched her eyes shut tighter and prayed for sleep. But before she could finish, a sharp hiss made her eyes fly open, and she bolted straight up in bed.

On the ceiling, in the corner opposite the one her bed was pushed against, crouched a creature that seemed spawned by darkness itself. Its shape was...human. Two legs and two arms, though they were hazy, as though their edges weren't truly defined. Green glowing eyes were slits in its thin head, and its feet were resting against the wall as if gravity had no power over it.

Wendy's eyes locked with the creature's, and Wendy felt trapped in its gaze. Try as she might, she couldn't pull away.

"Nana," Wendy whispered. She should scream. Wanted to scream. But there was no air left in her lungs with which to do so.

As soon as the word had left her lips, the creature sprang straight at Wendy. Only when fingers, cold and powerful, wrapped around Wendy's neck, did Wendy remember how to scream. Before she could make a sound, though, Nana launched herself at the attacker.

The creature snapped its head toward Nana. Too late, though. The dog bit down hard on the creature's leg, and it let loose a bloodcurdling scream. Nana pulled, and something ripped. Then the dog attacked again.

This time, the dog leaped at its upper body, and Nana's jaws clamped down on what should have been the creature's shoulder. Instead of fighting the dog, however, the creature dissolved, and Nana's jump continued over Wendy, where she hit the wall. Wendy pulled her dog close and hugged her tight as she searched the room, which was once again lighted only by the moonlight. The creature was gone. Not a swirl or whorl of green light was left.

Wendy trembled as she held her dog close. Nana, who didn't seem any worse for having jumped into the wall, growled at the air, pushing her body back against Wendy. And for once, Wendy didn't mind. Nana could squish her for all she cared, and it would be better than ever seeing that terrifying monster again.

But no, *monster* wasn't the right word. As frightening and new as the creature had seemed, there was something eerily familiar about it. It had been something powerful...

Power. There was only one other source of power on the island besides Peter. Actually, not sources. Rather, they were beings.

Everything snapped into place—the power, bright and pulsing, of the non-corporeal entity that had hovered above her in the night. Peter had once said that the fae could be very dangerous if they were no longer frozen in time. But if the island was healing, how had this one changed?

More importantly, why had it wanted her dead?

Wendy was up in a moment, running out the door before her courage fled her and her legs gave out with shaking. The last place she wanted to be frozen stiff was in the middle of the clearing outside. She needed to get to Peter.

The walk that took one whole minute on an average day seemed never ending tonight as Wendy stumbled in the dark toward the treehouse stumps. Her legs were shaking so badly that when she put them against the trunk and fell inside, she couldn't get herself upright again. All she could do was sit on the floor and sob. Thankfully, Nana, who had stayed right on Wendy's heels, needed little assistance to follow.

"Wendy!" John cried, his words slurring slightly as he rubbed his bleary eyes. Still, to his credit, he stumbled out of bed and knelt beside her. "What's wrong?"

Peter was on her other side in a flash. "What happened?" His voice was strong and clear.

"A fae..." Wendy did her best to stop sobbing, but when Peter put his arm around her shoulders, she collapsed into him and cried even harder. "A fae was in my room. It attacked me..." She broke down again but was just aware of her surroundings enough to feel Peter go absolutely still.

"Was it in human form?" he asked, his voice so low it was nearly inaudible.

Wendy shook her head, but then she remembered. She pulled a scrap of embroidered blue and gray fabric from her pocket and handed it to him.

"I found this on my bed as I was getting out. It's not mine." She let out a slow breath and pressed her face against Peter's chest. He took the fabric in one hand while stroking her cheek with the thumb of his other hand, but the movement seemed almost forced.

"John," he finally said, gently forcing her to sit up, "you keep her company. She can sleep in my hammock while I'm gone. And I want you to stay awake until I get back."

John, who seemed functionally awake by now, nodded, his

face shadowed in the low light of the dying embers in the fireplace. Most of the boys were awake, but they must have been too frightened to get out of their beds because Wendy heard only whispers rather than their usual noise. Michael ran to her and crawled into her lap, and Wendy was thankful for the feeling of his sturdy little body in her arms. But then, Peter's words sank in.

"Where are you going?" she whispered, her blood running cold once again.

Peter turned, and his gaze was dark. "To see Tiger Lily. She's gone too far this time." Then he marched over to Tinkerbell's tunnel. "Tink!" he snapped. "Get down here."

A scowling Tinkerbell appeared a moment later. "Peter, what in the depths—"

"I need you to get Tiger Lily," he said, already standing below the stump. "Have her meet me in the sunflower field."

Tinkerbell rubbed her eyes. "Wait...right now? In the middle of the night?"

Peter's glare only darkened. "Yes, now. And hurry." And then he was gone.

Wendy did her best to lie down and sleep after he'd gone. But all she could think about was how desperately someone must want her out of Neverland.

CHAPTER 4
ONLY A BOY

Peter's heart beat erratically as he sped toward the sunflowers. He'd have to play this carefully. If the fae were able to change form, it meant that Neverland was far worse than he had initially thought. And if Neverland was that far gone, there was little left standing between the fae and those they would hold responsible for its fall.

And if everything fell, he wouldn't be able to help Wendy at all.

By the time he reached the sunflower field, the moon was mostly gone, and the sky was nearly pitch black. A large, rounded boulder sat in the middle of the field, and it was on this that Peter alighted to wait for Tiger Lily. He'd spent hours on the boulder recently, getting the sunflower seeds ready to grow, and he was doubly grateful for their success now as he waited. If this conversation was going to go his way at all, he needed everything to appear at an advantage. He took a deep breath. Including himself.

"Peter?" In the dim light, he could see the outline of her tall, regal form descending toward him.

"I'm here."

She landed and looked around. "I'm assuming there's a

reason we're meeting all the way out here in the middle of the night?"

"What do you see here?" Peter demanded, gesturing at the field.

She snorted. "Nothing. It's dark."

Peter rolled his eyes and waved his arm. Thousands of fireflies gathered in a floating veil above them. The army of light made Tiger Lily's eyes glitter.

"What do you see now?"

"A field of baby sunflowers."

"Exactly. You don't see death or cracks in the earth. Everything is green and new."

She nodded slowly. "So I do. I've seen such all over the island."

Peter nodded. "Exactly. Neverland is healing. Which is why I want to know why one of your people attacked Wendy in fae form tonight."

Tiger Lily sucked in a sharp breath. "They did what?"

"You heard me." Peter folded his arms across his chest. "And tried to kill her."

Tiger Lily was silent for a long time. She turned slowly and gazed out at the fields once again.

"Tiger Lily," Peter finally growled, unable to wait any longer. "If your people are going to flaunt the rules just as I'm getting Neverland to heal—"

"I didn't know we could shift back." In the weakly, yellow light of the fireflies, Peter could see her lips tighten. "And I certainly didn't send anyone to break any more rules. You can rest assured that I will deal with such immediately tomorrow."

"Any more?" Peter arched an eyebrow. "If you're talking about Wendy and Jay—"

"I'm talking about you, Peter." Her voice hardened slightly. "Of course, Wendy and Jay are something to consider. But whether you want to discuss it or not, you were the one to shed Jay's blood."

Peter's mouth fell open. "I was protecting you and Wendy!"

"And I'm grateful for that." Her voice was annoyingly pacifying, as though she were talking to Curly or Michael. "But your intentions don't change what happened. You can't change the laws of this world on a whim, even in Neverland. The truth of the matter is that you drew blood. No matter the reason, it happened. And now you have to deal with the consequences." She stood slightly taller. "Of course, that brings us back to Wendy."

"This is not her fault."

"Perhaps, perhaps not. But you need to remember, Peter. My people are...passionate. And while they see the healing going on around them, they're also vividly aware of how long it's taking. And as Jay is gone and Wendy's still here, that's something to consider. I can only guess that the ability to shift between forms took the attacker by surprise. Their first reaction was most likely to blame her. I can almost guarantee you that the attack was one of fear."

"That doesn't make it right."

"No, and I'm not excusing it. The last thing we need is more rule breaking. But you also have to consider the fact that progress might be hampered because a rule is being broken. And as there's no ongoing violence, that leaves only one option." She fixed her dark eyes on him, and Peter squirmed in spite of himself.

Then she took a deep breath. "But I do owe you and Wendy much for coming to my rescue. So in an attempt to bring our little groups together, I suggest a celebration."

Peter blinked. That was...not what he'd been expecting.

"We'll have it tonight at the camp. Bring the Darlings and the Lost Boys. Come at sunset and come hungry."

"Very well," Peter said slowly.

"But," Tiger Lily said, her voice sharp once again, "consider

39

this. If the island truly doesn't improve significantly...and soon, something will have to change. Drastically. Or I can't promise that my people won't do something drastic on their own accord."

"I understand."

Instead of flying away, however, she simply studied him. When she spoke again, her voice was softer. "I have to admit, though, that it amazes me."

"What?"

"You don't seem to care at all about what will happen to you as Neverland falls apart. Your lack of natural self-preservation is a curious one." Tiger Lily tilted her head to the side and put her finger to her cheek. For several long moments, she studied him. Finally, she straightened and gave him an indulgent smile. "Although, I suppose, you are only a boy." And with that, she flew off.

Peter shivered as he soared high above Neverland. No, there wasn't a chance in the world of forgetting that. It had been bad enough when they'd chosen to focus on him all those years ago. But now that Wendy was their target, Peter had no choice. He had to fix Neverland whether Neverland wanted to be fixed or not. Then maybe...just maybe...Wendy could stay. Uninvited, images of what could be, spending eternity with Wendy at his side, flashed before his eyes. If the fae would leave her alone, there was no reason for Wendy to go. Not if the island was fixed and everyone was happy.

His heart beat faster as he made his way home. It wouldn't be easy. There was much about the island that, while his creation, Peter didn't understand. He would do it, though. He had to.

If only he knew how.

CHAPTER 5
PLAY

P eter returned from whatever errand he had gone on just as the sun rose. He didn't say much to Wendy or the boys except that she would be sleeping in the treehouse with them from then on. His eyes were bright with a nearly feverish light as he uttered something about Color Canyon and left the treehouse yet again. The boys complained, saying he'd promised them fun, but he looked so determined that Wendy did her best to distract them with breakfast. Then she set to hanging her new bed, which was a former Lost Boy's discarded hammock, and told the horrified boys to straighten theirs.

Wendy would have been scandalized by such a thought when she first came to Neverland. Sleeping in the same room as a boy her age bred the kind of gossip that could make one untouchable in Ashland. But she felt no shame now, only relief. The thought of being alone, even for an hour, made Wendy shake nearly as hard as she had when the fae apparition had visited her.

A few hours later, when Wendy had the boys playing a noisy game that involved lots of spinning, John pulled her aside.

"You don't have to sleep in here, you know," he said.

Wendy shook her head. "John, if you knew what I saw—"

"That's not what I'm saying." John put his hands on Wendy's shoulders. "Wendy, we can leave anytime. All you have to say is the word, and we're gone."

Wendy felt a tug at the bottom of her dress. She looked down to find Michael.

"We don't have to stay," he said softly. "I like flying, but I don't want you to be scared."

Wendy sighed and closed her eyes. She wasn't ready. That had been the deal, after all, staying until she knew where she was going. Kaylem. Destin. Vaksam. There were so many possibilities, and despite her hours spent staring at her maps, she didn't have the first idea of where she was going to go. Because leaving Neverland meant growing up. And not just growing up, but doing it alone. She wasn't going to marry the man her parents had chosen, and by now, there was no way to shield them from the shame that would have come from having their nearly grown daughter run away. She refused to go back and make their lives worse.

But she couldn't stay here either. Now that it seemed the fae were beginning to shift back, Wendy had no doubt they would turn on the boys eventually if Neverland continued to grow worse. *She* might not be ready, but the longer she stayed, the more danger she was putting the boys in, both her brothers and the Lost Boys.

"You're right," she said, giving her brothers a weak smile. "It's time."

"Give me one more night before you go."

Wendy and John looked up to see Peter once more. His entrance had been nearly silent. His face was pale, and his green eyes too wide.

"Why?" Wendy asked.

"Peter's back!" someone shouted before he could answer, and the boys nearly crushed Peter in their enthusiasm.

Peter gave his boys what looked like a forced, tired grin. "The fae have set up a celebration for tonight to thank us for saving Tiger Lily," he told them. The boys whooped and hollered, but Peter met and held Wendy's gaze. "It'll be fun." These last words were uttered like a plea.

Wendy couldn't tell what, but something inside her broke.

"Wendy," John started, but Wendy shook her head.

"One night," she told him in a low voice. "We can stay for one more night."

Peter swallowed and nodded. And though Wendy couldn't give a logical reason for it, she was glad.

THE SPRINGS that had been wound tightly throughout Wendy's entire body began to slowly unwind over the remainder of the day. No more apparitions appeared, and the morning was bright and clear. A brief thunderstorm had started and stopped just after Peter had come home from meeting with Tiger Lily, and the air smelled of sweet rain. Wendy filled her lungs with one deep breath and then another as she closed her eyes and breathed slowly, the fear of the night melting away in the brilliant sunlight that covered her face. Maybe this last day would be different. After all, she had helped to save Tiger Lily from Jay. And Peter had said that this particular celebration was meant to thank both her and Peter for their part.

Her stomach turned slightly, as it always did when she thought of the privateer who had been Peter's best friend. He'd been her friend, too, she'd thought. Perhaps, he'd meant to even be more. Not that he'd had the time to pursue any intentions he might have harbored. Still, she'd trusted him. He'd found her when Tinkerbell had abandoned her and tried to get her killed over the swamp, and he'd treated her injured ankle.

In the conversations they'd had during his stay in Neverland, he always made her feel appreciated and worthy of attention. But then he'd betrayed them all in his desperation to convince Peter to save his dying mother with the power of the Neverstar.

But no. Wendy shook her head to clear it of such morbid thoughts. As much as she had respected Jay—at least, before he'd betrayed them—and as much as she cared for Peter and Neverland, it was all going to be gone soon. She might as well enjoy herself tonight with the knowledge that she was about to kiss it all goodbye.

That was easier said than done, though. As Wendy helped Peter prepare the boys for the celebration on the fae's plateau, she had to bite back tears as she finally admitted to herself that this would be her last night with them. And not just the Lost Boys, but John and Michael as well.

"Wendy, what's wrong?" Curly lifted into the air so he could look Wendy in the eyes. "Your face is all red, and your eyes look really wet."

"Oh," Wendy laughed nervously as she tried to quickly dry her eyes on her sleeve, "I'm just thinking about how much I love all of you."

Curly looked at her as though she'd lost her mind. "That's weird. But all right." He shrugged. "Do you want to see me do a trick?"

The boys were far less excited about the celebration when Wendy announced that they would all have their baths. But Peter and Wendy somehow succeeded in scrubbing the little boys down, and Nibs and John were too horrified by the thought of being scrubbed down to even consider protesting. Wendy spent the majority of the time doing her best to live in the moment, pretending she wasn't leaving first thing in the morning, and for the most part, she was successful. She only faltered when their party drew close to the fae plateau, and her heart galloped in her chest.

"What's wrong?" Peter asked softly as the boys went whooping and screaming into the fae camp, terrorizing everyone there as they did.

Wendy let out a breathy laugh. "I'm not exactly popular here."

Peter chuckled. "Considering you helped save Tiger Lily, I think you've been forgiven."

"Forgiveness seemed forgotten last night."

"We're here for Tiger Lily to show her thanks. No one's going to try anything stupid in front of her." His fingers brushed hers, then pulled back. And though Wendy knew he was only being careful, the retreat still hurt a little inside.

He cleared his throat and gestured to the camp. "Shall we?"

Wendy forced a smile and nodded. Her smile became real, however, when she found the boys not wreaking havoc for once, but dancing as the fae played a kind of music she'd never heard before. Drums and voices and pipes mixed in a lovely cacophony, and it wasn't long before Wendy found herself tapping her feet to the rhythm as well.

Even better was the food. The fae had prepared foods from all over the world. Spices lit her mouth up like explosions, and combinations of sweet and salty tickled her tongue until she was sure her senses would be spoiled forever.

She couldn't be too comfortable, however. The looks she received from a number of the fae were cold and hard. There was one fae in particular that made Wendy tremble. His eyes glittered as they followed her, and his clothes were missing a chunk of fabric, strangely similar to the gray on the fabric Nana had torn from Wendy's nighttime visitor the night before. As if reading her thoughts, the fae gave her a cruel smile.

Wendy nearly fainted.

"What is it?"

Wendy jumped at the sound of Peter's voice only inches from her ear.

"That one." She nodded at the fae. "He's the one who attacked me."

Peter frowned. "You're sure?"

"Look at his shirt. See that tear?"

Peter's frown deepened. "I'm going to talk to Tiger Lily. You go ahead and wander. Just stay in the camp."

Wendy didn't have to be told twice. Thankfully, as Peter went in search of Tiger Lily, she wasn't too worried that the fae would come after her. He had joined those playing music, and his attention was already back on the music.

Just to put some space between them, however, Wendy decided to walk the outskirts of the encampment. She was leaving tomorrow, so she might as well see a little more of the camp in the dying light of the sun. She'd been to the fae camp numerous times, of course, but never had she gotten so close to the huts or seen their fire pits. She'd just leaned down to examine a colorful glass bead that was buried in the dirt when a familiar voice caught her attention.

"Why are we celebrating her? I thought we wanted to get rid of her!"

It was Tinkerbell's voice. Wendy would know that pout anywhere. She wanted to run so she wouldn't be seen, but the voice was coming from the hut she was standing beside. So she stood as still as she could and prayed they wouldn't notice her.

"We've already talked about this." It was Tiger Lily this time. "Peter knows he must fix the island. So you don't need to worry. We will deal with Wendy when the time comes, but not tonight."

Wendy tried and failed to quiet her breathing as she pressed herself against the hut's animal skin wall and made herself as small as possible. Thankfully, neither of the fae seemed aware that she'd been eavesdropping, and a few minutes later, she decided it was safe enough to follow them back to the main celebration. She watched Tiger Lily carefully after that, but the fae leader showed no sign of knowing she'd listened in on her conversation. That was good. What was even better was when Tiger Lily announced that it was time to gather, and the entire camp and its visitors came together in a circle around the central bonfire. Wendy's attacker didn't even glance at her as he seated himself on the other side. Still, Wendy shuddered and scooted closer to Peter.

"Storytime is the best!" Pop announced as he pressed himself against Wendy's other side.

"How do you know it's storytime?" Wendy asked.

"Oh, the fae like to complain." Curly rolled his eyes. "But they actually like it when we come to these things. And they always end with stories."

"You don't give us much choice," Tiger Lily said in a bemused voice as she took her place in the center of the great circle.

"See?" Curly grinned at Wendy. "They love us."

Peter sat between Wendy and Tinkerbell. He'd been strangely quiet all evening. Not that Wendy blamed him. Every second was bringing them closer to an end they couldn't deny. No matter how either of them felt about it, Wendy couldn't stay in Neverland forever.

"Tonight, we have guests." Tiger Lily spoke, gesturing to the Darlings. "So it's only right that they hear the story of our origins."

To Wendy's surprise, every boy leaned in and listened just as carefully as the fae. She glanced at Peter to see if this was normal for the boys, but he still seemed too lost in thought to notice.

"Back before the spark of Neverland was ever lit. Before we were sealed out of our own land, and before we chose this form," Tiger Lily said, gesturing to herself she spoke, "the fae were many. There were hundreds of us. We lived in a world where we were the artists, and the realm was our clay. We would cross the bridge from our world to the humans' and roam at will. We sought beauty, light, and power. Unhindered by flesh, we could take whatever shape we wished and return home with our discoveries and create what was most beautiful there."

Tiger Lily's dark eyes sparkled as she stared up into the starlit night, fierce and exquisite as if she were peering through a window into her old land. "We were glorious, and we made our home so as well. Nothing was too great. In less than a day, we could recreate what took the humans decades. And ours was always better. Bigger. More glorious in its magnificence."

Wendy shifted in her seat. Tiger Lily was speaking of a world full of the other. Wendy had always dreamed of seeing worlds full of other. Other cultures, foods, clothes, music, and mannerisms. But after her taste last night, she had no desire to partake in anything the fae's world had to offer.

"...first laid eyes on the Fortress of Destin."

Wendy snapped her attention back to Tiger Lily. Destin, King Everard and Queen Isabelle's land, was by far the most powerful kingdom in the western realm, but she knew less of their history than she liked.

"We'd seen the Fortress countless times. The bridge between worlds was in Destin itself. But we'd never experienced such pure, unadulterated..." Tiger Lily's eyes brightened. "Power."

Wendy shivered.

"Nearly five hundred years ago was when the Destinian king first heard that our people were near. So he invited us to tour his great Fortress to dine and speak with them." Her eyes darkened. "But when we were inside, they turned on us. The majority were slaughtered."

Wendy blinked. That was strange. Usually, the Destinian kings were known throughout the western realm as benevolent rulers and welcoming hosts. They often acted as negotiators and peace-keepers between other kingdoms at war.

"Those of us who escaped were doomed to wander the earth. We had no rest from the continuous change our bodies were forced to bear in their human forms. For if we didn't don them near humans, we were chased and hunted." Tiger Lily's voice fell to a near whisper. "We nearly gave up all hope. Until..." Her eyes brightened once again. "We found the Neverstar."

"We know what happened then!"

Everyone turned to see Tootles. He had risen from the ground and was standing with his fists on his hips and his chest puffed out. "Wendy, tell the story! Tell it!"

"I'm sure Tiger Lily would know better than me." Wendy let out a nervous laugh. "I only know what I was told."

"But you told it so well the other day!" Pop was standing now, too. "Oh, please tell it the way you did! And we'll help!"

Wendy looked desperately at Peter for help. She'd come here hoping to make peace with the fae, not to aggravate them more. But Peter was no help. Instead, he had a small smile on his face as he watched the boys.

"Tell it, Wendy," he said, turning so he could face them better. "Let the boys have a little fun, too. This is their story, as well."

Wendy laughed nervously. "It's hardly accurate."

"It's fine," Peter said, his voice oddly authoritative.

The fae did not look convinced, but since Peter left Wendy no choice, she took a deep breath and began.

"Once," she started slowly, "there was a little wolf named Slightly. And he lived in a magical land called Neverland."

Slightly stood up, leaving his perch on her lap, and began to hop around on all fours, howling like the other boys had taught him to. And nervous or not, Peter and Wendy laughed as well. It was a rich sound, breaking through the tension of the night. It also gave Wendy the courage to tell some more.

"Neverland had day and night. A warm, yellow sun to light the day."

Top stood up and hovered over them.

"And a soft, silver moon for the night."

This time, Pop went up and hovered by his brother.

And before long, all the boys were running or flying or moving about in some way. Nibs and John, who had somehow grown inseparable in the last few weeks, exchanged suspicious glances when it was their turn to jump into the story, but whether it was Peter's deep laugh or the smiles of the fae that were beginning to slip past their tight lips, they took their places as well.

Tiger Lily looked amused as well, but the way her eyes continued to flicker to Peter wasn't comforting. Tink appeared to be utterly miserable.

But, Wendy reminded herself, this was her last night in Neverland. She would do her best to put Tiger Lily and Tinkerbell out of her head. Tonight, she would focus on her boys. She glanced back to realize that Peter was grinning like he hadn't in days.

All of her boys, she amended silently to herself.

THE BOYS WERE STILL jubilant when they all arrived back at the treehouse that night. Even John and Nibs were laughing as the little boys flew in circles around Wendy and Peter.

"Boys," Wendy laughed, "it's time for sleep. It's far past your bedtime."

"We're not tired!" Top shouted. "We want a game!"

"Yes! A game!" the others chimed.

"Boys—" Wendy began.

"Oh, come on, Wendy!" Michael sulked. "We're leaving soon enough."

The boys all came to a stand-still and turned to stare.

Wendy froze, and she looked at Peter in a panic. They'd agreed to wait to tell the boys until the next day. Wendy wanted the boys to have the day to get used to the idea, but Peter had pushed for a later announcement, although Wendy was rather sure it was just another attempt at getting her to stay longer. Peter, however, was studying her with a strange expression and was no help at all.

"It's all right, Wendy." Curly came up and put his hand on Wendy's arm. "We know you're leaving."

Wendy's throat grew tight, and her eyes pricked. She did her best to force a smile, but it felt more like a grimace. "But how did you know?"

Curly gave her a sad smile. "There are six of us, not including Michael and John. That's a lot of ears."

Wendy choked on a laugh as a sob tore its way through her throat.

"But why are you leaving?" Tootles whimpered, coming up to cling to her other arm. Apparently, not everyone knew as much as Curly thought they did. "Did we do something bad?"

"No, my boys!" Wendy knelt down and wrapped her arms around them. "I'm only leaving because I want you all to be safe. And as long as I'm here, I'm not sure how safe you can be." She thought again of the fae's hands around her throat, and she shivered.

"That's stupid." Pop kicked a leg of the table. "You're the one keeping us safe."

"She means from the fae, you dummy," Nibs scoffed. "The fae don't want her here because they think she's too grown up. Who do you think attacked her the other night in her bed?" He turned and glared at Tinkerbell as she perched herself in the corner.

"What?" Tinkerbell sneered back. As Tinkerbell and Nibs

continued to make faces at each other, Top pulled on Wendy's skirt.

"Why can't we all just leave Neverland? You and Peter can take care of us in the Old World. We can all be together, and we won't even mind growing up. Will we boys?" He looked at the other boys.

Wendy's throat ached, and her voice threatened to break and betray her. Peter, who had been staring at Wendy throughout the conversation, opened his mouth, but it was Tinkerbell who spoke first.

"I'll tell you why. Because Neverland is tied to Peter's heart through the Neverstar. If Peter leaves Neverland any more, he knows he's going to grow up." She looked defiantly at Peter.

"It won't come to that," Peter said softly. "I have a plan."

"You always have a plan." Tinkerbell rolled her eyes and went on. "If Peter grows up, he'll break Neverland's first rule of no growing up. Neverland will die."

"Poo to Neverland." Curly sneered. "I've had enough of it. It's been around for too long anyway." He looked up trustingly at Wendy. "We don't need it if we have Peter and Wendy."

"And just where do you suggest *I* live?" Tinkerbell snarled.

"About that going to bed," Wendy interrupted loudly. "We still haven't come to a decision."

Tinkerbell rolled her eyes and darted up the tunnel to her bedroom, and Nibs didn't look convinced in the slightest. But Michael, easily distracted, jumped up and down. "So, do we get a game?" Slowly, the others began to clamor for a game once more as well. Wendy glanced at Peter, but he seemed more lost in thought than ever, that enigmatic expression on his face once more.

It was up to her. Wendy studied her boys for a moment longer, indecision roiling in her stomach. Her maternal instincts said they needed to go to bed. Her job was to take care of them, and taking care of them meant making sure they got enough sleep before the heartbreaking day they would face tomorrow.

But then again...how much longer did it really matter? She wouldn't be here to institute bedtime tomorrow night. Peter and his boys would go on doing what they'd always done. And even if these boys remembered her lessons, there would soon be new ones, and they wouldn't know or care whether Wendy had let their predecessors stay up late one night.

"Very well," she closed her eyes and shook her head. Still, she smiled indulgently when she opened them again. "What do you want to play?"

The boys erupted in an explosion of sound. Pop wanted to play Neverland again. Top wanted to be pirates. But when Tootles called out, "Let's play house!" the boys surprised Wendy with their overwhelming agreement.

The boys never agreed on anything.

"Play house with us," Curly said, his hand still on her arm.

Wendy forced a smile, though she felt like dissolving into a puddle of tears. Of all the games to play... "That's a new game we haven't played before," she managed to say, her voice breaking twice. "Tell me how it works."

Curly beamed. "Pretend you're cooking. The boys and I will be...us. You're the mother. And Peter's the father. And we'll all be a family like in the Old World."

It was all Wendy could do to swallow and nod faintly. She looked at Peter, but he was still staring. This time at the ceiling.

"Come, Peter." Top tugged on his arm. "Play with us."

"Yes, play!" The boys' voices went up in a chorus of pleas. When Peter finally did look at them, his eyes were rimmed red, but he nodded, and when he spoke, his voice was husky, deeper than Wendy had ever heard it.

"All right, we'll play."

The boys cheered and immediately began to run around. "Pretend to cook, Wendy! Like mothers do at home!"

Wendy laughed. "I don't have a stove!"

"Peter, make her a stove!"

"And pretend you're coming home from working!"

"Yes, and you've brought sweets!"

"All right, all right." Peter raised his arms above his head and went to the opposite side of the room, where Wendy's bed was. Just inches from Wendy's feet sprouted vines that wound themselves into something that looked very much like a real stove. When he was done, the boys pushed Peter to the opposite side of the room.

"We're ready now!" Pop yelled. "Slightly, you're the baby. Go sit by Wendy."

"I'm home." Peter pretended to close a door behind him. "And I brought treats."

The boys yipped with delight when he held out his arms, which actually held little candied cherries.

Wendy laughed. This game was so strange. It was so much like what she wanted deep down, even the part where the boys ran around, wreaking havoc in their joy. To her surprise, however, Peter's playing didn't end there. He continued walking as though he really had returned from a hard day's work. He came to stand behind her and wrapped a hand around her waist and placed his chin on her right shoulder. Even through her dress, she could feel his warmth, and Wendy momentarily forgot how to breathe.

"What's for dinner?" he asked, swaying her slightly from side to side where she was pretending to cook. "I'm famished."

The boys watched in delight.

"Tell him it's maple apples!" Tootles called out.

Wendy laughed and turned to face him. She expected him to pull away when she did, but instead, he only pulled her tighter against him, still swaying from side to side as though they were nearly in a dance.

"Turnips." She grinned at him. "And onions."

The boys let out a collective groan, but Peter smirked and drew her just a hair closer.

"Mm, my favorite."

The boys let out howls of laughter, but Wendy hardly noticed. He was looking at her lips now. She was sure of that. And as his mouth was about four inches from her face, it was very hard not to look at his.

"Did you miss me?" he asked softly.

"Always," Wendy breathed.

"Then why don't you stay?"

Wendy paused, caught off guard. Was this part of the game? Or did he mean something deeper? Better to play along and see.

"And how do you plan to keep me?" she asked, laughing breathlessly.

"For you," he said, leaning down until she could feel the heat of his face on hers, "I would do anything."

It was a stupid thing to do. She should have known she was playing with fire. Both of them were. The boys might have asked for such a game, but Peter and Wendy were the older ones. They knew better. And yet, as he held her close, still swaying in their half dance, his breath soft against her face, Wendy did what all sense screamed at her not to do as she leaned forward and brushed her lips across his.

The kiss was brief. So brief it could hardly count as a kiss. At least, that's what Wendy thought. But from the shock on the boys' faces, it seemed she had been wrong.

Peter pulled back to look at her, his eyes wide, his arms still wrapped around her.

What was he thinking? Was he angry? Or just surprised? He should definitely be angry, as he'd warned her before that kissing definitely wasn't allowed. And yet, he was still holding her close. And slowly, so slowly, he brought up one hand and brushed her cheek with the backs of his fingers. And to her even greater surprise, he began to lean down and put his lips against hers once more.

What broke the trance was neither the boys nor the sound of Wendy's heart trying to pound its way out of her chest. It was the horrified shriek of a little fae.

"Peter!"

Slowly, blinking as though coming out of a dream, Peter turned to face Tinkerbell. Her eyes were wide, and her mouth was open.

"Peter," she said again, whispering this time. "What have you done?"

CHAPTER 6
CHILD

Time had seemed to freeze as Peter's lips touched hers. For years, he had wondered what it would be like. But even all of his imaginings, as practiced as his mind was in seeing what wasn't there, couldn't have prepared him for the way his soul quaked in his chest. A chasm might as well have opened inside of him, deep and wide. But out of the abyss, there wasn't darkness or fear. Only...

Depth.

If Peter had longed for Wendy before, it was nothing compared to what he wanted now. In years past, as he'd sat listening to her stories through an open window, he'd hoped and prayed for the opportunity to talk to her. And the longer he'd stayed at that window, the more he'd wondered what it would be like to show her the crystal rainbow, or to take her to meet his boys, or to swim in the ocean with the dolphins.

But this was so much more. His chest was gripped with pain as he stared at her stupidly, unable to express the way his world had expanded exponentially in the blink of an eye. Before this moment, he'd wanted a piece of Wendy's life for himself, whatever he could get from the sliver of time the Maker would keep her on earth. He'd done his best not to think about tomorrow or the next day or the next. Living in the moment had been all he could do, hoping she would just stay a little longer.

But now? He wanted everything. Every laugh and every tear. Every memory and dream. Every day. Every night. Every touch and every sigh uttered by her soul. He wanted it all.

Still, even in his silent struggle, something nagged at the back of his mind telling him he couldn't have that, no matter how much he wanted it. For the life of him, he couldn't remember why. That is, until he looked at Tink.

The rage on Tink's face was enough to shake him from his stupor. And if her rage didn't, her actions did.

Tink was a blur of light as she crashed into Wendy, knocking her away from Peter and to the ground. Peter snapped out of his trance fast enough to grab the angry little fae and yank her off of Wendy before Tink could go at her a second time.

"Tink! Stop!" he yelled. The boys huddled at the edges of the room, looking wildly back and forth between Peter and Tink, and Peter briefly hoped John would choose to stay with his brother instead of throwing himself in front of Wendy as well. The last thing Peter needed was the responsibility of protecting two people instead of one.

"What have you done?" Tink cried again. "You idiots! You've ruined everything!"

Wendy, seeming unharmed, scrambled to her feet. "I..." She looked back and forth between Peter and the fae. "I didn't mean to. I swear. It just happened..." Her voice trailed off, and she looked nearly as shaken as Peter felt.

"This is why I didn't want her here!" Tink shouted. "I told you, Peter. I told you the first night we met her to leave her alone. And now she's ruined everything!" She glared at Wendy. "You little harlot. You couldn't keep your body to yourself. You had to throw yourself at him, and now you've done more harm than Jay ever could have!"

"I told you!" Wendy shouted back, her cheeks coloring. "I didn't do it on purpose!"

"You'll never be satisfied." Tink was sobbing now, seething through her tears. "You're trying to change everything when it was never broken. You wanted Peter to grow up. That's all you meant to do in coming here!"

"I didn't want it to happen! It just did!" Wendy pushed past Peter and stood nose-to-nose with the fae. Her blue eyes burned into Tink's as they glared at one another. "But you're too young to understand. And you never will because you're determined to be a perpetual child for the rest of eternity!"

"And you aren't?"

"No!" Wendy shouted, her voice echoing through the room.

Then it was silent, all except for the shrill sound of Slightly's crying. Peter stared in horror at Wendy, and so did the boys. A few seconds later, though Wendy still breathed heavily as though she'd been running, her fatal error seemed to dawn on her as well. She turned and met his gaze in horror as Tink began to smile.

"Tink, don't—" Peter began. But without a word, Tink flew over to the stump and left.

Peter wanted to cry.

CHAPTER 7
WHAT IF

J ohn and Nibs talked in whispers as Wendy and Peter hurried to put the boys to bed. Even in her fear and angst, it broke Wendy's heart the way their wide eyes searched hers for answers when she had none to give. She was supposed to have had one more night and morning with them. There would have been one more sunrise and a few more hours of laughter. But now that Tink had gone to tell Tiger Lily of Wendy's rash words, for that's precisely where Wendy was sure Tink had gone, Wendy knew it wasn't to be. As soon as the boys were well enough rested, Wendy would need to take them away from this place forever.

"Wendy," John said when she came to tell him good night, "maybe we should just go home now. Before they can do anything to get back at you."

"We all need sleep." Wendy forced a tired smile. "I'm not sure we'd even make it over the rainbow if we left right now. Especially Michael."

John's frown deepened, but he nodded and leaned back in his bed.

"I think John's right," Nibs said in a soft voice. "You don't know what they'll do to you."

"Peter will keep me safe." Wendy brushed his hair out of his eyes. "Now, go to sleep. I'll see you in the morning." It was probably a lie, but she couldn't bear to tell him otherwise.

"Peter," she called softly once all the boys were in bed. But Peter didn't answer. Instead, he sat in silence on her hammock, brushing the rose petals on her pillow lightly with the tips of his fingers. And though she wouldn't admit it for the world, it terrified her that he looked as scared as she felt.

"Peter," she said again, going to him. She knelt on the ground beside his knee. It was easier to stare at his foot than his face. "I want you to take me out tonight."

He blinked several times as if waking up, and slowly turned to look at her. "What for?" he asked.

"I know they're not going to let me stay," she said softly, aware that several of the boys behind her were listening. "But I just want one more night..." She let the words die, but there could be no mistaking the meaning behind them. One more night of Neverland.

One more night of Peter.

Looking ten years older than he had earlier that evening, Peter looked at the boys before nodding and taking her outstretched hand. He pulled them up through the stump and was about to seat her on a nearby boulder when a twig snapped.

Wendy nearly screamed but stopped when Moon Flower stepped out of the brush.

"I heard what happened," she said softly. "I thought you two probably needed a few minutes to say goodbye."

Wendy threw herself at the fae and wrapped her in a tight embrace. "Thank you," she whispered as her eyes misted over.

"I'll keep them safe." Moon Flower fixed her gaze on Peter now and sent him a glare. "Just don't do anything else foolish. Or Tiger Lily will have your girl ousted here and now."

Wendy expected Peter to make some sort of remark about

how she wouldn't dare. But to her shock and chagrin, he only nodded and lifted into the air, pulling Wendy along behind him.

They didn't go far. Peter paused near the foot of the rainbow and then brought them down into a little hollow that was surrounded by a thick copse of trees. They weren't far from the fae camp, but the hollow was deep and hidden by dense branches and made the treehouse feel a million miles away. The waning moon shone down on them through a single break in the ring of trees as Peter landed and seated himself on the lowest branch of the biggest tree. Wendy landed beside him.

For a long time, neither of them spoke. He only held her hand in his and rubbed the backs of her knuckles with his fingertips.

How had it come to this? They'd been so careful. There was so much Wendy wanted to do and say that she'd held back, and it had seemed like Peter had felt the same way. And in one stupid breath, she'd ruined it all.

But no, that wasn't true either. This trouble had started the moment Wendy had first set foot in Neverland. Almost as if she wasn't supposed to be there at all.

"Let's play a game," she blurted, her throat so tight the words hurt to say.

His gaze moved up to hers, and his eyebrows rose. "A game?"

She nodded and tried to smile. "We both know I won't be here in the morning. Besides," she let out a strained chuckle, "children play games. That ought to be safe enough for your rules."

Peter sighed but nodded. "Very well. What game would you like to play?"

Wendy looked up at the stars as they twinkled above, as if all were right with the world, and there was no civil war in Ashland, and Wendy's oldest dream wasn't about to die forever. "Let's play the what-if game."

Peter let out a gusty breath. "Wendy—"

"Please, Peter." She took his fist in hers and held it close. "If I'm about to lose you forever, at least give me this."

Peter winced when she said forever, but after a moment, his shoulders drooped. "Very well. What do you want to know?"

"What would happen if Neverland ceased to be today? What would you do?" She forced a laugh. "Would wheat farming be a top priority?"

To her surprise, Peter gently lifted the necklace he'd given her and studied the stone, the tips of his fingers brushing the hollow of her neck as he did.

"If Neverland were to disappear tomorrow," he said softly, "I would take you to the nearest holy man I could find. I'd have him marry us on the spot."

Wendy's heart was racing so fast it pounded in her ears. She'd known there was something between them, something beyond the friendship he tried so hard to tout. But she had, apparently, misunderstood the depth to which his affections ran.

He reached up and took her jaw gently in his hand and turned her face toward his. His green eyes pierced hers and trapped her in their gaze. "I'd throw myself before your father and beg his forgiveness for stealing his children away from him."

"You didn't steal me." Wendy sat up a little straighter. "And you saved me from Reuben."

Peter laughed softly. "I never said I was wrong. I only said I'd beg his forgiveness."

"Why?" Wendy breathed.

"Because you would never be happy anywhere but that farm. And if I wanted to get a job with your father, I'd probably need his forgiveness first." He tapped her nose. "Now, stop interrupting and let me finish."

Wendy blushed.

"We'd take all the boys with us and build a house somewhere

on your father's land with twenty rooms and the biggest kitchen you ever saw."

"Twenty?" Wendy let out a strangled laugh. "Even with my brothers, there are only eight."

Peter arched an eyebrow. "And how do you know we wouldn't find any more along the way?" He wrapped a hand around Wendy's waist and drew her close so she was leaning into him.

Funny, if Reuben had tried this, despite his impressive size and stature, not to mention his incredible good looks, Wendy knew deep down that she would have felt uncomfortable, like she didn't belong. But here in Peter's arms, as she leaned her head on his shoulder and her own shoulder touched his side, she felt no intimidation. She knew without a doubt that he wouldn't try to force her to do anything against her conscience, nor would he pressure her to change what she believed was right.

Even if it meant leaving him.

"I would give you as many beautiful babies as you wanted," he whispered, resting his forehead against her head, his hand tightening slightly around her waist.

Wendy felt one tear roll down her face. Then another. She'd tried to keep herself from indulging in such fantasies because she knew they could never be. But having a family with Peter, the kind with Lost Boys and their own children...

Please, she pleaded silently with the Maker as the tears continued to fall. *I don't know how. Just...please.*

"And you would be the best mother ever to walk the world," Peter continued. "You'd tell them stories every night before we tucked them in. And I'd work so hard you'd have all the paper in the world to write those stories down so no one would forget."

Something wet landed on Wendy's left arm, but it wasn't one of her tears. She pulled back slightly to find tears rolling steadily down Peter's face as well.

"We'd grow old together," he said, his voice breaking in the middle. "We'd look at all the beautiful sunsets and imagine up stories about their magic. And when the Maker called me home, I'd die in your arms the happiest man that ever lived."

A sob escaped Wendy's chest. Then another. The flood that had been dammed up by the rules of Neverland and her fear of growing up broke loose as she wept into Peter's shirt, clutching it as she covered it in tears. He cried, too, though his pain was quieter than hers.

They sat that way, holding one another and crying until there were no more tears within them. Then she leaned limply against him, and he held her close until the night was too dark to even guess at the hour.

Wendy had hoped to spend the night there, soaking it all up so it would be too much in her heart for the memory to ever die. But before the sky began to gray, the earth began to rumble.

"Peter?" she asked, but he shook his head.

"It should be over in a moment."

It wasn't over in a moment, though. Unlike the other tremors they'd grown used to on the island, this one quaked harder than she'd ever felt it. And it didn't stop.

"What's going on?" she whimpered, clinging to him to keep from falling off the tree. He lifted them off the branch and up above the treetops. As they watched, the island below them continued to shake. Then, to their left, an explosive cracking sound interrupted the rumbles of the tremors. Wendy's mouth fell open as she looked up at the crystal rainbow and watched it crack in half.

CHAPTER 8
PROBLEM

They were still staring in horror at the broken rainbow when a noise to their right made them turn, and Tinkerbell flew through the branches.

"Tiger Lily has summoned you," she said, keeping her eyes on Wendy. Not once did they flick to Peter. "Everyone's waiting in the camp."

Wendy turned to Peter. Surely he didn't mean to take her there. Not in the wee hours of the morning with the rainbow looking as though it might topple at any moment. But instead of arguing, he only nodded to the ground, and Wendy was reminded of his reaction to Moon Flower's words only hours before.

She trembled but allowed him to lead her up out of the trees to the north end of the island. He wouldn't let the fae hurt her. He was the one with the power, after all.

Wasn't he?

Wendy's stomach clenched as the circle of fae came into view. Wendy realized as they descended that there were more fae than had even been there the night before. Peter's answer, when she'd once asked him how many there were in total, had been four dozen. At the time, that hadn't felt like a great deal, particularly as

Wendy hardly ever saw more than twenty together at a time. But now, as they neared the circle gathered around the fire, she could see that forty-eight fae were far from a few.

They landed in the center of the circle, close enough to the bonfire for Wendy to feel its heat.

"Wendy Darling." Tiger Lily stood. Instead of her usual simple braid, she wore a headdress. It was made of bone-covered leather stretched over what looked like the skull of some great cat. Fangs reached out toward Wendy, and the empty eyes seemed to stare down at her from atop Tiger Lily's head. She also held a staff of wood, carved with figurines and dotted with pieces of stone and what looked like more bone sticking out from its sides.

"You have broken one of Neverland's most sacred laws," Tiger Lily continued, "and the fae collective has condemned you."

And though Wendy knew it was probably foolish to challenge the fae, she couldn't quite let it go without a fight. Of course, she already knew she'd be leaving. But the misery on Peter's face was more than she could bear in silence.

"And, pray tell, what am I guilty of?"

The firelight's reflection seemed to dance in Tiger Lily's eyes. "You are guilty of growing up."

Wendy lifted her chin. "And what proof have you that this has been my doing? Jay was here for weeks. How do you know for certain that this isn't the repercussions of having a shipful of men on and off your shores?"

Tiger Lily's mouth tightened. "Was tonight's expression too subtle for you?" She indicated to the rainbow.

Well, she did have Wendy there. It hardly seemed a coincidence that the rainbow had broken just hours after Wendy had kissed Peter.

"I'm leaving in the morning." She lifted her chin proudly. "It's already been decided. Even the Lost Boys know I'm going."

"No." Tiger Lily shook her head. "You're leaving now."

Wendy turned back to look at Peter to see his reaction. But instead of the annoyance or anger that she expected to find, she saw only listlessness. Or rather, the death of hope. And why shouldn't he feel hopeless? After all, Wendy would mourn the loss of the soul who had set her free. Life would be hard. She would miss her family and friends and everything she knew and loved. She would meet her challenges, though. She would rise to find her path, as her best friend, Moira, had once said.

For Peter, though? This was life. Taking in homeless boys as he danced around the bidding of the fae. And though Neverland was a fun adventure to visit and enjoy, Wendy couldn't imagine life repeating itself forever. At least, until he went into the Old World enough to no longer be able to deny his manhood. Or would the fae even grant him that freedom after this? Based on what Tink had said, Wendy guessed not.

A seething, hot rage began to simmer in Wendy's stomach as Tiger Lily spoke again.

"Your first charge will result in your immediate expulsion from Neverland. And you will never come back."

"And my second?" Wendy challenged. She felt a tug on her elbow and looked back at Peter.

"Wendy," he whispered. "Don't."

She turned back to Tiger Lily. "And my second?"

Tiger Lily's face hardened into a sneer. "If Neverland suffers irreparable damage and the star dies, then you will feel the wrath of the fae from the day this world falls until the day you die."

Wendy should be frightened, particularly considering her last experience with the fae in their natural form. But resentment at the way they had treated Peter and the way they planned to treat him seemed to strip her of all common sense and self-preservation. Because instead of bowing out, as she could feel Peter silently begging her to do as he tugged on her arm, indignation boiled over. She took a step forward and raised her voice for all to hear.

"Who are you," she demanded, "that you have the right to dictate a boy's entire life, stretching it over eons until the world ends or you simply grow too bored to continue?"

The ring of fae was silent.

"Pardon me?" Tiger Lily finally said in a low, terrible voice. But Wendy was too incensed to take heed.

"You may think you have some sort of righteous hold on this place." Wendy gestured to the world around then. Then she pointed up to the top of the mountain. "To the power of the star. But I've heard and seen enough to know that you have no such claim."

"I wouldn't—" Tiger Lily began, but Wendy continued.

"You have lied to and manipulated Peter his whole life! You have required him to grant you access to anyone he might wish to love or be loved by. You've denied him the gifts of change and human dignity for your own selfish gain!"

"Wendy!" Peter hissed, but Wendy yanked her arm free of his hand and closed the distance between herself and Tiger Lily until they were face-to-face.

"You," she spat, "are too cowardly to face death. So you suck the life from others so that you may live."

"And that," Tiger Lily snapped, "is enough." She began to raise the staff, but before Wendy had the chance to see what she wished to do with it, Peter had whisked her up into the air.

"I'll take care of the problem, Tiger Lily," he said, his voice flat as if he hadn't slept in a week.

Wendy turned to face him. The problem?

"Do," Tiger Lily called up to them. "Or I will have to do so myself."

CHAPTER 9
THAT MAN

S top it!" Wendy tried to yank her arm away from him. "I'm not finished!"

"Wendy, think of your brothers," he whispered in her ear.

Wendy froze, allowing Peter to tow her away, not stopping until they reached a small clearing on the mountain not far from the Neverstar's cave.

"Why did you just sit there?" Wendy cried as soon as he had put her down. "Why do you allow them to manipulate you like that?"

Peter ran a hand through his hair and sighed. "It's not that simple."

"It is exactly that simple!" Wendy went to him and grabbed his arms, forcing him to face her. "You owe them *nothing*! You've given them a life more than five times what they ought to have had. You've protected and provided for them. And for what?"

Peter plucked a nearby flower and twirled it in his fingers. "Wendy—"

"Run away with me!" Wendy pulled him to a standing position. "We'll bring the boys with us! Leave this place behind, and let's start somewhere new!" Her voice dropped to a whisper. "They don't own you."

Peter just stared at her. There was a longing in his eyes, and sorrow of unimaginable proportions. His hands moved to her waist, and he pulled her against him. Hope and thrill flared in her blood as she began to imagine all that could be if he would just keep her in his arms and never let go. He closed his eyes and rested his head against hers.

"I'm sorry, Wendy. I can't."

Wendy sprang back, fighting the urge to throw up as disappointment threatened to crush her.

"You're not the man I thought you were," she spat, doing her best not to cry.

His jaw hardened. "Because I can't be a man at all, Wendy."

"But you could be!"

"Look," he shouted, pulling her close once again and glaring down at her. "I need you to know something here and now. I cannot leave Neverland. What part of that don't you understand?"

Wendy opened her mouth, but no words came out.

"Furthermore," he continued, "I can swear to you now that I will never marry you. Even if you stayed in Neverland, it never would have worked. So you need to get that idea out of your pretty little head now. No matter how much scheming and plotting and hoping you indulge in, I will never be yours." His green eyes darkened. "You knew that when you came here, so I'm not sure what you think will change now."

Wendy tried to speak, but her words were little more than a choking sob. "Then why did you even bother?"

Before she could continue, though, he wound his left arm around her back and held the flower he'd plucked up to her nose.

And the world faded away.

CHAPTER 10
CRY

P eter felt something die inside of him as Wendy's head hit his shoulder. Breaking her had never been part of the plan.

Once upon a time, he'd been sure that the horrible man Wendy's parents had picked for her would break her. Or maybe it would have been slow, the drawn-out death of the spirit he loved so much. But in his attempt to steal her away for himself, he'd done something far worse. He'd seen it in her eyes as he'd sworn he would never marry her. The Wendy he'd known and...if he was honest with himself, had come to love, would never be his again.

He flew back to Ashland as slowly as he could, but he crossed the barrier between lands far too soon. Tink had been right when she'd said that any more significant time spent here would make him a full-fledged adult. He had to do this quickly before he gained any more time than he had to. With each breath he took, he inhaled the smell of her hair and drank in the warmth of her form curled against him. Each breath was one less that she would be in his life.

When she had asked him for the what-if game, she couldn't have known what kind of pain had filled his chest. She was asking him to articulate everything he could never have. Because if he gave her what she wanted, heart and soul, she and her brothers would never even make it back to the farm. Tiger Lily wouldn't take kindly to losing Neverland, and Peter wouldn't be able to protect them.

The window to the Darlings' nursery was still open when he arrived at the farm. This was strange, as Wendy's father was a man who valued his security. But then, he peeked inside to find Wendy's parents stretched out on Wendy's and John's beds. As if he didn't feel guilty enough already. The children had been gone for weeks, and their parents were still sleeping in the nursery, as if being there might bring them back. Well, Peter thought as he gazed down at Wendy's sleeping face, at least they'd get one wish granted. Hopefully, he could bring the boys in the morning. Now, in the peaceful gray of the early morning, he regretted not stopping for the boys on his way back. But the way Tiger Lily had looked at Wendy had chilled him to the bone, and at first, all he'd been able to think about was getting her out of Neverland.

Peter inched the window farther open until he could fly in silently. Then, staying an inch off the ground so he wouldn't make a sound, he laid her gently on Michael's bed.

An angry voice inside his head told him to kiss her. She'd already done it not once but twice. The damage was done. What would it hurt to take one more as a memento?

But no. Whether or not he meant well in doing it, he'd broken her heart. It wouldn't be right to steal a kiss without her permission.

Oh, how he wanted to, though.

In fact, he'd better make sure she didn't hold on to any hope. Fighting back nausea, he dug the thimble she'd given him out of his pocket and placed it in her palm. As he did, his eyes fell upon the green necklace he'd given her.

He should take that with him. As long as she had it, he knew she would miss him. Better to cut all ties. Break everything at once so the pain of healing could begin. And yet, as his hand hovered above her, he couldn't do it. Whether it was for pride or fear, he couldn't say. Pride because she'd treasured that necklace, and giving it to her had made him feel like...

Well, like a man.

And fear. Fear because he knew that one day, when Neverland did fall, whether that was now or five centuries down the road, he wanted someone to have something to remember him by. And if anyone would remember his existence, it would be Wendy.

Leaving the necklace where it was and hating himself for it, Peter closed his eyes and headed for Neverland.

THE SKY WAS A LIGHTER gray when Peter got back to the treehouse, passing three fae watchmen in the process. Sent by Tiger Lily, he was sure, to confirm he'd obeyed.

Not that he cared right now. A new wave of dread washed over him as he neared the stump only to hear Nana's frantic barking from the little rose cottage that still stood mockingly in its clearing. He'd somehow forgotten Nana. Hopefully, he could get Wendy's dog back with her brothers before the Wasaaca flower released her from its clutches. The last thing she needed after all he'd put her through was to be separated from her beloved dog.

"I kept her locked up because she was going crazy." Tink flitted down from the low branch of a tree to stand before him demurely.

Peter glowered at her until she looked down at the ground. "I tried to warn you," she whispered. "But you wouldn't listen."

"Tink—"

"It was for the island, Peter. And my people." She peeked up at him through wet lashes. "And you."

"I hope you know," Peter said with as much control as his exhausted mind could muster, "that I will never trust you like that again."

"But—"

"Never again." Peter straightened his shoulders and finished the walk to the treehouse.

"She says she's keeping the boys here," she called out tearfully behind him.

That got him to turn around.

"What did you say?"

Tink hunched down even more under his wrathful gaze. "She says when she knows the island is truly healing, she'll let them go home."

Peter stared at her for a long time but said nothing. Eventually, he silently resumed his walk to the stump. But in his head, he let out a scream of frustration. Would the attacks never end? Not only had Wendy been banished, but Peter, Michael, and Nana were now hostages. Actually, Peter had a feeling they all were.

To make matters worse, before his feet even touched the treehouse floor, he found John and Nibs awake and waiting for him as the little boys still slept.

"Where's my sister?" John asked.

Peter paused. "I had to send her home," he finally said quietly, hoping not to wake the little boys yet.

Nibs gaped, and John's eyebrows shot up. "You did what?" he sputtered.

Peter glanced back at Slightly's crib. The little boy was stirring already. "Tiger Lily threatened Wendy last night. She made it very clear that she would hurt your sister if I didn't do what she wanted."

"The blazes she would!" John snapped. "You're Peter Pan! You hold the power of the Neverstar!"

Peter groaned, kicking himself mentally once again for not remembering to bring the boys along with him. But he'd never seen Tiger Lily so incensed, and in the moment, had lost track of all concern except keeping Wendy alive.

"Yes, I do have the star," Peter whispered. "But you don't understand how powerful the fae are. Even if we shrugged off all of Neverland right now and let the star die of old age, I wouldn't be able to protect you. Or her." John opened his mouth, but Peter cut him off. "And just think. Even if I did dismantle the world to protect Wendy, would she have wanted you and Michael to be hurt in the process?"

John glared up at him.

"Well," Peter prodded. "Would she?"

John gazed over his shoulder at Michael's bed for a long moment. "No," he finally muttered. But then he crossed his arms and puffed his chest out. "But wait until I get the chance to get my hands on the fae."

"You won't do anything of the kind."

"But—"

"Because if you don't want Tiger Lily to haunt and torment your family every waking moment for the rest of their lives, you're going to wait patiently until I can fix this and take you back safely." Peter glowered down at him. "Do you understand?"

Nibs nudged John, and John huffed. "Fine. But just so you know, I blame all of this on you." With that, he walked over to Michael's bed and knelt beside him.

If only he knew how much Peter blamed himself, too.

Peter's body hurt as he lowered himself slowly into his hammock. But as he closed his eyes, he felt small hands on his face. Raising his head, he found himself staring into the bright brown eyes of Slightly.

While the fae were learning they could change form once again, the little boy must have grown tall enough to crawl out of his crib. Peter rubbed his eyes. An escaping toddler was just what he needed right now.

"Happy." Slightly held out his blanket to Peter. Peter blinked at it a few times before realizing he didn't recognize it.

"Where did you get this?" he asked, more to himself than the child. But Slightly just held it out again. When Peter saw the star stitched into the side, he recalled where he'd seen the blanket before. Slightly's "happy blanket," Wendy had called it as she'd sewn the thing together. But Peter had been so tired when she'd finished it, he'd hardly noticed.

"Happy," Slightly repeated. This time, he pressed the blanket against Peter's face, where the tears had begun to roll down again. "Make happy."

Peter snatched Slightly up in his arms and pulled him close, praying that the little boy wouldn't see him cry.

CHAPTER 11
DONE

Wendy awoke to the smell of bacon the next morning. Gerty was clinking the pots and pans loudly, and there was a hum of voices outside her door. Without opening her eyes, Wendy strained to hear what they were saying.

"...let her be," her mother said. "If she's that tired, perhaps she's sick. Pushing her will only delay her telling us even more!"

"But we need to know about the boys!" her father replied.

The boys. Why did they need to know about the boys? Wendy groaned and rubbed her eyes. It was unusual for Michael and John to sleep this long. She could already tell how late it was by how warm the sun was on her skin through the window. When she finally pried her eyes open to squint at Michael's bed, panic hit her like the ground when falling from a horse. She was in Michael's bed. But where was Michael? She twisted so fast she nearly hurt herself to look at John's bed. Which was empty as well.

Where were the boys?

Wendy's brain felt heavy, like a dense fog had settled between her ears. She slowly sat up and tried to remember just why she was so late to rise as well. What was happening?

Wendy's door opened, and her parents peeked through. Their eyes widened, and what looked like tears shone in the corner of her mother's eyes. When they saw that she was awake, however, both descended on her like rain.

"Wendy?" her mother said, caressing her face like she was a child again. "How are you feeling?"

"Um...tired." Wendy rubbed her eyes again and blinked at her parents. "Why?"

"You wouldn't wake up." Her father's voice was tight. He sat on the other side of the bed. "We tried several times after we found you."

Found her? "Where was I?"

Her parents looked at each other, and her mother's mouth fell open.

"You..." Her mother swallowed. "You don't remember? Wendy, you've been gone for seven weeks!"

Wendy froze. Seven weeks. But where...Ugh. Her head was still fuzzy. Why did she feel like she'd taken one of her aunt's old nasty sleeping draughts?

"Where did you get that necklace?" her father asked, pointing at her neck. Wendy looked down to find a green gem hanging from a leather cord around her neck. She frowned as she reached up to touch it. But the moment her fingers hit the smooth green stone, a spark lit in the back of her head, and it set her entire mind on fire with memories that burned holes through the fog and ate through the veil that was blocking her thoughts.

Green like Neverland.

Wendy groaned and held her head in both hands as the last two months came back to her, everything from leaving her parents behind to Peter putting that blasted Wasaaca flower in front of her nose. No wonder she felt as terrible as she did. Then she realized she was holding yet another item in one of her hands. A silver thimble. Why was that there?

"Wendy," her father said, putting a hand gently on her cheek, "where are the boys?"

Wendy was out of the bed in an instant, and ran to the window as if Peter might still be there. He wasn't, of course. Instead, she looked down at the farm, bathed in the late morning sun. Panic made her bones feel hollow as she thought back to how she left them behind to say goodbye to Peter. And on its heels was a burning shame. Wendy put the thimble on the dresser and backed away from it, as though it were a sin she could leave behind.

"Neverland," she whispered, turning slowly back to her parents. "The boys are still in Neverland."

WENDY'S MOTHER fell back onto the bed, and her father gripped the bedpost until his hands turned white.

"Neverland?" he whispered. "You were actually in...It exists?" He looked at his wife. "But Amos..."

"Moira was right," her mother breathed.

"Amos told the truth." Wendy gave him a sad smile. "I'm just sorry I ever tried to find out." And she was. If she hadn't been so rash, her brothers would be safe. They would still be here on the farm, helping her father and teasing her to death. Their safety would have been worth every agonizing second of any marriage to Reuben.

"I'm afraid to ask," her mother said breathlessly, "but who took you to Neverland?"

Wendy gave a hard laugh. "Peter Pan, of course." Back when she'd been convinced he was strong enough to move on and let go of the past. All he needed was some help, she'd told herself. If he had a shoulder to lean on, he would have the strength to let go of the fae and move beyond them. He'd saved her, and she could save him.

But he was too much a boy. And that was how it would always be. Instinctively, Wendy looked to Nana's corner, where she slept with her blanket beside Wendy's bed. Another wave of regret washed over her as she realized her best friend had been left behind as well.

"Are the boys safe?" her father asked, seeming to recover himself enough to stand up straight.

Wendy frowned at the window. "I think so. For now, at least. But not for long." She looked back at her parents, determination gathering in her bones. "I have to go back." Then something dawned on her that she'd missed before. "You said Moira was right. How did Moira know we went to Neverland?"

Her parents looked at each other. "We searched all we could. The entire town was looking. We went down every road out, covered every square foot of the fields." Her father swallowed. "But when Moira heard that you flew out the *window*," he said the word as though it was a shamefully scandalous admission, "she immediately insisted that you'd flown away to Neverland." He rubbed the back of his neck and shook his head slowly. "We just couldn't..." His voice trailed off.

"How do we get the boys back?" her mother, always the practical one, asked in a thin voice. "And please tell me it doesn't involve sending you there."

Wendy gave her mother a sad smile. "Like I said, I have to go back." Then she gasped and looked down at her clothes. "Father, I need you to leave."

"Why?"

"Because I need to change so I can shake all the stardust out of my clothes and hair, so I have as much as possible to try to get back with." Wendy doubted there would be enough. And even if there was, she didn't know how to get past the barrier. Jay did, but he'd been in and out with Peter lots of times. Still, she wasn't about to let what little she could find go to waste. She had to do something.

After her father had gone, walking out of the room as though he were in a dream, Wendy's mother told her what had happened since she'd gone, as Wendy shook everything from her hair to her clothes out over the bed she'd been sleeping on.

"After you left and the searches were given up on, your father and I threw ourselves into research." Her mother drew in a shuddering breath. "We knew we hadn't imagined seeing you fly out the window. And yet..." She looked at Wendy and shrugged. "What could we say that wouldn't make us sound crazy? We were afraid if people knew how you'd been taken, they would stop looking, and no one would help us."

"Then how did Moira find out?" Wendy took off her necklace and tossed it onto the blanket. She'd throw it away if she weren't afraid it might have more dust stuck to it.

"You know Moira. She wouldn't leave us alone until she knew all the details. Then she ran off and said something about asking her husband..." She looked at Wendy with questioning eyes, but Wendy could only shrug. So her mother sighed and resumed her story. "Anyhow, we did everything we could think of. We even went to talk to Old Amos, but he was so upset when he heard that you were missing that we couldn't get anything out of him, and he disappeared the next day. No one's seen him since."

Wendy paused. That didn't sound like Amos at all. She gave her old clothes one more shake over the bedspread then pulled on a new dress to replace them. A pathetic smattering of fine silver dust twinkled here and there on the bedspread, but Wendy already doubted it would be enough to get back, even if she knew how.

"Mother," she sighed and let her shoulders droop. "I can't tell you how sorry I am. For running away and for taking the boys with me. Then for staying away—"

Before she could finish, she was wrapped in her mother's arms again, the way she hadn't been since she was a little girl. And she found herself sobbing into her mother's sleeve as her mother held her there and stroked her head.

"Your father and I have begged the Maker's forgiveness for trying to push you into an unhappy marriage. The magistrate took another wife, not a fortnight after you were gone, and since then, we've seen the kind of man he really is."

Wendy realized her mother was trembling, too.

"We would have hated ourselves if you were ever yoked to that kind of man. We only wish we'd trusted your judgment and not been so desperate..." She pulled back and drew in a shaky breath. "Can you forgive us? If we'd listened—"

"That doesn't matter." Wendy gave her mother a squeeze and began to pull on her shoes. "I know you were only trying to do what you thought was best. What matters now is getting the boys back. And I'm not going to stop until I do."

After helping her gather a pathetic amount of dust from the bed cover and placing it in a small glass bottle the size of Wendy's thumb, her mother left to go get her some breakfast. Exhausted, Wendy fell back into the bed and stared up at the tree branches through the window. Her head still pulsed with the remnants of the Wasaaca flower.

As she'd been speaking with her parents about the evils of Reuben, Peter's words had come back to her as well, all the things they would never do.

Part of her wanted to mourn. When he'd first uttered the words, they'd nearly crushed her with their finality and lack of remorse. But now she was beyond any fickle promises of a boy. She was done playing pretend. Wendy was going to defy the fae and get her brothers back. And she was going to let Peter reap what he had sown.

CHAPTER 12
WHAT THEN

As soon as Wendy was dressed and fed, as her mother refused to believe that Wendy could have possibly been well-fed while she was in Neverland, Wendy and her father went outside to ready their horses. They would go to Moira first. Then Wendy would chase every possible path that crossed her mind. Anything to get them back.

As if nature wished to emphasize her many, many mistakes, the silence was nearly overwhelming when she stepped outside. There was no sound of little paws trotting beside her as she saddled her horse, only the crunch of her own boots on the gravel. For a moment, she laid her head against her horse's neck, closing her eyes and breathing in deeply.

"I'm glad you're here, girl," she said, rubbing the horse. "I've managed to lose nearly everyone else."

But there wasn't much time for self-pity. Wendy sighed and mounted her horse and then joined her father on the main road.

For a long time, they were silent. Wendy's father kept sending her long glances, but Wendy stared straight ahead. She'd forgiven her mother. And she was convinced that she'd forgiven her father, too. But there was no way in the world she was ready to talk to him about what had happened. The words he'd said, and the things he'd done...

No. When her brothers and dog were home, and her mind was less cluttered by all the "what ifs," then maybe she would be ready to talk. And the Wasaaca flower. If her head ever cleared of its effects, it would be a miracle.

"You would think she would have contacted us by now if she'd found something." Wendy's father finally broke the silence as they reached the edge of town.

"Moira's nothing if not diligent," Wendy said, trying to ignore the stares and exclamations rising up from the people who saw them. Of course, they would cause a scene. She and her brothers had been declared all but dead for nearly two months, and here she was again, riding with her father as though nothing had happened. "She might have learned something but didn't want to tell you until she could confirm it was true," Wendy continued in a lower voice. At least, that's what she was banking on. Her mother's story of Moira's reaction gave her hope that Moira knew something. It was a thin hope, but as Wendy needed something to cling to right now, it would have to do.

"And what do we tell them?" he asked in a low voice, keeping his eyes forward.

Wendy swallowed. Usually, her father was the one in charge. He always knew what to do and say. Even if Wendy didn't always necessarily agree, her father was steadfast and confident. But ever since the word Neverland had crossed his lips that morning, he'd seemed a shell of his former self. But Wendy's head was still too fogged up from the sleeping flower to figure out what to do about it.

"Tell them nothing for now," she replied quietly as they turned a corner. "I'll be leaving again, eventually, and we can't have anyone interfering."

Her father nodded and then gestured at the cottage on the

corner. He and Wendy dismounted and tied their reins to the garden fence. A goat munched on grass in the corner, and several chickens scurried away, squawking as Wendy and her father walked to the door. Several people outside the yard stopped and stared, and a few called out, but Wendy just straightened her shoulders and knocked on the door.

Several moments later, the door opened, and Moira was there, drying her hands on her apron. When she saw Wendy, her pretty pale face went even whiter than usual.

"Moira," Wendy began, "I'm sorry—"

But she didn't get any further into her apology because Moira had yanked her inside and clung to her as she began to sob.

"I'll, um...go see what Alim is about." Wendy's father removed his hat and strode back out. He had always been wonderful when Wendy or her mother cried. But multiple women blubbering at once filled him with terror.

Wendy just hugged her friend back as the potency of loneliness hit her like a horse's kick. She'd missed Moira in Neverland, but apparently, she'd been lying to herself about how deep her longing went.

"When you didn't come home from Neverland, I thought something could be wrong." Moira hiccuped into Wendy's shoulder. "I knew you might be gone for a few weeks, but I knew you would never leave your parents that long. Something had to be wrong."

Guilt gnawed at Wendy's stomach and made her feel nauseated. Every day she'd procrastinated in Neverland was a day of torment for her parents and her friends. Each day had also been one more day she could have taken her brothers and come home, and they wouldn't be in danger.

"I'm sorry, Moira," she whispered, hugging her friend more tightly.

Moira pulled away and dried her tears with her apron. "I'm

sorry," she shuddered. "Let me bring you to the parlor. We can talk there." She took Wendy by the hand and led her out of the entry to a small, cozy room with two red, slightly faded stuffed sofas and a table. It was a nice house. Small but clean and well furnished. It seemed Alim had, in spite of Wendy's fears, actually grown up. Wendy wished she could say the same for herself.

Moira led Wendy to the first sofa then ran back out to grab a tray of tea and biscuits. When they were seated again, Wendy took a deep breath.

"My parents said you seemed like you knew something when you heard that we had flown out the window." She leaned forward. "They said you knew we had gone to Neverland. And that you had said something about asking your husband...something?" Ugh. If only she could get the fog out of her head. If she ever saw Peter again, she would tell him what she really thought of his abominable sleeping flower.

Moira frowned. "Alim has lots of stories he learns when he travels with his father to gather trade. I was hoping he'd heard something, so I ran to ask him."

"What did you find?" Wendy asked.

Moira opened her mouth, then paused. "Wendy, what's wrong?"

Wendy looked at her tea. "My brothers are still in Neverland. And I have to get them out."

Moira choked and sputtered as she set her tea down. "I think," she coughed, "I'm going to need you to go back to the beginning."

So Wendy told her everything. From Peter's first appearance to her father's ultimatum to Peter's invitation to Neverland.

Well, perhaps not everything. When it came time to talk about Wendy's desire to return, she left some particulars out and focused on her inability to form a cohesive plan for what to do when she returned. But her silence on the subject didn't seem to fool her friend.

"You're leaving something out." Moira raised one eyebrow delicately as she poured cream into her tea.

Wendy bit into a biscuit.

Moira nodded to herself. "That's what I thought. You fell in love with Peter Pan." Moira had never been one to mince words.

"That doesn't matter now." Wendy cleared her throat and sat straighter. "What matters is getting my brothers back."

"What happened?" Moira asked softly.

Wendy studied her teacup. It was made of the delicate bone porcelain from the east, with delicate red flowers painted in patterns, and little purple leaves beneath each one. "He couldn't do for me what Alim did for you," she said softly.

"It sounds to me," Moira said slowly, "as though there might be more than one reason for his actions. Especially if Tiger Lily was threatening you."

Wendy took a deep breath. "Like I said, it doesn't matter anymore. What matters is getting my brothers home. We came to ask if you'd found something."

"As a matter of fact, I did." She frowned slightly and pushed a dark curl out of her face. "Or at least, I thought I had."

Wendy leaned forward and gripped her teacup until her fingers hurt.

"I asked Alim if he'd ever heard anything about Peter Pan or the Lost Boys or the fae. Everything Amos used to talk about when we were young. I knew when your parents said that you flew out the window, it must have something to do with Peter. At least, with the stories. It was the only way to explain it all. Especially after your encounter four years ago."

"You said I dreamed it up."

Moira pursed her lips. "Your parents said you flew out the window. As they're both reasonably sane and had no other reason to lie, that was all I had to work with."

Wendy gave her friend a sheepish grin. "Did Alim tease you?"

Moira let out a bark of laughter. "He knows better than to try to come between you and me. And as everyone knew you and your brothers had disappeared, he said he would ask around the next time he went out to trade."

Wendy's heart tripped over itself. "And?"

"Most people laughed at him. He nearly gave up until he was approached by a man from Destin, who said King Everard himself was nearly killed by the fae a number of years ago."

"Tiger Lily said something about being chased from the Fortress!" Wendy frowned. "But...that was nearly five hundred years ago!"

Moira shrugged. "Either way, the man was absolutely sure he knew what he was talking about. So the first thing I did when I heard the story was to write a letter to the king himself."

Wendy gasped. "You wrote to King Everard?"

"Wendy, I spent years teasing you and trying to talk you down from your fantasies. And I can't tell you how horrible...how responsible I felt when I tried to pressure you into marrying that nasty man—"

Wendy launched herself from her seat and wrapped her friend up in a fierce hug. "You have done nothing but the best for me," she whispered. "And I owe so much to you. So don't ever doubt that you are the best friend who ever walked the world." Then something occurred to Wendy, and she sat back, her hands still on Moira's shoulders. "Wait. You said you wrote to him. Did he ever reply?"

Moira shook her head. "I'm afraid not. And I sent the letter with the fastest courier I could find, so he should have received it at least two weeks ago. Long enough to have sent an answer back."

"Unless he thought it wasn't so pressing." Wendy frowned. "If I were the most powerful king in all of the western realm, I probably would have better things to do than chase down a foolish girl and her brothers who ran away from home on their own accord."

"It was all I could think to do."

"And it was splendid." Wendy touched her friend's cheek. "You know, now that I think about it, I wonder if there would be any books in the magistrate's mansion on it. The fae were obviously in more places than Neverland, especially if they tried to overthrow the king of Destin."

"Take care, Wendy." Moira's voice was full of warning. "Reuben didn't take your absence well. He married within two weeks of your leaving, but he refused to speak with your father for weeks. Everyone knew about it."

Wendy frowned. "I don't have any other choice. We're not near enough to another region to use their magistrate's library."

"Wendy!" her father called from the door. "Are you ready?"

Wendy and Moira stood.

"I mean it this time," Moira said, glaring through red, shining eyes. "If you decide to go running off again, the least you could do is leave me a note letting me know when you'll be back." She sniffed. "Or if you will."

"Moira, you are the best friend a girl could ask for." Wendy hugged her friend and kissed her wet cheek before leaving with her father. "If I disappear again, my mother will tell you everything she knows."

Moira waved and gave her one more hug before letting her go. Thankfully, people had gotten bored during Wendy's chat with Moira, and the street was clear when she and her father left again.

"Find anything that will help?" her father asked as they mounted their horses.

Wendy took a deep breath. "Possibly. But I'm going to have to do something terrible to pursue it."

Her father looked so startled that Wendy hurried to assure him.

"It's nothing dangerous. I'm just going to have to ask our beloved magistrate if I may use his library."

"I'm afraid that might be a bit difficult."

Wendy turned to study her father. "Because I left?"

He sighed, looking deflated. "Not exactly. After you left, he said some rather..." His jaw hardened, and the fingers wrapped around his reins grew tight. "Indelicate things about you. And I might have let him know how I felt about such language pertaining to my daughter." He paused. "With my fist."

Wendy stared at her father in shock. And then, before she knew it, laughter bubbled to the top. She laughed until she cried, and her father joined her. The absurdity of it all was unbelievable. Peter Pan had sworn never to marry her, and her immovable father had punched the most powerful man in their region.

What had begun as laughter, though, turned into a deep shudder as the weightiness of their situation settled on her. She felt frustrated and powerless. How had everything gone so wrong?

Peter had let the fae beat him. Even if he had brought her back for her own safety, the coward had turned his back on all that could have been. He let the fae use him and control his boys through their manipulative ways. He'd sworn never to marry her, which wouldn't have been nearly as insulting if he'd never encouraged her feelings in the first place. What had he been thinking, giving her a necklace and then taking her out and showing her the rainbow he'd made in her honor?

But no, this wasn't about her. This was about getting her brothers back. She would deal with the repercussions after.

"It doesn't matter whether Reuben wants to see me or not," Wendy growled. "I'll knock on his door until it falls off."

Her father studied her for a moment then let out a tired chuckle. "If nothing else, your mother and I didn't raise children of weak constitutions." Then he looked down at the ground for a moment. "Wendy, I want to talk about what happened the night before—"

"Did you happen to hire a young man named Kassin?"

Her father stared at her for a moment before answering. "I did," he finally said. "When he told me who sent him, I had no choice." His shoulders slumped. "It was my only link to you. Unfortunately, he was able to tell me little."

"Is he still in town?" Wendy's heart picked up speed. She'd asked about the young man she and Peter had helped, a former Lost Boy, as a way to put off her father's questions. But now she felt excitement bubbling up in her chest. How had she forgotten about him before this?

"Actually, he's still on the farm. He works out in the north fields." Her father frowned. "Why?"

Wendy hesitated. It still felt so strange to talk of stories her parents had considered nonsense for years, though they clearly believed her now. "Kassin was one of Peter's Lost Boys from a long time ago. He left Peter and came to this world but ended up falling into crime. Peter and I found him, and we sent him here."

"Yes, that's what he told me." Her father nodded. "He and his wife live in one of the old houses on the east side of town, just at the edge. She's expecting, if I'm not mistaken."

Despite her apprehension, Wendy smiled. So he had married the girl after all. That hadn't been the case when she'd first met him, but her father didn't need to know that. The less the scandal of their origins was known, the better for their little family. Of course, that wasn't what Wendy needed to know now.

"I'll need to talk to him," she said. "Perhaps he can help me find more dust."

"Wendy," her father said as they crested the last hill, "before we get home, there's something I want to—"

"I'm sorry, Father," Wendy said, forcing a smile. "But I'm exhausted, since I was up most of last night. I think I'll just hurry home and get some sleep so I'm a better conversationalist at supper." And with that, she nudged her horse into a run. Guilt ate her from the inside, but she couldn't do it. She couldn't have this discussion yet. Not when her head was filled with every heavy thing she'd ever encountered in the world.

It was silly, she chided herself as she quickly fed and brushed her horse, all the while missing Nana more than ever. What was one more deep conversation in the midst of everything else? And yet, the idea of rehashing the night she'd run away with Peter was more than she could bear. Just another reminder of all that had gone wrong.

When she was done taking care of her horse, Wendy gave the animal a final pat and made her way inside. A storm was coming, and the air was sharp and crisp and held the promise of snow. Wendy slipped past her mother and hurried up to the stairs, threw herself into her bed, and covered herself with the blankets to stare out the window.

It felt so wrong to be snuggled up in her warm bed, safe and fed. But she needed silence to figure this out, where parents couldn't interrupt her to ask well-meaning questions, and no one would try to help.

She'd counted herself blessed the last time escape had presented itself. But her only villain last time had been an unwanted suitor. Her brothers weren't in danger, and there were no angry fae with desires for revenge.

What a gift it would be to run away *now*.

As if planning such a desired escape, fetched the little bag from her dresser to it, loosening the drawstring and plunging her hand inside. Her fingers landed on something small and smooth, and she pulled out the little bauble Jay had given her before leaving Neverland.

If you have need of me, press it between your hands, and the sand will point me back to you.

What if she found Jay first?

Better yet, what if they went to Neverland together? He was sure to have enough stardust. Peter had always said he was the kind of person to plan ahead like that, to always have another plan.

She should have considered it before, but her mind had been too foggy from the Wasaaca flower's effects. Now that she was thinking more clearly, she wondered.

Of course, now that she really thought about it, she remembered that the bauble could only call Jay from Neverland. It couldn't signal him from anywhere else because it needed stardust.And she wasn't there. Well, then, she'd just have to find a way to contact him in this world.

Unfortunately, she also realized she didn't know the name of his uncle or his uncle's company. Ashland had more ships than nearly any other country in the world. Finding him could be like searching for one particular fish in an ocean. It would be far more expedient to call him from Neverland if she could get there first. For even if she found out where his uncle's company was located, there was no guarantee Jay would be there. In fact, he was probably still out at sea, searching for a cure for his mother's palsy.

That was too risky. By the time she discovered him, Neverland might be gone. Still, who better to take on the fae than Jay? He knew Neverland better than Wendy, and he, unlike everyone else on the island, was mature enough to understand why she had to do what she had to do. She was sure of it.

Well, that settled it. Wendy would have to find enough stardust to return to Neverland on her own and then use the bauble to call Jay directly there. Only if all else failed would she go to the closest port, and she wouldn't stop searching until she'd found him.

Wendy smiled. It felt good to have a plan.

Unfortunately, her euphoria wasn't long-lived. Her plan was

risky. At one time, she'd been sure she could trust Jay. Now she wasn't sure of much at all besides knowing that she needed to save her brothers. But if partnering with a charming man of questionable morals meant getting them back, then so be it. Wendy's heart beat faster as she began to think of all the possibilities. Jay knew Neverland nearly as well as Peter did. If he helped her, she just might stand a chance at getting the best of Tiger Lily and her fae.

Peter wouldn't like it. But Peter had given up any right he'd held before to have any influence on her decisions.Then what?

What if she and the boys survived this awful nightmare? As much as she wanted to stay at the farm, she knew she couldn't. Already, there were too many reminders of what had been and those she'd lost and those she was losing still.

Perhaps...just perhaps, she thought as the soft, warm blankets began to make her sleepy, she could talk to Jay about letting her stay on just a little longer. She wouldn't wish to impose herself upon his hospitality, of course. But he'd seemed to enjoy her company in Neverland. Maybe he would allow her to travel with him to his next destination once the boys were safe. Maybe not knowing where she was going would be best. She certainly hadn't been able to make her decision before with weeks and weeks to decide. If he allowed her to trespass on his generosity just a little more, maybe she could find out where, after all this was done, she truly belonged.

CHAPTER 13
BOOKS

After her visit with Moira, Wendy threw herself into searching for a way to get back to Neverland. For three days, she searched for Amos, but as her parents had said, she could find no trace of him. He seemed to have vanished into thin air. This, of course, only made the loss of her brothers more poignant. Not only had Amos been her most important link to returning to Neverland, but he was her friend, too.

She also tracked down Kassin, the young man she had met on her night excursion with Peter, the night they'd argued about teaching the Lost Boys manners.

"Wow," he said when she finished telling her tale. "All that happened in Neverland?" He'd been pitching hay in the barn when she'd found him, and now he turned the pitchfork thoughtfully in his hands. "Huh."

"I need to get back to Neverland to get my brothers," Wendy said. "If I could find enough stardust, would you be able to tell me how?"

Kassin frowned and started to pitch again, but slower this time. "I'm afraid leaving is easier than coming. To leave, you just keep flying until you reach the edge. To find it, though..." He grunted. "Peter takes us all there the first time. And when we leave, it's because we don't plan on going back."

Wendy groaned and rubbed her eyes. "That's what I was afraid of." After remembering how Jay had gone in and out with Peter in his searches, Wendy had hoped that perhaps, there had been another boy at some time who had done so as well. But at the moment, the only answer she'd received was a big pile of nothing.

"Besides, I don't know where you think you'll find dust here."

"I saved as much as I could from my clothes and pockets."

Kassin shook his head, making his thick brown curls shake, too. "Probably won't be enough. Not if Neverland's struggling the way you say it is. You'll need more dust than that to make it all the way to Neverland."

"You wouldn't...happen to have any, would you?" she asked sheepishly.

He gave her an apologetic smile. "I don't. But if I did, I'd give it to you in a heartbeat."

Wendy's shoulders slumped. "Well, I guess that's it then. I'm left with no other choice."

He frowned again. "And what would that be?"

Wendy gave him an unhappy smile. "I was hoping to avoid it, but I'm afraid I'll have to use the magistrate's library. If I could find anything that will help me get back to Neverland, at least I would know where to start."

He put his pitchfork down and leaned against the top. "That shouldn't be a problem, should it? I thought the magistrate's library was open to the whole town."

"Oh, it usually is. But most of the town hasn't rejected his romantic advances multiple times."

Kassin stared for a moment then let out a belly laugh that was so loud and long that even Wendy had to smile. "Wish I'd been there to see that pompous..." he paused and glanced back up at Wendy, "...donkey get turned down."

Wendy gave him a wry grin. "It was a good show. I'm just hoping I don't have to view the fallout for myself."

Five days after returning to the farm, Wendy stopped and ate lunch with her mother in the kitchen before heading to the dreaded chore. Her search had been sorely slowed by inclement weather, and she was determined to make the best of the day before it began to rain again. They enjoyed a simple lunch of cheese slices, fresh apples, some cold bacon strips, and her mother's freshly baked rosemary bread. Wendy savored each bite of that hot bread. She'd imagined it up in Neverland for their meals several times, but nothing could make it taste quite like her mother's.

"Your father says you've been avoiding him," her mother said as Wendy finished off her plate.

The bread that had tasted so soft and buttery in Wendy's mouth a moment before was suddenly dry and bitter. With some difficulty, she swallowed.

"I've been busy trying to find the boys."

"I know." Her mother began to peel an apple. "But I've watched you two, and you've had lots of time to listen to him, even if you don't want to speak about it."

Wendy went over to push her leftovers into Nana's bowl...only to remember that Nana wouldn't be there to eat them.

Why did that realization hurt more every time she made it?

"Want to tell me why?" her mother asked.

Wendy took a deep breath and closed her eyes. "I wish I could. I just..."

"You just what?"

Wendy searched for something she could say that would explain her resistance to her mother. She wished she could show her parents the weight of guilt that sat on her shoulders. She'd made a choice. Or many choices, rather, and their consequences felt like they were crushing her soul beneath them. These devastating effects could have been stopped long ago, but she hadn't really paused to think about the complications such an escape would create.

"I'm struggling," she said slowly. "There's more pain than I know what to do with. And I'm afraid I don't know how to take any more."

"I see." Her mother was thoughtful for a moment. Wendy studied her plate as she waited to hear what her mother had to say.

Mary Darling was well known throughout the city as a beauty, even in her early fifth decade. Her coloring was darker than Wendy's, and though her hair was beginning to gray, she was still spoken of as a very handsome woman. And though she was quite striking, Wendy had always been convinced a large part of her mother's allure came from her poise and grace. Confidence seemed to surround her.

Wendy wished she could be like that.

"I think," her mother said softly, "that what he wants to tell you will actually give you peace. It might answer some of your questions, at least."

Wendy smiled and nodded wanly, but secretly was convinced that she *didn't* want one more deep conversation right now. Nothing that pulled her focus toward anything other than her brothers. Because that meant she would have to try sorting out the turmoil in her heart about what was and what might have been and what she had once wanted.

Compared to all that, thinking about getting back to Neverland seemed simple.

"Well." Wendy put her plate in the water bucket to soak and pulled her shawl off the hook on the wall. "I'm going to visit the magistrate's library. Hopefully, I can find something about the fae or stardust in there."

"Do you want your father to come with you?" her mother asked.

Wendy shook her head. "I heard he and Father haven't seen eye-to-eye lately."

Her mother gave a dark chuckle. "And you think you'll do better?"

"I'm hoping he won't be at home." Wendy wrapped her shawl around her shoulders. "I ran into one of the servants at the market today, and she said Reuben would be gone this afternoon. I'm hoping someone will just let me in like anyone else. Then I can be gone before he gets back."

"Make sure you take the horse." Wendy's mother left the table, where she was chopping apples, and glanced through the window at the sky. "Silas swears there's going to be another storm."

Wendy looked out at the sky, too. It was mostly blue with some puffy clouds here and there left over from their rainshower that morning. It certainly didn't look like stormy weather. But doubting Silas had never done anyone good, so she did as her mother asked and went to ready her horse.

She would leave now and get to the magistrate's mansion in about an hour. Usually, it would take half that time to reach the mansion by the main road, but Wendy wasn't taking the main road. She was taking a back road so there was no chance of running into Reuben along the way. According to the servant she'd run into that morning, a distant acquaintance from when they'd been children, Reuben and his wife should be gone for six hours before returning. That would give Wendy more than enough time to at least see if there were any books that could help her.

As she rode through the empty, brown countryside, Wendy went over what she knew already in her head.

She needed more stardust to get back to Neverland.

Or she needed to find Jay.

Each seemed as impossible as the other.

She could get stardust by either finding a fallen star or by getting stardust from someone else who had been there as well. And since finding a fallen star made the word unlikely comical, she would have to get the stardust from someone else.

So what was left? Running to the nearest port and asking every sailor in sight if they knew of a man named Jay? She didn't even know his uncle's name or the name of the company.

She would do it in a heartbeat, if that was her only choice. But perhaps, even if it didn't have information on stardust or Neverland, Reuben's library might have something on Ashlandian shipping companies. That would be useful information for a magistrate to have, would it not?

Her heart leaped a little as she sent up yet another prayer that *something* would work out.

Perhaps, unlikely as it was, she could find Jay.

Why did that thought make her happy? It shouldn't. Not after the stunt he'd pulled with abducting Tiger Lily. She could feel grateful for his offer of help, hopeful even. But not warm inside the way she was feeling now.

But then, a rebellious voice inside whispered, *he didn't kick you out of his home and swear never to marry you, either.*

Very well, maybe Jay had been a royal pain in the backside when he'd abducted Tiger Lily. But, unlike someone *else* Wendy refused to think about, Jay had been man enough to admit his mistake and move on.

By the time Wendy arrived at the mansion, new clouds had not only appeared but were beginning to thicken up, just as Silas had predicted. She would have to be fast. That wasn't a bad thing, though, as the last place she wanted to be was in the mansion when Reuben returned.

All of her confidence, however, melted when she rang the bell, and Reuben was the one to answer it.

"MISS DARLING." He filled the doorway with his wide, well-framed shoulders. "To what do I owe this pleasure?" He smiled just a little too widely, and his dark eyes were just a little too bright.

Wendy had never wished more for Nana to be by her side.

Still, she did her best to stand tall. "I'm sorry to disturb you, but I need the use of your library."

He tilted his head and studied her. Raindrops began to hit her shawl, and thunder rumbled in the distance, but he didn't step aside or invite her in.

"Doesn't the irony strike you?" he asked. "You spurned the hand that offered for you because you believed you had the answers. And now you come seeking them."

Wendy felt her face flush hot. She had been right to reject this man, and his response now was enough to prove that. And yet, for some reason, his charges brought her shame.

"I apologize for disturbing your afternoon," she said in a low, even voice. "But I need use of the town's library." She said the words slowly, emphasizing the town's ownership over his.

"Oh, I know. I was informed this morning."

The servant. Wendy bit back a curse. Drat that woman. She'd set Wendy up, probably under the orders of her current employer. His ego wouldn't allow Wendy to return home quietly. He would do his best to get his revenge first.

"The books belong to Beddington," Wendy said, trying not to

convey what she really thought of him. "I have every right to read them."

"Yes, but they're in my house. And I'm not obligated to allow anyone into my domain at any hour of the night." He put his hand over his mouth and yawned.

"But it's only afternoon!" Wendy protested. Another clap of thunder exploded in the distance.

"Please, dear."

Wendy and Reuben both turned to see the woman that Wendy assumed to be his wife. It was Missy, a girl one year Wendy's senior. She was a pretty girl, but Wendy didn't know her well beyond that, as she had been raised on one of the outermost farms. Still, she had always seemed nice enough, and Wendy's heart fell a little as she realized what kind of life Missy had been roped into.

"Let her at least stay through the storm." Missy came to stand just behind her husband. "This storm will be a dangerous one."

"Did I ask you to predict the future?" he snapped.

She winced. "No."

"Then let me handle my private affairs, please."

Missy gave Wendy an apologetic look before nodding and retreating into the house. The magistrate took a deep breath and straightened. "As you can see, I'm very busy." He paused, and a strange smile crossed his face. "Unless, of course, you'd like to discuss this more privately."

Wendy's blood ran cold. Searching the shipyards for Jay it would be then.

"No, thank you." She took a step back.

He put one foot outside the door, his shiny black boot thumping loudly on the wooden porch. "I really think we're mature enough to put our differences aside," he said. "Come. Talk with me." His eyes burned into hers. "We'll sort through all our misunderstandings quickly enough." He rested a large hand on Wendy's shoulder.

She jerked her shoulder away and glared at him. "We're done here."

"Then, if that's the case," he said, stepping back into the doorway, "I never want to see you on my steps again."

"Oh, don't worry. You won't."

Reuben's eyes widened before he slammed the door shut. "Tell me if she comes again!" she heard him shout from inside.

Wendy couldn't run fast enough to the stable where she'd left her horse.

She'd known the man to be cruel. But not like this. Her shoulder still tingled where he'd touched it, and she fantasized scrubbing it with lye soap then and there.

Instead, she mounted her horse, and for one brief moment, she considered heading to the main road and making a break for home. Anything to get her away from the monster who had once been her intended. Before she could continue to think about how much she despised the man, an exceptionally loud crack of thunder brought her back to her senses. She needed to find shelter. She couldn't ride all the way home in this, or she and her horse would be struck by lightning before getting halfway there.

As she brought her horse to stand in the door of the stable, it occurred to her that she might hide in the stall with her until the worst had passed. But no. That was too risky, especially after the way Reuben's gaze had traveled up and down her person like a man starved for companionship. And, unfortunately, the mansion was nearly as remote as her farm, so there were no other buildings nearby that didn't belong to him. She had to get away.

Wendy patted her horse and tried to offer her soothing words as she looked around for somewhere to hide. Even at the stable's entrance, her hair and clothes were fast becoming soaked, and her poor horse's mane was dripping steadily. From the sound of the approaching thunder, the worst of the storm hadn't even arrived. The best option she could see was a ravine about three hundred yards away. There was a little stream at the bottom, and it was surrounded by trees. Of course, being near trees wasn't ideal, but at least she wouldn't be the tallest thing in the hills either. She pushed her horse into a gallop.

The animal bolted, lightning close behind, thunder on their heels. The rain stung Wendy's face as they blazed through the sheets descending from the heavens. She had to slow her horse, though, as they neared the ravine. Sending the animal careening down into the trees could kill them both, or at the very best, render the animal lame if she wasn't careful. As she slowly coaxed the animal into the brush, however, she got the distinct feeling of being watched. She looked up to see what looked like a shadow dart behind a bush. Fear and hope made her freeze for one brief second. Had Peter found a way to send his shadow back? Was he looking for or after her?

Her hope melted into fear, though, as she made it halfway down the ravine, and the shadow stepped out from behind the trees, where she found herself, once again, staring at Reuben.

"What do you want?" she called over the storm, trying desperately to keep her horse calm so she didn't go sliding down into the muddy creek bottom.

"I want to make it very clear that you overstepped your bounds," he said, the dark, wet locks of hair drooped down over his face making him look even angrier than he had appeared back at the mansion.

"There's no law that says a woman must marry a magistrate when he offers," Wendy spat back, hoping her voice sounded more confident than it felt.

"Maybe not on the books." He took a step closer, making Wendy's horse whinny and toss her head. "But you need to understand your place. Something it seems no one thought to teach you growing up."

"What does it matter to you?" she cried over the noise of the storm. "You were chosen to represent us to the king. Not to rule over us!"

"Does it matter?" He held his arms out and looked around. "The king has his hands tied up in a war with his own people, and the prince is too busy pining over that idiot traitor of his to care what happens to some worthless farmer's daughter in the south."

Wendy tried to move her horse backward, but the slope was steep enough, and the ground muddy enough, that they couldn't move anywhere fast. Reuben closed the distance easily and had reached up to grab her wrist when he fell back and let out a cry.

CHAPTER 14
KING EVERARD

Wendy watched in awe as tongues of blue fire ran up and down his arms and legs. Reuben screamed, but to Wendy's amazement, not even his clothes seemed to burn. The strange blue flames danced on his skin like a garment he couldn't remove, keeping him on the ground without seeming to actually harm any part of his body. But as he writhed, a movement in the corner of Wendy's eye made her look up, and when she did, she let out a little cry.

A man was walking toward them. He wore all black, and his face was hidden by the hood of his cloak. His left hand was turned palm up, where bright blue flames danced upon it. When he reached Reuben, he gave a slight flick of his wrist, and the blue flames jumped off of Reuben and back into the man's hand.

"Who are you?" Reuben cried as he scrambled back up the muddy ravine, slipping twice.

The man threw off his hood. His blond hair was cut short, and the muscles in his neck and the size of his shoulders made Reuben look like a child in comparison. He had a square jaw, and his mouth was set in a grim line. Though older than both herself and Reuben, he was one of the handsomest men Wendy had ever seen. He also gave the impression of being the most dangerous man she had ever met. For more fearsome than the set of his jaw and the flames in his hand were the blue flames that danced in his eyes, pulsing and rhythmic as they burned every bit as brightly against his storm-gray irises as stars against the inky black sky.

"My name is King Everard Fortier," the man said in a rich, deep voice. How did something sound so velvety smooth and so threatening at the same time? "And," he said, leaning toward Reuben, the fire in his hand nearly blinding and his mouth turning up at the corner in a terrible smirk, "we're going to keep that a secret, aren't we?"

Reuben once again stumbled backward. "Yes. Yes, of course!" With that, he sprinted up and out of the ravine faster than Wendy knew was possible.

Wendy looked back at her rescuer. "You're..."

"Yes." The man who had identified himself as the most powerful king in the western realm extinguished his flames and gave her a gentler smile. He whistled, and a horse, midnight black, joined him. He mounted easily and took up the reins. "But I'm not supposed to be here, according to your king. So let's get ourselves somewhere dry and solve this problem now, shall we?"

"My farm is about half an hour in that direction if we take the main road." Wendy pointed southeast.

"Then let's go." He moved his horse to a canter. Speechless, Wendy could only nod and follow.

As they crested the ravine, lightning and thunder exploded above them and made her jump. Did the great king, renowned for his wisdom, really mean for them to travel all the way home in the storm?

As if answering her silent question, he motioned for her to follow him.

"In the storm, Your Highness?" Wendy balked.

He turned and gave her a grin, which was slightly fierce.

"We're not taking the road." Several other men on horses joined them, seeming to appear out of nowhere, each man wearing full armor with an arsenal of weapons all over his body.

"Everything clear?" the king asked one of the men closest to him.

"It is, Sire," the man replied.

"Good. Stay behind us. And you," the king turned and looked at Wendy, "are coming with me." He came close and lifted her horse's reins from her hands. Before she could ask what he was doing, they shot off into the most disorienting gallop Wendy had ever been on. Trees whizzed past in a blur, and though she could hear her horse's hooves beneath her, she felt as though they were flying. She'd never even flown this fast in Neverland.

She could tell that the rain was still falling by the moisture on her arms and face. But the wind in her ears was so loud that the sounds of thunder seemed distant and nearly gone. Her head and stomach felt funny, and after several minutes of this unusual mode of travel, she began to feel like she might fall off. But just as she was about to ask him faintly if they could slow down, he drew their horses to a stop, and she found herself in front of her barn.

The storm was still raging, but Wendy was too dazed and confused to even mind.

"How..." She looked around her in shock. In a matter of minutes, they had made the journey that should have taken at least half an hour.

"I don't like taking longer to get somewhere than I have to." The king gave her a wry smile. "Would there be someplace for us to speak?" He glanced up at the house. "Alone, perhaps?"

Wendy had to catch her breath before she could answer. As her senses caught up with her body, Wendy realized that this was the answer to their prayers. The king hadn't written to Moira. He'd come in person. That honor alone was inconceivable.

And yet, the fear wasn't completely absent. She'd known this man for possibly ten minutes. Everything about him exuded danger. He had to be above forty years, and yet, that only made him more threatening. From the way he held himself to the weapons that covered him down to his sheer size, her common sense told her to be frightened. And then, there were those fiery eyes.

He had, however, also saved her, and if anyone was equipped to help her save her brothers, it would be him. So she did her best to swallow that fear and gesture to the animal barn, his men behind them.

"You can put your horses there," she said, pointing to a few empty stalls at the end of the large building. "We use the upper level to store food and supplies, so you'll find all you need for the animals in the stalls themselves."

"I thank you." The king nodded to his men, who wordlessly tended to the horses, but he waited to speak again until he and Wendy were alone once more.

"I can bring them something to eat," Wendy said, watching through the windows with some guilt as they stationed themselves out under the eaves.

"They'll be fine, thank you." The king sat on two stacked hay bales and gestured for her to do the same. Wendy sat, but she felt small and vulnerable as she looked up into his face. He watched her expectantly.

"I'm sorry," she finally said. "I'm not familiar with court etiquette. This seems hardly a fitting welcome for a king who's traveled as far as you have."

"Nonsense." The king rested one of his legs on another bale. "I invited myself. Your friend is the one who asked for guidance and was kind enough to send a map. I was the one who chose to come."

"Well...thank you." Wendy smiled. "To say I'm honored would be the grossest understatement."

"Tell me," the king said. "How did you return without your brothers? When your friend wrote, she said you had all disappeared, and she believed you had gone willingly with a young man to a world that doesn't exist."

Wendy sighed and had the sudden desire to crawl into a hole. "I'm afraid I've been the cause of all this trouble. And now I've put my brothers in danger because of it." She covered her face in her hands and leaned her elbows on her knees. "I never meant it to be like this."

"While I don't seek to persuade you from just blame," the king said, "I'm curious to know what would drive someone like you to make such a drastic choice as to leave your family. You seem at least reasonably rational." The corner of his mouth quirked up, as though this were funny for some reason.

Wendy sighed. "That man you threatened in the ravine? My parents wanted me to marry him."

"I see." The flames in his eyes seemed to dance with more fury. But, of course, that could have simply been Wendy's imagination. "That in itself doesn't seem as if it would have been a prudent match."

"No, but my father was desperate to see me married well before winter. He's worried about the war, and the magistrate seemed the perfect match to provide for me."

The king rolled his eyes. "He *would* be a magistrate. Serves Xander right," he muttered.

Wendy didn't know what to make of that, so she went on. "The more I came to know the man, however, the less I wanted to be married to him. And when my father threatened to lock me in my room until I changed my mind, I took the first chance to escape that I could find."

"Which was running away with a boy you hardly knew?"

It sounded so bad when he put it that way.

"Not a complete stranger," Wendy hedged, not able to look

the king in the eyes. And she told him, as sparingly as possible, of course, about their interactions before, and about Amos's stories and how she had somehow known in her heart that Neverland was real. Then, upon his prompting, she told him about Neverland, leaving out, of course, all the parts about Peter's particular attentions to her. It felt funny enough telling another adult about such a place, and a king, no less. But his face didn't show an ounce of surprise as her story unfolded. When she finished, she frowned.

"I don't know how or why the star is able to create such a world. But I know the fae wanted a place of their own since they were cut off from their own home." She shivered slightly as she remembered the ferocity in Tiger Lily's face during the story of how the fae and Neverland had come to be.

"I'm curious, though..." she said, pausing to study the king. "Tiger Lily said the king of Destin attacked them while they were in the Fortress."

The king snorted. "Hardly. Every time they've come to the Fortress, they've seemed intent on nothing short of bloodshed."

Wendy nodded. "That makes much more sense to me. Only...I was curious because of the time disparity."

The king frowned. "How so?"

"Well," Wendy said slowly, "Tiger Lily says they fought with you, but that would have been over five hundred years ago."

Even in the storm's gray light that filtered in through the windows, Wendy could have sworn the king's face went white. He sat up slowly. "Did you say...five hundred years?"

Wendy nodded, unsure of what his reaction meant.

"Garin." He closed his eyes.

"Garin?" Wendy repeated.

The king's jaw tightened, and he opened his eyes and drew in a shaky breath. "I'm afraid these fae aren't the ones who attacked my family after all." He stood and went to look out a window at the gray fields. "At least, not my wife and children."

"I'm sorry," Wendy said, "but I'm afraid I don't understand."

The king nodded and swallowed before turning to face Wendy. "Just over five centuries ago, the fae were free to wander the earth. They would travel around the world, collect all the beauty they could find, and then return to their own realm and recreate that beauty in whatever way they wanted. Nothing was permanent, not even their own bodies, but that was the way they had been created. They were meant to find the beauty in the earth and enjoy it. We didn't know it for a long time, but their bridge to this world was actually in the southern part of my kingdom. They discovered the Fortress one day and were overwhelmed by its beauty. And," he added in a darker voice, "its power."

"I've heard the Fortress of Destin is..." Wendy paused. "Special?"

The king nodded and pulled a knife from somewhere on his person and began to examine it. Wendy stared at its jagged blade. How many weapons did the man carry around with him?

"A thousand years ago," he said, "my ancestor saved the starving people of the land from their king, whose descendant now rules the kingdom we know as Tumen. As a reward for his bravery and sacrifice, the Maker gifted him with not only an unusual strength," Ever held out his hand, and a ball of blue fire appeared hovering over his palm, "but also a home which would help him guide, protect, and rule his people in wisdom and love. There's power in the very stones of the Fortress, and that power is extended through the Fortier line."

He lifted his hand, and the blue flame grew. Then he reached over and touched the edge of Wendy's wet cloak. Immediately, steam hissed and rose from Wendy's wet clothes. In no more than three seconds, her clothes were completely dry. She looked up in amazement as he removed his hand.

"The Fortress's spirit is also in the air around the building. But even more than that, it follows its children wherever they go. In a way, the Fortress seems to me almost an extension of the Maker Himself." The king paused and watched the blue flames thoughtfully for a moment before extinguishing them and shaking his head as though to clear it. "But that's beside the point. What I meant to say is that more than anything in the world, even beauty, the fae love power. They crave it. And when they sensed the magnitude of power that resides within the Fortress, they decided to take it for themselves."

He paused, and when he spoke again, his voice was quiet. "That night, they murdered every human in the Fortress except my infant ancestor. He survived only because the Fortress changed the heart of one fae and turned him against his own people." He cleared his throat. "Garin became a guardian for the Fortier line for five centuries. He raised the young king until he was old enough to use his strength to seal the fae back into their own world through the bridge in the southern forest of my kingdom. These fae must have escaped my ancestor and wandered the earth until they found that star."

"If your ancestor sealed up their bridge, and Peter's fae were in Neverland," Wendy asked, "how did they attack your family?"

The king frowned. "That would be due to the indiscretion of my father. But that's another story for another time. What I'm here to tell you is that fae are some of the most dangerous creatures in the entire world. Largely because they're not from our world."

"Is that why you're here?" Wendy asked. "To keep them from escaping?" Although it should probably concern her that he was there for the fae and not for her brothers, Wendy could completely understand why anyone who had come into contact with the fae before would wish to make sure they were never unleashed upon the world again.

"I want to come with you," the king said, standing taller. "To help bring your brothers home, and to make sure the fae cannot escape again."

Wendy gasped. "That would be...incredible!" With the king's help, she could rescue her brothers and the Lost Boys from the fae, should they wish to come with her. Tiger Lily didn't stand a chance against the king. "But..." Wendy paused. "Do you know how to get there?"

"I was hoping you could tell me."

Wendy's shoulders slumped. "I don't," she said slowly, the hope she'd entertained just moments before deflating inside her. "I'd hoped to talk to an old friend...the one who used to be a Lost Boy. But he disappeared after hearing that we were gone, and we haven't been able to find him." Then she paused. "Now that I think about it, how did you find me? No one from my family could have known I was in the ravine."

"Your friend included a well-drawn map with directions to your home, and for that, I'm more grateful than I can say. But as for you..." His brows furrowed slightly. "It's strange. You leave a trail of power behind you. I went to your house first and then tracked you using that trail."

Wendy frowned and looked down at her dress. It was still wrinkled, but at least it was dry. The only source of power she could think of would be the stardust. But that would have washed off days ago—

"The bottle!" Wendy yanked the little bottle out of her reticule and held it up. Inside glimmered the pathetic remnants of dust she'd managed to shake out of her clothes and hair. At the sight of the bottle, the flames in the king's eyes leaped. He held out his hand, and Wendy carefully handed it over.

"This is definitely it," he said, slowly turning it in his hands. Then he smiled and handed it back. "I think I know how to find your friend." But just as Wendy was about to respond, his eyes flamed. He was on his feet, and in one move, had her behind him. His sword was in his hand, and he crouched, his stance like that of a feral cat.

"What's wrong?" Wendy whimpered.

The king didn't turn. When he spoke, his voice was low and flat. "Something else is here."

CHAPTER 15
NOT EVEN PETER

A s he said the words, a green whorl of light flew up into the air, hissing. Wendy screamed as it dove straight for them. It was like the night she'd experienced in Neverland, but this was far worse. There was no hesitation. Its legs were nothing but mist, and its head and arms were green and oddly shaped, its glowing green eyes without iris or pupil still locked onto the king.

But just before it reached them, King Everard threw a ball of fire up into the air. The fae stopped, its body beginning to thicken as it sank toward the ground, its eyes trained on the blue flames. Then with flick of his wrist, the king threw the knife directly into the center of its chest.

They couldn't rest, though, because seconds later, another fae was in the air, shrieking as it hurled itself toward them. This time, King Everard threw three blue balls of flame into the air, one after the other. Wendy worried one might catch the barn on fire, but all were aimed perfectly and floated rather than falling. This fae didn't become distracted as easily as the first had. The king, however, had expertly aimed the third ball to force the fae to the left. That slight movement was enough for the king to plunge his sword deep into the fae's side, which had also thickened with his distraction. This one landed on the floor on top of the other.

The king stood and cleaned his sword on a bale of hay, but Wendy couldn't stop trembling.

"Don't worry," the king said gently, laying a hand on her shoulder. "There aren't any more. Not around here, at least."

"But..." Wendy shivered uncontrollably. "Where did they come from?"

"They've been following you." The king picked his dagger up from the ground, where it had fallen, and he wiped that clean, too. "I had to draw them out before I could kill them, though."

"They were following me?" she echoed stupidly.

"My guess," the king said, gently leading her from the barn, "is that the fae want to know where you are at all times in case they feel the need to use you against Peter in the future." The rain had stopped, though the sky was still overcast and the road muddy. "Now, if you get your horse, we'll go find this Amos fellow."

By the time they left the barn, the storm had stopped. The world was still shiny and wet, but the threat of being struck by lightning was gone. Wendy peeked into the kitchen to tell her mother of all that had transpired since she'd left just a few hours ago, but her mother wasn't anywhere to be found, nor were her father or Silas. Only then did she remember that they'd expected her to be at the magistrate's home for several more hours. So with nothing left to do, Wendy returned to the king, and they mounted their horses once again. The king's guards followed at a distance.

"We'll return to the square," the king said as they made their way to the road. "That's where I felt it first."

"I don't mean to be impertinent," Wendy said as their horses clopped along the road, "but how do you...know? You said you tracked the trail of my stardust."

"Those of us who have great power are often very sensitive to it," the king said. "When I was a boy, my childhood nemesis used that against me. She was powerful as well, and she would purposefully try to overwhelm me whenever we were together. It grew so terrible that my mentor, Garin, had to teach me how to build walls inside my mind to keep her out."

"That's terrible," Wendy said. "Does she still try today?"

"She's dead."

"Oh."

"Of course, that's what happens when you try to kill the Fortress's queen." The king turned and gave Wendy a sideways grin. "Who happened, at the time, to be my future wife."

"Oh," was all Wendy could say again. How she longed to know that story. But it seemed a bit forward to ask about now. So instead, she went back to the trail of power. "I'm curious, though. In Neverland, too much water would wash away our stardust, like when we went swimming."

"It's faint," the king said. "So, your friend must have a concentrated amount of dust like you do."

Wendy stared at him, and her heart doubled in speed. If Amos had more dust...*Please let there be more dust*, she prayed silently to the Maker.

Soon after that, they entered Beddington and went to the square. Wendy watched in awe as the king located Amos's old place of honor among the pile of crates he would sit upon, and then decided with confidence that they must follow the highway that led southwest out of town.

They rode in silence for a while. Despite everything that was going wrong in her life, Wendy tried to bask in the fact that she was being personally aided by the most powerful man in the western realm. Possibly the world. Unfortunately, the cold kept her from enjoying it too immensely. The air was noticeably colder than it had been when she'd left for Neverland, and as Wendy drew her cloak around her snugly, she wished she'd thought to change into something warmer before gallivanting off on this mission.

"I notice you didn't bring a carriage with you," she ventured as another gale of wind grabbed her curls and tossed them up in the air. "Is that expected of the kings of Destin?"

The king threw his head back and laughed. The sound boomed around her, making her bones quiver with its force. "No," he said, still chuckling, "it's not expected. But my father always taught me that too much comfort makes a king soft. And a soft king cannot be a dangerous king."

Wendy blinked up at him. "Should kings be dangerous?"

He gave her a strange smile. "When they need to be."

An hour later, they reached the town of Wheaton. Wendy had been there often enough, generally accompanying her father as he met with other farmers to discuss seasonal conditions. It wasn't much different from Beddington. There were a few streets with shops and merchants, and the rest was mostly made up of tiny farms that only grew one or two crops per year. But it seemed strange that Amos should come here of all places.

If Wendy had been the one to lead the search, she would have stopped and asked people if they had seen a man that fit Amos's description. But Wendy was not in charge, nor was she foolish enough to make this suggestion. Instead, she watched the king work. His brows creased, and several times, he stopped his horse and closed his eyes. She could only guess he was...feeling the trail left by Amos's stardust.

"I don't wish to sound at all ungrateful," she finally ventured as the light began to lessen, and he closed his eyes for the fifth time since arriving in Wheaton, "but my parents think I'm at the magistrate's home. I'm afraid they'll worry if I'm not home by dark."

"They're good parents," the king said, the flames in his eyes dancing more brightly. "And they won't need to worry." He started forward once more. "I've found him."

They came to a corner in the market that was filled with stacks of crates that smelled of fish. And what she saw broke her heart.

Amos wasn't sitting on the crates as he did at home, hands on his knees and leaning forward in anticipation of something good. Instead, he was splayed out on the ground, his head against one of the crates, his arms and legs limp.

"Amos!" She scrambled off her horse and fell at his side. His face was too white, even for his usual complexion.

Could he be dead?

"Something's wrong!" She turned to the king. "I need to find a healer! If you could—"

The king laid a large hand on her shoulder and gently moved her to the side before putting both his hands on Amos's head. Then he closed his eyes and took a deep breath. The now familiar blue fire danced over his hands. But as with Reuben, Amos's skin didn't appear to burn.

Amos let out a cry and jerked to the side.

"Try to keep him still," the king said. "It will take longer if he moves."

Wendy took both Amos's wrists and struggled to hold them to his sides, all the while coaxing him, pleading with him to lie still. But he didn't want to stay still.

"Wendy!" he cried out over and over again. "I need to tell... Wendy! Wendy, I need...I need..."

His cries grew softer, and his jerking slowed as the king's flames began to wane. Then finally, the king opened his eyes at the same time that Amos did. Wendy gasped. All signs of the opaque white were gone from his irises, and his color was visibly improved, even in the duller light of the evening.

"How did you do that?" she whispered.

The king gave her a smile. "Just another part of the Maker's gift to me. But now, I suggest you ask your friend here how we can help you."

"Amos, what are you doing here?" Wendy asked. "My family has been looking all over for you!"

"I was looking for you, Wendy!" Amos sat straight up, seeming so consumed with whatever he had to say that he didn't even notice the king who had healed him sitting beside them. His eyes were wide, and his words were fast. "When I heard that you'd disappeared, I knew you'd gone to Neverland. I knew it. And I knew you'd be in danger, so I tried to go to your parents to tell them I was going after you. But my blasted eyes are...were so bad, I took the wrong road, and..." He paused as he began to dig through his clothes. "It must be here somewhere..." Then he stopped and looked at her. "But you're back now." He said this slowly, as though her presence were just dawning on him. Then he glanced at King Everard. "Who's he?"

"I'll explain later," Wendy said quickly. "What's important is that my brothers are stuck there. I have to get back to them. That's why I came to find you. I was hoping you could help me."

"I told you, I don't remember the way." He pulled a small, brown drawstring pouch from his faded vest and sighed as he gazed down at it. "But when I heard you were gone, I had to try. I knew Tiger Lily wouldn't take kindly to you. And I thought it was all my fault for painting up such a pretty picture of the place I ran away from."

"It's not your fault. It's my own." Wendy gave him a wry smile. "I tried to run away when I should have faced my problems here. Besides, I'm back because Tiger Lily liked me just about as much as you thought she would."

"But that's neither here nor there right now." Amos shoved the little drawstring pouch into Wendy's hands. "What matters is that I have more dust for you. And you can use it to get back to them."

Wendy blinked at him. "If you don't know the way, though..."

He shook his head. "I'm an old man, Wendy. It's been too long. But you were just there. All you need to remember is how to dream of Neverland."

Wendy shared a confused glance with the king. "I'm not sure what you mean."

"I don't know if they're still there," Amos said, "but when I was a boy in Neverland, there were these twin brothers named Pop—"

"And Top!" Wendy cried, recalling Peter's story of how the twins had returned to Neverland.

He nodded. "And they were the first ones who discovered that Lost Boys could return to Neverland using their dreams." He leaned toward Wendy until his nose was only inches from hers. "Use the stardust." He shoved her hands, which were holding the bag, toward her. "I've been saving it all these years, hoping I could remember the way back. But I know now that you were meant to have it."

Wendy's mouth fell open as she opened the drawstring. Then her heart immediately fell. True enough, in the dull light, she could make out the familiar glitter of the stardust inside. But it was dirty, so unlike the pure, nearly translucent, sparkling layer of dust she was used to in Neverland.

"It's not much," Amos said sorrowfully. "But it should be enough to give you one chance."

Wendy took a deep breath and pressed the bag against her chest. "Thank you, Amos. It's more than I dared to hope for."

"Could I accompany her?" the king asked. "She has a little dust of her own."

Amos shook his head. "I'm afraid you cannot visit in your dreams unless you've already been there. Now, if you could find the barrier on your own, perhaps..." He looked at Wendy.

"I'm afraid I don't know where it is. Peter went in two separate ways, and I was never sure just where those ways were," Wendy said, rubbing her face. "To be honest, I didn't even know how I was going to get back at all until I found you."

"Then," the king said, "it seems you'll have to go on your own." He frowned. "It makes me uneasy that you should deal with the fae without protection. They'll be even angrier at your return if you're there against their wishes."

"I'll have to do my best to stay out of sight." Wendy tilted her head thoughtfully. "All I need to do is find the boys and get them to follow me out of the barrier. After that, I'll be able to get us home."

"If you can," the king said, "please try to collect some stardust for myself. I need to see that these fae aren't a danger to our world, and I can do that better by examining the nature of their world." He studied her for a moment. "Although, I get the feeling that they won't let you leave Neverland alone for very long. We may not have to go anywhere to meet them."

This wasn't exactly what Wendy wanted to hear, but she'd seen enough by now to trust that the king knew what he was talking about.

They set off for Wendy's home after that. One of the king's guards, who seemed to have appeared out of nowhere, held Amos in front of him, the man healthier but seemingly weak from hunger. Something Wendy's mother would fix in no time.

"I suppose I'll head home once you're in Neverland," the king said as they watched the sun touch the western horizon. "But I'll leave two of my men at your parents' home until you're all back safely."

"That is most generous," Wendy said. "But are you sure you

can spare them?" And, of course, she didn't say it aloud, but would they really be as skilled as the king? There was no point in getting everyone home if the fae were just going to kill them all there, her parents and the guards included.

"If Neverland is crumbling, as you've said, there's a good chance the fae won't easily forgive you for being a part of ruining their land. They'll come after you and all you love."

Wendy squeezed her reins more tightly.

"My men were present during our last battle with the fae. So they're familiar with how to handle the fae, should they appear. Besides," he added, "if these miscreants somehow managed to escape my ancestor's attempts to send them back to their world, it's my responsibility to make sure they can't do to anyone else what they tried to do to my line."

Wendy felt she should argue this point, merely for the sake of propriety and this king's strange sense of responsibility for something he didn't cause. And yet, with the thought of returning to Neverland alone looming over her, she decided to simply be grateful. After all, soon she would be all on her own again with not even Peter Pan to save her.

CHAPTER 16
NEVERLAND

When they arrived at Wendy's house, just as the sun set, the king acted as though he dined in humble farmhouse kitchens every day. Wendy's parents, however, were more than a little confused and overwhelmed by his presence, and it took no less than ten assurances on the king's part to convince them to stop making a fuss about supper.

As they ate, Wendy's mother attempted to keep everyone's plate filled (although Amos emptied his at least four times), while Wendy explained how she would attempt to return to Neverland that night. King Everard then informed them of his intention to leave his guards there until Wendy returned.

Wendy's parents just watched and listened with ever-widening eyes.

"I wish I could stay until the problem is resolved," the king said apologetically. "But your idiot king doesn't want me in Ashland for the time being, and while he'll not be looking for me this close to your southern border, I'd prefer not to create an international incident until I need to."

"International incident?" Wendy's mother dropped her serving spoon.

The king gave them a strange smile. "I have no problem provoking your nitwit of a king, but I prefer to wait until such a ruckus is absolutely necessary."

"If...if you don't mind me asking...Your Highness," Wendy's father said, clearing his throat. "While I'm more humbled and grateful for your help than I can express, I can't for the life of me understand why you would come so far and risk so much on the account of peasant children who aren't even your subjects."

The king smiled, but it was tinged with sadness. "My family was nearly destroyed by the fae. Twice. I've seen what they're capable of, and no one else deserves to suffer the way we did." He squared his shoulders. "I suppose I also feel responsible. There are few humans in this world who have survived contact with the fae, and even fewer who can do anything about them." Then his smile widened slightly, and his eyes glinted. "Also, it gives me great pleasure to take care of your king's problems without his knowledge."

"Oh?" Wendy's mother asked, glancing nervously at Wendy.

"I attempted to help him in stopping your lovely little civil war before it began, and he thanked me by refraining from sending me any more invitations." The king scowled. "You'll be in much better hands when his son takes the throne, I can guarantee you that."

Wendy's parents exchanged a terrified glance and went back to eating their corn, applesauce, and ham. It wasn't until after supper, when Wendy had gone up to her room to change clothes and gather what she thought she might need for the trip, that her mother seemed once again capable of speaking.

"You're leaving without talking to your father, I take it?"

Wendy's hands froze over the handkerchief she was folding. Her shoulders drooped, and she closed her eyes. "I need to do this quickly, Mother. Every second they're in Neverland, the boys are in danger."

"Wendy, it will only take a minute." When Wendy didn't respond, her mother sighed. "I know it might bring up painful feelings, and we take full responsibility for that. But if you don't let him explain himself, and you don't come back this time, it's going to kill him."

Wendy scrunched her eyes closed as her last fight with her father came to memory. He'd broken something inside of her that day. And in its place, Peter had helped her make something new.

Until that had been broken, too. Wendy glared at the thimble, which Peter must have returned. It sat on the dresser, where she'd left it after waking up that morning. She should throw it away and forget everything between herself and Peter that had ever happened, along with the stupid necklace she couldn't seem to remove, no matter how much she chided herself. But then again...She tossed the thimble back in the reticule. Maybe she would have a chance to throw it at Peter's head.

"Wendy," her mother said again.

Wendy's insides felt like the black, choppy waters of midnight, breaking up on the rocks in the mermaids' lagoon. The last thing she wanted to do was think about this right now. She'd worked hard to bury Peter in the mire of her mind as she searched for a way to save her brothers. She didn't need this distraction right now.

"Please," came a deeper voice this time.

Wendy turned to see her father standing in the doorway. Her mother nodded at him and stretched up on her toes to kiss his cheek before leaving them alone.

Wendy went back to packing her reticule.

"You almost died, you know. As a baby, I mean."

Whatever Wendy had expected him to say, it wasn't that. Against her better judgment, she stopped and looked up at her father. "Excuse me?"

He sat on Michael's bed, interlaced his fingers, and stared down at them.

"You know your grandfather didn't want me to be a farmer."

"Yes."

"Well, it wasn't without good reason. You couldn't know this, but the year you were born was almost as bad as this year has been." He rubbed his neck and grimaced. "My marriage to your mother wasn't the advantageous match your grandparents had been searching for. And then, to bleed the wound more, I used all the money I'd saved up for what they'd hoped to be an education of enlightenment, and I bought this farm." Her father gestured to the window. "Of course, I didn't own as much of the land back then. And it didn't look nearly so nice or so ready to produce. In fact, it was the saddest little farm you'd ever seen. And what's worse, I was a terrible farmer."

"What?" Wendy cried. "But you're known far and wide for—"

He held his hand up. "I am now. But back then, I was doing something I'd neither apprenticed for nor even spent more than one or two summers doing for other farmers. I tried to run a farm of my own. And I was terrible."

Wendy frowned. "How does this relate to my near death?"

"That second winter was worse than the first. Even the best farmers lost animals to the extreme cold, and many were forced to eat their supply of planting seeds, potatoes, and other foods they'd saved to turn into crops the following spring."

When he looked up at her again, his eyes were full of tears. "You can't understand the agony that gripped me when I looked at my wife, thin and pale, and my child crying for milk your mother couldn't make..." He swallowed hard and rubbed his eyes with the palms of his hands. "You can't imagine, Wendy, the regret and fear and guilt that permeated my life and infected my bones when I knew everything in front of me was my own fault."

"What happened?" Wendy asked, too engrossed now to even pretend to pack.

"One of our neighbors died. His son sold all his possessions, for a steep price, of course, as so many people had so little. By some miracle, he had a single stubborn goat that was making it just fine through that monstrous winter. But I had to give his son all my planting seed for the beast. And only because the Maker saw it fit to give my family what I couldn't, we survived. All our crops the next year were grown in thanks to the families in Beddington that donated what few extra seeds they could spare the next spring. They felt sorry for us and scraped up anything extra they could find."

"That's why you give grain to everyone else now," Wendy said softly.

Her father let out a long, shaky breath. "I never meant to chase you away," he whispered. "I only wanted you to be fed and warm. But I was wrong in placing my faith in Reuben, and I can see that now." His voice hardened. "When I see the way that man treats his poor wife, it fills me with anger down to my core." He got up and took Wendy's hands in his, rubbing them with his thumbs as he had when she was a little girl.

"Thank you," Wendy blurted out.

He looked up at her in surprise.

"For telling me, I mean." She shook her head and sighed. "I might also be a little stubborn...sometimes. I suppose."

He gave her a warm smile, then leaned down and pressed his forehead against hers and closed his eyes. "I know you have to go. But please, please promise me you'll do your best to get back. You and the boys—Oh!" He stood up and reached down into his boot and pulled something out. When it came into the glow of the candlelight, Wendy could see that it was a long, thin knife.

"I've seen the machete that boy carries with him," her father said gruffly. "I figured you should have a knife of your own."

"Thank you," Wendy said, taking the knife carefully. It wasn't nearly as large as Peter's machete, but Wendy felt better having it already.

"I have gifts as well," came a deep voice from behind them.

Wendy and her father turned around to see Amos, Wendy's mother, and the king standing outside the threshold. The king came forward, and from beneath his cloak, he produced a small drawstring bag. When Wendy opened it, she found what looked like a dozen miniature casum balls inside.

"If you need to escape or fight the fae," the king said, "these will help. Crush it in your fingers and throw it into the air. It will explode there, creating a temporary burst of light."

"To distract them," Wendy said. "Like you did in the barn."

"Precisely." Then he removed his cloak. He tore the bottom off along a seam and then handed the now much shorter cloak to her. "Wear this, too. I had one made for every member of my family after the fae attacked our home. It hides power, so the balls of light will be safe until you pull them out."

Wendy wanted to reject the gift, for it was all far more than she could have hoped for. But in her time with the king, she guessed that he never made a decision without being absolutely certain about it. So she simply accepted the cloak with her sincerest thanks.

"Do you know what you'll do once you're there?" he asked.

"I'll have to see where the boys are," she said, tucking her new gifts into her reticule. Then she put her cloak on. "I'll try to simply get them out, but I doubt it's going to be that easy."

"It rarely is." A small smile lit his lips. "But the Maker shall provide a way to do what he wishes you to do."

Wendy thought of Peter's promise never to marry her, and her insides seemed to twist in on themselves. "I hope so."

"I know so," he said firmly.

After some disagreement as to how they should make their

attempt, it was decided that Wendy would lie down, and her mother would spread the stardust all over her body. Falling asleep with her parents, Amos, and the king watching wouldn't exactly be easy, but her father refused to leave her side, and the king wanted to watch to see if he might sense a portal opening, something he could follow through in case Wendy didn't come back.

As she lay back against the pillows, Wendy tried to focus on the thoughts she had once used to lull herself to sleep, but almost immediately, she tried to shake them from her mind. The dreams that had once been precious now mocked her. There would be no happily ever after with Peter Pan. No more adventures in Neverland, not the kind she wished for, at least. He would never again smile at her or decide she was worth growing up for.

Because, apparently, she wasn't.

"She's not sleeping," her father whispered before her mother hushed him. "But what do we do if she doesn't sleep?" he asked, slightly louder this time. Before Wendy could open her eyes to glare at him, she felt a calloused, heavy hand on her head. And as if someone was pouring a sleeping draught straight into her head, a wave of cozy warmth ran down her ears and neck and shoulders until it encased her entire body. It was the kind of heat that one might doze off to while sitting in a warm windowseat on a summer afternoon, or in front of a fireplace in the winter, and for a moment, she thought she saw the slightest flicker of blue flames in the corners of her vision.

Neverland. She needed to focus on Neverland. It's how she would get there, after all. Terrified she might be too late, Wendy forced herself to retrace every step of her journey to Neverland the first time, as much as she could remember. Hand in hand with Peter, the stars twinkling above them and the sparkling sea below. Back when Neverland was healthy and beautiful, and the crystal rainbow lit the night sky as Peter flashed her his ornery smile. But just as she was about to fall into a deep sleep, something made her side tickle, and she was horrified to feel her eyes open in response.

It was dark in her room, and no one stood above her anymore. Wendy's heart crashed into her stomach. She'd ruined everything. She hadn't been thinking of the journey to Neverland at all when she'd fallen asleep. She'd been thinking of Peter. And now all the stardust was gone. Just as she was about to roll over and begin crying, though, the sound of a frog croaking shook her from her sorrow. Was there a frog in her room?

Wendy sat up and realized that she wasn't in her room, after all. Rather, she was sitting in what felt like...sand? As her eyes adjusted, she could see dark waves lapping at the shore beside her, and on the other side, against the backdrop of cloud cover, she could see the purple outline of a mountain.

Wendy was in Neverland once more.

CHAPTER 17

HELP

P eter leaned against the stump and let it pull him into the treehouse, nearly landing on Slightly at the bottom.

"Who left the baby under the stump?" he called over the noise from the boys, who seemed too busy chasing each other with sticks to notice his return. Nana, who was always in a foul mood since Wendy had left, barked at Peter and dove to place herself between him and Slightly, who was still sitting on the ground, completely oblivious to the fact that Peter had almost fallen on him.

"He's getting a tooth!" John called back above the ruckus. "All he does is cry all day and demand Wendy."

Peter bent down and picked the little boy up and peeked inside his mouth. "How do you know?" he asked.

John rolled his eyes and left the fort he'd created with Michael and Pop. "See how he's drooling? And look here." John dipped a handkerchief into the bucket of water they had to fill at the stream and drag back every day, now they could no longer reliably conjure up food and drink at will. Then he walked back to Peter and handed the handkerchief to Slightly. The little boy immediately stuck the rolled-up cloth into his mouth and began to gnaw on it.

"See?" John smirked. "Teething. I was six when Michael started to teethe, so I remember." Then his smirk darkened as he studied Peter's face. "What's going on?"

"Tinkerbell!" Peter yelled over the chaos. He hated having to even say her name. After she'd betrayed Wendy's kiss to the rest of the fae, he'd wanted nothing more than to kick her out. Unfortunately, he also knew that without her, he couldn't keep the boys safe while he was gone all day, even with John and Nibs's help.

Before the island had begun to rot, Peter would have taken off and left the boys—well, not Slightly, but the rest of the boys—without a second thought. But now, as everything seemed to fall apart, he was too nervous to leave them all alone. So instead of sending her away, he'd chosen to simply ignore her as much as possible when she wasn't absolutely necessary.

Slightly let out a wail, and about half a minute later, Tink appeared at her door, yawning.

"What's he mad about now?"

"That's where you've been?" Peter called over Slightly's wailing. "Really?"

"If you haven't noticed, the boys are a little tired of being inside. It gets kind of grating." She took Slightly from him with a huff. "If you want them quieter, you'd better let them out."

"It's not safe anymore, and you know it. Now take him up to your room until he calms down," Peter said.

"Peter—"

"Just do it, Tink!"

She looked slightly taken aback. In the past, she would have let him have it for that kind of speech. But his silence must have been effective, because after a moment of glaring, she simply pursed her lips and did as he said. That, and the fact that if Tink hadn't told on Wendy, she wouldn't have to deal with the boys at all because Wendy might still be there to help.

Only after Tink was gone was he was able to take a deep breath and focus on John again.

The boy had grown quieter since Wendy had left. He smiled less and chided more. Only six days had passed since Wendy had gone, and it seemed all the boys had changed in the same way Slightly had gained a tooth. Or maybe it was just that without Wendy, Neverland seemed bereft of something Peter hadn't realized it needed.

"I'm going to talk to the fae tonight," he said in a low voice. I'm going to ask them to let you and the other boys go, but I doubt they will."

"So they're just going to keep us here until it all collapses?" John snapped.

"I don't know what they think they're doing. But I'm going to be frank with them tonight, and I think they'll see that they don't have much choice." He looked up at the other boys, who were mostly looking at him now as well. "When the boys are asleep," he added softly, "I want to talk to you and Nibs. We've got to make a plan."

John studied him for a moment. It was funny. The boy had been against Wendy coming from the start. He'd been the one begging to leave since arriving in Neverland, and he was often the one to point out how little Peter knew about young children. But now that Peter found his life blurring into one endless day, it occurred to him that John had become his most valuable asset. In spite of his resentment for what had happened to Wendy, he was helpful with the boys, often more dependable than Tink these days, and he was far less trouble. If he'd been a few years older, Peter would have been able to forgo Tink's help altogether.

It was odd to think about, but Peter realized he would miss John when it was time to say goodbye. His throat tightened so much it hurt every time he imagined that day. And it was coming far faster than he ever could have imagined.

When the younger boys were all snoring in their beds, Nibs and John slipped out of their beds and came to stand by Peter's hammock. Nibs, while not as familiar as John with the needs of very small children who were in the habit of growing, was also a great help with distracting the boys. And he, like John, had come to act as an extension of Peter himself.

"What is it, Peter?" Nibs asked, rubbing his freckled face. "John says you're going to tell the fae something new?"

Peter drew in a long, deep breath. "I don't know how to tell you boys this, but...Neverland will be gone soon."

John just nodded solemnly, but Nibs's mouth fell open. "What?"

"I've tried everything I know to save it. Wendy's gone. Jay's gone, but it keeps getting worse."

Nibs, big boy that he was, looked like he was about to cry. "But...where will we go?"

"I'm going to try to make a deal with the fae." Peter frowned down at his hands. "If they let me bring you all to the Darling farm, the star and I will move to the plateau. If I don't have to care for all of Neverland, I can probably restore at least the plateau and the canyon for a while. Several years, at least." He turned to John. "Do you think your parents would be able to find homes for the boys?"

A deep crease formed between John's brows, but he nodded.

"But we'll miss you, Peter," Nibs whispered, his face a ghostly white.

Peter reached up and rumpled the boy's hair. "You boys are everything to me. So I have to get you out of here when I can." He looked them both in the eyes. "Deal?"

"Deal, Peter," Nibs said in a subdued voice.

John, however, continued to study him. Finally, he shook his head and began to walk away.

"What is it?" Peter called after him.

John turned, and for a long moment, he stared at the ground. "She trusted you, Peter. With everything. And you let her down."

Peter had to swallow hard as the boy turned and walked away. It was better not to let them see how much that hurt.

"Wait here for me," he said, standing and pretending John hadn't spoken. "I'll be back soon. And don't do anything rash while I'm gone." He glanced down at Nana, who glared at him from beneath Michael's hammock. "You, either. Someone has to be the grownup here."

The dog snorted, which under better circumstances, would have made Peter chuckle. For now, though, he simply told the boys to wait for him.

"Tink," he called up through her little tunnel that led to her room.

A moment passed, but just as he was about to call out again, the little fae's head popped out from her bedroom entrance. "What?"

"Is Slightly asleep in there?"

She huffed. "Yes, on my bed. What do you want?"

"Bring him down here and put him in his bed. Then I want you to go to Tiger Lily and ask her to call a council."

Any resentment Tink might have harbored for their conversation earlier in the day melted from her face as Peter's words seemed to sink in. "What will you tell them?" she whispered, crawling out of her door.

"You'll hear when I get there. Now bring Slightly down and make sure they're all there in half an hour."

She nodded faintly before going to do as he said.

Peter left the tree with a strange sense of finality. It wasn't peace, exactly. An ache radiated out from his heart down to his fingertips and toes as he thought about what he was about to do. He flew silently up to the mountain's pinnacle and into the cave at the very top.

The star was still there as she had been the last time he'd seen her. But the walls around her no longer glittered with the reflections of her beauty. Her luster had dulled so that there was hardly a sparkle left, and she no longer turned in her place of suspension between the floor and the ceiling. Her jagged arms stuck out as though they were trying to hold on, rather than twirling in their glorious dance as she had done only a month ago.

"Are you sure you're at peace with this?" Peter asked, coming to sit beneath her, the way he had as a boy. "Once we do this, there's no going back."

It will slow the decay.

Though Peter heard the voice in his heart, rather than with his ears, the words seemed to echo dreadfully around him.

"How much longer do we have?" Peter asked after a long pause.

If they do as you ask, months. Perhaps a few years if they don't demand much.

"And if they don't agree?"

One thing at a time, Peter.

Peter pulled his legs up to his chest. "Can I tell you something?"

You know you can tell me anything.

He took a deep breath. "I'm afraid of death." Then he let out a dark chuckle. "Death was such a part of my childhood. Everyone died. But now that I've cheated it for so long, I don't know how to face it anymore." He looked up at her. "Does that make me a coward?"

The Maker will show you a way. She paused. *Eventually, death is a part of every human's way. But not all death is the end.*

"Maybe I wouldn't fear it so much if I had more to show for

it." Against his better judgment, he allowed himself a small indulgence, drudging back up in his mind the night he'd sent Wendy from Neverland. Before he'd been forced to take her home unconscious, she'd pleaded for him to play the what-if game, and unable to refuse her, he'd given in.

And all the what-ifs came flooding back.

What if he'd simply been a boy who had fallen in love and asked her father for her hand in marriage? What if he'd married her and gotten to fall asleep with her by his side every night? What if she'd carried his children, and he'd been a real father, not some clueless boy who was playing pretend?

What if he'd gotten to die, surrounded by his wife, children, and grandchildren, gray-haired and ready to pass from this world to the next?

Slowly, he rose from his seat and bid the star good night. He had work to do.

On the way north to the plateau, Peter was tempted to stop by the memory gems, but he knew better. The images were beginning to fade as the amethysts began to lose their color. The faces of his Lost Boys were leaving him, too.

No. It was better to stay the course. The fae should be ready by now. So Peter flew faster.

"Peter," Tiger Lily greeted him as he landed in the center of the fae circle. "Welcome."

Peter suppressed a shudder as he recalled the last time he'd been here surrounded by all the fae. It had been less than a week ago, but it felt like a lifetime. Wendy had been beside him, and she'd nearly gotten herself killed trying to defend him.

Now he was just trying to keep them all from dying.

"Thank you for meeting me tonight," he said, turning in a circle to make eye contact with most of them. "I know it was unexpected, but I've come to a realization today that I don't think can wait."

The fae began to murmur amongst themselves, but Tiger Lily hushed them all with a sharp word. Then she turned back to Peter. "Which would be?"

"I've talked to the Neverstar, and we've realized that Neverland is too far gone to save."

The fae leaped into the air, some shouting, some arguing, while others began to shift into their green mist forms. Tiger Lily held up a hand, though, and everything came to a stop.

"So what do you propose to do?" she asked in a dark voice. "You promised you would create a land where time stopped." She held up her hands. "As you can see, that promise is no longer being kept."

"It's been five hundred years," Peter said. "Far longer than any of us should have lived." Then he drew in a long, shaky breath and had to work hard to force his next words to spill from his lips. "I mean, Neverland has been wonderful. A gift. Do we really want this limitless existence forever, though? Nothing to mark the passing of time, nothing special. Just...existing?" He ran his hand through his hair. "It's a beautiful lie. But I can't keep patching it up."

"A lie for you, perhaps," Tiger Lily said in a calm voice. "But for us, it's life. It's the closest existence to our old world that we've been able to find, and giving it up would be like death itself to us."

"I don't know what you don't understand about this!" Peter cried, throwing his hands in the air. "Jay and Wendy are long gone, but I can barely keep the boys fed. At the rate we're losing stardust, we're going to lose our ability to fly in a matter of weeks. Maybe days." He huffed. "I can't even control the animals anymore. Tootles was nearly attacked by the crocodile yesterday."

"I can tell you exactly what's going on." Tiger Lily stood taller. "Wendy may be gone in person, but in spirit, she's here as much as she ever was."

Peter shook his head. "What?"

"That girl has left a mark on your heart. She doesn't have to set foot in Neverland ever again to cause damage because she lives on inside you. If you want to heal the island, you must cleanse her from your soul."

"I can't do that—"

"You *can* and you *must*, Peter!" Her voice boomed across the plateau. "You must keep your word!"

"I have!" Peter shouted back, Wendy's anger during their last meeting with the fae suddenly seeming quite logical. "For five hundred years, I've done everything you've ever asked!"

"Does a promise have limitations?"

"I was eight years old when I made it!" Peter roared. "I gave you what you wanted. When will you consider it fulfilled?"

"What more do you want, Peter? To marry her? To grow old and fat and die? We made you a god!"

"Gods aren't held against their will!"

"We never chained you down," Tiger Lily smirked.

"Wendy was right about you. About everything. And I'm done with it." Peter rose into the air and started to fly away, his plans for a compromise all but forgotten. He was going to get the boys out. No matter what he had to do to protect them, it couldn't possibly be worse than this.

"Peter!" Tiger Lily's voice boomed behind him. "If you dare to leave or even try to smuggle a single boy away out of Neverland, I'll spend the remaining years of my life on this earth hunting them down and tormenting them until they beg for death."

Peter froze in the air and turned slowly. "What did you say?"

Tiger Lily's lips curled into a terrible grin. She'd gotten him, and she knew it. "And I will make sure Wendy suffers more than all the others put together. I'll give her just enough freedom to find what her heart desires. Then I'll dash it to pieces. Over and over again, I'll destroy everything she's ever wanted or hoped for. Then I'll haunt her and her children until my dying breath if you leave so much as one leaf of this land unprotected."

Peter gave her his most withering glare and then flew back to the treehouse as quickly as he could. But instead of going inside, he went to Wendy's cottage for the first time since Wendy had left. The roses had wilted to an ugly brown, and parts of the walls and roof were falling off. But Peter went inside and knelt beside the bed anyway.

"I don't know what you have planned," he told the Maker, tears running down his face. "But I need some help. And I need it fast."

CHAPTER 18
STEALING THE NEVERSTAR

Wendy frowned at the flat, empty rock in front of her. "I want eggs and strawberries," she said again, louder this time. And again, nothing happened. She felt the slightest snap in the air, like the static that made her clothes spark sometimes. But no food appeared.

Wendy took a deep breath and tried to swallow the panic that was threatening to come loose.

It had all seemed simple enough last night when she'd arrived. After taking shelter in a little cave on the south shore of the island, she'd pulled Jay's little glass bauble out of her reticule and rubbed it just the way he'd told her. She had no idea how long it would take him to reach her, so after summoning him, she had decided to sleep for a few hours so she could stay awake later and watch so she could signal the ship when it did arrive.

But now, as the sky began to gray with early morning light, the breakfast she'd planned on imagining up for herself didn't appear, and Wendy realized that unless she could scrounge up something to eat, she'd be hungry until Jay arrived.

As she left the cave, careful to stay out of plain sight in case Peter or the fae were nearby, Wendy tried to figure out what had gone wrong. She'd been gone less than a week! Had Neverland really gotten so bad in just a few short days? Her stomach twisted as she thought about her brothers. Were they starving? How long ago had the food quit coming?

Then a new sort of fear gripped her. Had Jay's bauble even worked?

His directions had been simple. Hold the glass—which was in the shape of a flattened ball—in the palms of her hands, press against it. The sand inside, which was taken from Neverland's shores, would call him back to the island. It had all seemed so simple at home. But if Jay never came...

After doing as he said, she stared at the horizon until her eyes hurt, as though she could will the ship to appear, all the while, racking her brain to come up with another plan. What if she went back for King Everard? He'd said he would wait a few hours before leaving. Then she sighed. Even if she did find him, there was no guarantee she could take him back with her. She'd come through a dream, rather than on the water or through the air, as Jay and Peter traveled. The king wouldn't be able to dream his way there because he'd never been to Neverland in the first place. Besides, if the stardust was this weak, she wasn't sure they'd be able to fly back even if she could figure out the way.

Dawn's golden light brought little relief. Instead, it brought Wendy horrors she hadn't even considered. Far from the generally healthy forest she'd left behind, the majority of the island was now dead and colorless. The trees, flowers, and even the weeds were something between gray and brown, and the air, which had been filled with the chatter and buzz of birds and bugs, was nearly empty.

As she waited, Wendy did her best to get close to the tree-house, but more than once, she nearly stumbled upon a fae and had to dive back into the brush to stay hidden. They were keeping watch, it seemed, in a loose circle around the boys. Which meant, as Wendy had feared, Tiger Lily must be holding the boys hostage.

Wendy's former place of refuge had become a nightmare.

She needed to get the boys home. All of them. From John and Michael to Nibs and Slightly, every Lost Boy needed to escape this horrible place. Then, even if the fae did attempt to follow her back home, King Everard's guards could protect them until the king was able to help her decide what to do.

Of course, this meant leaving Peter behind.

Wendy stared wistfully at the tree before shaking her head. No, he'd chosen this path. If he'd just defied the fae and had chosen to come with her, he could have met King Everard as well, and they could have figured out what to do about the fae by now. But he had insisted on taking care of Neverland and the fae himself. Wendy's eyes pricked as she recalled his last words.

EVEN IF YOU stayed in Neverland, it never would have worked.

No. She swallowed her tears. He'd made his decision, and now she had to make hers.

As SHE WAITED, Wendy plotted. She did her best to think of everything that could possibly go wrong, and tried to think up ways to correct those possible mistakes. But she was no war strategist, and though she eventually worked out a plan, based on what she knew of Neverland's changes, by the end of the day, she was sure she might just lose her mind. To make matters more dire, fog like thick smoke had rolled over the water, making it nearly impossible to see anything more than ten yards away. Even if Jay did answer her call, how would he even find her?

She would have to come up with a new plan if he didn't come soon. If she was having such a hard time coming up with more than a few skinny roots to eat, Peter must be struggling to find food for the boys. They couldn't last much longer. Even Peter would have had to agree with her on that. But just as dusk began to fall, something sharp pierced the fog. Wendy nearly screamed for joy, stopping herself at the last minute as the rowboat headed her way, a familiar figure at its bow. When he and his rowers drew near and waved, Wendy held her finger to her lips and glanced back behind her. A fae had passed by not long before, close enough for noise to draw his attention if they made any. Jay nodded and helped her into the boat, which immediately turned around and headed back to the ship.

"Are you all right?" Jay asked quietly as they skimmed the water.

"Yes. But the boys won't be soon."

Jay nodded, but he didn't say anything else until they were on his ship and in his quarters. When they arrived, he ordered one of his men to immediately fetch Miss Darling tea and supper. Then he indicated for Wendy to sit in the good chair before seating himself on the other side of the table that took up the majority of the small room. He spread his right hand on it. His left arm, which Wendy hadn't paid heed to until now, was also placed atop the table. The bandaged nub, however, which had covered the remnant of the hand Peter had cut off, was no more. In its place sat a gleaming golden hook.

"Go ahead and stare," he said with a grim smile when Wendy looked away from it a little too pointedly. "It's my lifelong reminder never to let the drink take me again."

"You got here quickly," Wendy said, hoping to steer the conversation away from that awful day.

The corners of his mouth turned up, as though he was

attempting to hide a smile. "I...I might or might not have been keeping close to the barrier in recent weeks."

"You have?" That was strange. "But why?"

He opened his mouth as though to chuckle then stopped himself. "I was rather hoping you might call." Wendy stared at him, but before she could enquire further, he tapped the table with his fingers. "Now, while I can't express to you how delighted I am to see you, I'm guessing your need is rather urgent. So why don't you tell me what you need?"

Even now, in this dire moment, Wendy couldn't help admiring the width of his shoulders and the bright interest in his dark eyes. Her heart fluttered stupidly as she tried to recall just why she was here.

"You said something about the boys..." he said slowly, as if hoping to help her remember.

Oh yes, the boys.

"I need your help to get the boys away from this place," she said.

"Very well." Jay nodded as though this were a common request. "How shall we do that?"

Wendy leaned forward against the table. "You're going to help me break Neverland."

He raised his eyebrows. "Oh?"

Wendy smiled in spite of herself. "We're going to steal the Neverstar."

CHAPTER 19
WENDY DARLING

several minutes passed in silence. Jay got up from his chair and stared into the fireplace, and Wendy worried that the hammering of her heart in her ears might make it hard to hear him. When he did turn back to her, his brows were furrowed, but instead of telling her how stupid such a plan would be, as she half-expected, he gave her a resolute nod.

"I agree."

Wendy blinked at him. "You do?"

He sat down again as a sailor knocked and entered with a tray of tea and food. It took every minute of her mother's etiquette lessons to keep Wendy from scarfing down the food with Michael's gusto, instead forcing herself to eat tiny, ladylike bites. In her angst over her brothers, she hadn't realized how hungry she was.

"From the first day I met them, I believed the fae were using Peter," Jay said. "But Peter refused to listen every time I mentioned it. Once, I even asked to see the star, hoping to find some way to use her to convince him."

Wendy swallowed slowly. If anyone was in a position to see

the fae's abuses, it would have been Jay. He'd been in Neverland much longer than Wendy had.

"And he said no," Wendy finished for him.

Jay stabbed a stick of dry beef with his hook and brought it closer to examine it. "When Peter created a barrier between the rest of the island and Neverstar's cave, I don't think he ever meant to let anyone in." He shrugged. "As far as I know, you're the only one he's ever allowed inside."

Wendy was reminded of Peter's confession that he'd never even shown the star to Tink because he was afraid she'd do something mischievous. Of course, this reminder only filled her with a sickly guilt, which she did her best to ignore. This was for Peter's own good, after all.

"All that to say," Jay continued, "that the fae have used that star to control him since the first day. If he won't listen to you, then he's not going to listen to anyone. And he'll be forced to continue in this miserable existence until the star eventually dies." He paused and tilted his head slightly. "I'm curious, though. What do you wish to do with the star once it's in our possession?"

"From the way I understand it, our problem is this." Wendy put down her food and twined her fingers. "If it were up to Peter, he would have ended Neverland years ago. But he made that stupid promise to the fae, and they won't consider it fulfilled even though they've had five hundred years."

"So far, I agree. Go on."

Wendy nodded. "So if we could get the boys to safety, somewhere that the fae can't follow to get revenge, Peter could...How would you describe it? He could let Neverland go. The star wouldn't die because she wouldn't have to power Neverland any longer, and Peter would be free."

"Again," Jay said, "I agree. I'm wondering where you plan to take the boys so the fae can't follow, though." Using his shirt, he cleaned the spot on his hook where the meat stick had gotten oil on it. "As much as I'd like to provide that protection, my ship is made for travel and cargo. We're not a warship. I might be able to challenge the fae here, as they can't change into their old form. But if we were out in the Old World, where they could change form as they pleased, my men wouldn't stand a chance. And, unfortunately, they'll be waiting for that. As soon as we're across the barrier, they're free from all obligation of Neverland's rules, including the one about drawing blood."

"Oh, I don't mean for you to do that," Wendy rushed to say. "What I mean to say is that if we could simply get them out of Neverland quietly, King Everard can help us. He's apparently familiar with the fae and their dangers."

"And how do you propose we get the attention of the realm's most powerful monarch?" Jay looked again like he was hiding a smile. This time, however, Wendy was a bit annoyed. He looked much like a parent, listening patiently as their child explained the desire to complete some impossible feat.

This made her sit taller. "When I disappeared, my friend wrote to the king and told him of Amos's old stories, which included the fae. In response, the king came to Beddington—"

Jay's jaw dropped. "Wait, you're telling me that *King Everard* came to your hometown to hear about the fae?"

"I know. It's incredible. Really. But it seems that these fae are part of the group who attacked the Destinian Fortress and nearly wiped out the Fortier line half a millennia ago. Their descendants, or rather, those who weren't part of this group, returned to the Fortress recently and nearly killed the king and his family. So he's familiar with how to fight them. He's promised that if I return, he and his men will deal with the fae themselves."

Jay sat back in his chair and ran his hand over his face. "Wow...huh."

"The king has left two of his experienced soldiers at my

parents' farm. If we can get the boys back to them, they can protect us. And the king has said he'll do his best to help with whatever else we need."

"Peter won't like it," Jay said quietly.

Wendy bit her lip. She knew that, of course. But hearing him say it still hurt. "I know," she said. "But if it means getting the boys safe, he'll do it."

"And you know that how?"

"Tiger Lily is holding them hostage."

"And what do you plan to do with Peter and the star when you're all done?" Jay asked slowly, studying her a little too closely for comfort.

"I was thinking," Wendy said, tracing the grain of the wood in the table, "that perhaps....perhaps you could take the star to your mother. I'm sure Peter wouldn't mind, since he wouldn't be bound to Neverland's rules anymore. Then, once she was healed, he could take the star back and do whatever he wanted." Why did those words taste so bitter?

Jay's eyes brightened, and he sat up. "You would really do that for me? Even with all you and Peter..." He let the thought die, which sent another wave of shame across Wendy's shoulders and down into her chest.

"I don't want to betray Peter." She looked down at her food. "And honestly...I feel terrible about this." She looked back up, beseeching him, willing him to understand. "But I don't know what else to do." Her eyes pricked. "Besides. He swore nothing would come of us anyway. So it's not like it really matters."

The fire crackled, and the ship rocked quietly in the dark. But the splashes of Wendy's tears against her hands felt deafening. Her shoulders shook, and without her permission, the emotional flood she'd been pushing back broke loose.

I can swear to you now that I will never marry you.

The finality of Peter's words crackled in her ears and her

heart. When had she been idiotic enough to think that he could... or even would marry her? Because the hope had blossomed without permission long before that stupid what-if game she'd begged him to play.

She'd known growing up was against the rules. She'd come to Neverland specifically to avoid growing up and having to get married. So when had their fun and games become more than just that? Was it every time he'd touched the necklace he'd given her? Or the way he watched her with the boys, with that soft affection she saw reflected in his eyes for no one else?

"I'm sorry," she whispered, trying to dry her eyes with her skirt. In response, she was handed a lace handkerchief. But before she could finish drying her face with it, a hard, calloused hand took her face gently and lifted it up so that she was looking at Jay.

"Don't be," he whispered. His own eyes glistened, and his jaw was tight. He withdrew his hand and leaned back into his chair. "While I can't claim the same kind of...affection you have for Peter, he was...is a brother to me. And when he brought me back to the real world, I wanted nothing more than for him to stay with myself and my mother." He paused and swallowed, letting his gaze get lost on the wall behind Wendy. "But he wouldn't come. And I felt like my world was being torn in two as he flew back to Neverland."

"I don't know why I'm so disappointed." Wendy gave a shaky laugh. "I knew better, and I was still foolish enough to believe he might—" She stopped talking when Jay reached across the table and touched her lips with his finger.

"It's because we see what Peter is denying. He sacrifices so others may live, and there's an undeniable draw to those who put others before themselves."

"I'm sorry to distract you from searching for your mother's cure." Wendy hiccupped, and Jay poured her another cup of tea.

She took it gratefully. "I wouldn't have called you if I'd known any other way to save the boys."

"To be honest, I wasn't accomplishing much, drifting out in the ocean as I tried to sort through which legends and stories to follow and which to throw out as old fisherman's tales." He turned and gave the island a wistful look through his large window beside the bed. "Besides, there is the star. And I guess I hadn't quite given up hope..." He sighed.

"I'm afraid she's quite weak," Wendy said. "The island is no longer producing food."

Jay had been staring down at a loose button on his cuff, but at this, his eyes met hers. "Which means the star is not only weak. She's dying."

Wendy nodded. "I didn't know what else to do."

"You did the right thing." He gave her a small smile. "It's why I left you the whistle, after all." He took a deep breath and looked back out at the island, which was nearly impossible to see under the cloud cover. "We'll have to be swift. And there's also the problem of the fae. They won't take kindly to their paradise being dismantled."

"I actually have an idea," Wendy ventured carefully. "But I'll need your help."

At this, Jay threw his head back and laughed. "Of course you do. You wouldn't be Wendy Darling if you didn't already have everything sorted and planned."

Wendy's cheeks warmed, but she tried not to let the compliment go to her head and distract her. She could do that later.

"And then, when it's all done, you would take the boys with you?" Jay raised his eyebrows.

"Yes." Wendy nodded then paused. "Well, I mean, I would love to. Obviously, if they're determined to go with Peter, I wouldn't stop them, though I'm not sure how he would provide for them."

"And Peter?" Jay pressed.

"As I said." Wendy sniffed and straightened her shoulders. "He can do as he pleases."

Jay leaned back and crossed his arms over his chest as he studied her. "You really have given up hope of you and Peter—"

"Yes." Wendy sniffed. "He made his opinion of our chances crystal clear. And if he feels that way, I'm determined to be better off without him."

"Then why are you so desirous that he escape the fae?"

Wendy squared her shoulders. "I despise injustice. The fae did this to him, and if nothing else, it needs to end."

Jay watched her for a moment, his dark eyes full of interest but giving little away. Finally, he rose and stood, leaning against the table. "I believe you're right. But I also believe you've had too much time to think and not enough to rest. So I suggest I take you to your room for the night. We'll leave Neverland briefly to stock up on provisions, finalize our plans, then we'll return and carry them out."

"Stock up?" Wendy stood, too. "What for?"

He hesitated. "We might need more weapons if things go badly with the fae. I keep some basic defensive equipment about the ship, but only what you might need to defend against a small boat full of bandits. I'm afraid I'm completely unprepared for a horde of angry fae."

"Oh, I hadn't thought of that." It made sense, of course. Jay was a businessman, not a pirate. It was unlikely he'd have stashes of weapons all over his ship. "But what about the boys? If the island has died this much in less than a week, I'm afraid they won't have enough food by the time we get back."

Jay frowned for a moment before his eyes lit up. "I'll have my men deliver some of our pantry to the island first. We'll place it where Peter can't miss it. Then they'll be fed until we return. It should only be three days at most."

"That would be better than nothing, but..." Wendy's heart leaped in her chest. "What if we contacted King Everard? He could meet us and come back into Neverland with us!"

Jay grimly shook his head. "Not enough time."

"Why not?"

"Have you tried flying?"

Wendy frowned. "I did, but I didn't feel safe enough to try crossing the water. It felt too unsteady."

"If he's going home, Destin is south of Ashland, and he'll have to go through several kingdoms to get there." He nodded. "If Neverland has quit producing food, I'm not sure we'd be able to find him and then get him back in time. If we could fly, that would be one thing. But with the way the star is as we speak I'm honestly shocked you were able to fly back in at all."

"I didn't fly," Wendy said miserably. "I got in through a dream."

"Oh!" Jay looked genuinely surprised. "I didn't know that was even possible."

"Pop and Top figured it out."

Jay made a face. "I ignored them whenever I had the chance." Then his face became serious again. "To get to the nearest port, the king would have to travel for days."

"He's very fast."

"Yes, but we're not. At least, not without flight. By the time we located him, Neverland might already be gone."

This disappointed Wendy more than she could express. The thought of simply flying home and then returning again with the king had seemed like a dream come true. But as much as she wished to get the boys back tonight or tomorrow, giving up an unrealistic dream was undoubtedly an acceptable sacrifice if it meant her boys would be safer from the fae. Fetching the king wouldn't do anyone good if the fae killed them all first.

Jay put out the fire, closed the window curtains, then

stepped back out onto the deck, and Wendy followed him. The lights on the ship's deck were all dark, probably, Wendy guessed, so the fae wouldn't notice them. She had to feel her way along behind him. He must have sensed this because a half-second after she'd stubbed her toe, his warm hand was on her elbow, guiding her. She let him lead the way and hoped he didn't realize how fast her heart was beating. It was ridiculous, she knew. He was only making sure she didn't fall. Peter would have done the same.

Actually, no Peter wouldn't have. He'd been the one to put her to sleep and leave her instead.

Peter was a blockhead.

Jay led her down a narrow set of steps to a room below the deck that was full of men. This room was full of lanterns and merriment. One man was playing a lighthearted tune on a flute and another a fiddle, and the other men, of which there were probably two dozen, laughed and joked as they drank from large mugs. When Jay entered the room, however, they all jumped to their feet, and the laughter and chatter ceased.

"Gentlemen," Jay said, putting his hand on the small of her back. The touch was innocent but intimate enough to make her jump as he gently pushed her forward. "This is Miss Wendy Darling. She is our guest and will be treated with the respect you would pay my mother." He eyed a few of the younger men in the corner. "Am I understood?"

"Yes, Captain!" they all cried.

"I also want you to have Gustav gather enough food supplies from the pantry to last a party of..." He looked down at Wendy. "How many?"

"Nine boys," Wendy said.

"Prepare enough food to last nine boys four days."

"That's a lot of food, sir!" one of the men called out.

"We're going to restock tomorrow," Jay said. "So don't worry about the supply count. Just have it done and ready within two hours. We're leaving in three."

"Yes, sir!" they cried before springing into action.

Wendy gave him a grateful smile as he led her to a hallway at the end of the room. There were three doors on each side of the hall and one on the end. He led her to the last one on the right, pulled out a key, and opened it.

Inside, there was a small bed about half the size of the one at home, as well as a washbasin and tiny mirror. Red, cheery curtains hung from the round window in the wall that the bed was pushed up against.

"I apologize for the lack of a fireplace," Jay said as Wendy followed him inside. "Unfortunately, we never know who might book passage with us, and not all travelers are as trustworthy with fire on a ship as we would like them to be."

Wendy laughed. "It's perfect. To be honest, I'll probably be asleep before I could even think to light anything."

"We do keep some clothes for our passengers, just in case theirs are ruined out at sea. They might not fit well, but you'll find a clean sleeping chemise in that chest at the foot of the bed. It's not exactly cut to your size, but it will be more comfortable than sleeping in your clothes."

"I can't thank you enough." Wendy turned and walked back to the captain. "You've done everything I've asked and more. And you hardly know me." Why did she suddenly feel so shy?

The light from the lantern danced in his dark eyes. "You're not difficult to notice, Wendy Darling."

What did that mean? Wendy didn't even know, and her chest was wreaking havoc with her breathing.

Finally, Jay bowed his head and stepped backward. "I'll let you get ready, then." And with that, he and the light were gone.

Wendy didn't need the light to get ready. There was just enough weak moonlight making it through the fog and clouds that she was able to find a nightdress in the trunk, just as he had said. And though her brothers were still on the island, and she and Jay didn't yet have the star, for the first time in a long time, Wendy slipped peacefully into slumber without a single thought of Peter.

CHAPTER 20
NEVER WANTED

What is this?" Tink asked, staring at the crates of food sitting on the shore.

Peter shook his head slowly. He hadn't the faintest idea. Last night, the southern beach had been absolutely clear. This morning, he'd awakened and gone out to survey the island only to find this pile of food sitting out on the shore.

But that didn't mean he was about to let it go to waste. No, he'd prayed far too much lately for a miracle to leave the food here. He bent down and hefted a crate of oranges onto his shoulder. "There," he pointed, "grab that bag of bread."

Tink frowned but did as he said. "So we're just going to take it then?"

"Why not?" Peter grabbed a bucket of dried meat sticks as well, then tried to lift off the ground.

Only to come right back down. Drat.

"The food makes us too heavy to fly. We'll have to carry it all on foot." Peter paused to gather a few more drawstring bread bags and tie them across his chest, along with his bucket of meat sticks and crate of oranges. When he finally felt decently balanced, he started slowly back up the path.

"You're making me *walk* back up the mountain?"

"No one's making you do anything."

Tink snapped her mouth shut, grabbed two of the bread bags, and followed, though the pout of her lip made Peter roll his eyes. The stardust was continuing to weaken. She should just be grateful to have food, whether she had to carry it or not.

Several minutes passed before Tink broke the silence. "Think it floated in?" She sounded slightly breathless. "Like on a raft or something?"

Peter paused to readjust the weight of the orange crate on his shoulder and continued his walk up the trail. The more they talked, the longer their trek would take.

"Peter, wait!"

"You know the way," he called without looking back.

"But Peter..."

There was the sound of a package hitting the ground, then Tinkerbell flitted in front of him, directly in his path.

"Before you say anything," she said, holding her hands up in front of her, "I know you're angry with me. Furious."

Peter gave her a dark glare. "Whatever gave you that impression?"

"But you have to hear why."

Peter wanted nothing more than to push past the little fae and continue on his way. But his arms were getting tired, and the youthful, hopeful look in her eyes threatened to melt one of the many icicles that had grown in his heart around the place she had once occupied. "What is it?" he asked, putting the fruit down on the ground. "Make it quick."

"You didn't want me to tell Tiger Lily about Wendy's kiss." Tink looked down at the ground.

"How long did it take you to figure that out?"

"I'll admit, I was glad to be rid of her." Tink rubbed her elbow. "But I wasn't doing it to make you unhappy. I promise!"

"Then why did you do it, Tink?"

She shoved a tendril of platinum hair out of her eyes. "Two reasons."

"Three, since we've already established that you had a vindictive animosity toward Wendy, but go ahead."

Tink winced. "The first was my concern for Neverland." She gestured to their surroundings. "Which was clearly warranted."

"And the second?" Peter growled.

"It wasn't so much about getting rid of Wendy as...as it was showing you what was there first."

Peter crossed his arms. "Which would be?"

Tink took a deep breath, and for the first time, raised her eyes to his. "Me."

Not this again. Ever since Wendy had pointed out Tink's seemingly growing obsession with the strange notion of a romance between them, Peter had done his best to pretend it didn't exist. Then, after Wendy's expulsion, he'd done everything in his power not to talk to her at all. But it just kept coming back to bite him. Peter shook his head and lifted the food once more to make his way up the mountain.

Tink ran back and grabbed her bags before catching up with him again. "I know we couldn't have what Wendy wanted with you," she said in a hurry. "And I wouldn't expect it! But what we used to have...it was good! And I could help you restore Neverland in a way Wendy never could—"

"Tink, please don't."

"But, Peter, I love you!"

And there it was. Peter squeezed his eyes shut for a moment then opened them to stare at the path ahead of him. "And I've always loved you, too," he forced himself to say. "But as a sister! Or a little friend." He shook his head and continued plodding up the mountain. "I'm sorry if I ever made you feel that such a love could be possible between us, but I swear, I never meant to."

"Oh, I was like a little sister once," she snapped, her voice trembling. "But like a good little sister, I followed you faithfully. But I begged you—Peter, look at me!"

She stopped in front of him again and forced him to stop. He glared at her, but she spoke anyway.

"I begged you to stay in Neverland," she continued, meeting his glare, "because I knew what was happening to me. To us both! I never wanted to be this way." She held up her arms and waved her hands over her body. Which, to Peter's horror, now that he noticed it, was nearly as developed as Wendy's. When had *that* happened?

"To have these...these feelings," she continued. "And yearnings. But you wouldn't listen. You kept returning to the Old World like a sailor to a siren call."

"Tink, I..." Peter ran his free hand through his hair. "I'm sorry. Truly. I never meant to make you come with me. I always thought you just wanted to."

"I did! Because I trusted you to be as concerned for my well-being as your own!" She kicked a rock. "I never thought you'd be so selfish as to age me along with yourself."

"I promise, Tink, I was never trying to age you. I just..." Peter shrugged helplessly. "I never wanted to live forever. I was just grasping at whatever freedom I could whenever I had the chance."

"Well, congratulations," Tink snapped as tears ran down her cheeks. "You got what you wanted."

"That's not fair. I never wanted to hurt you."

"But you never wanted to love me, either!"

"I couldn't love Wendy the way she wanted!" Peter shouted. "You made sure of that! So what makes you think I could love you?"

Tink lifted into the air, tears streaming down her face. "Apparently, you can't." And with that, she turned and flew away, leaving the food and Peter behind her.

CHAPTER 21
CONSIDER

Sailing through the barrier was strange but exhilarating. One moment, they were in the warm, wet air that surrounded Neverland, and the next, Wendy was shivering in the cold winter gales that swept over Ashland's great Sharyn Sea. It wasn't really a sea. It was really a bay that separated Ashland's shining capital, Kaylem, from its biggest city, Solwhind. The thin strip of land beneath the bay that connected the two pieces of the kingdom was where Wendy's family lived. And, apparently, where Neverland was as well. And somehow, the ocean air felt even colder than Wendy's farm did when the sun hadn't yet risen. Wendy hoped pathetically that the sun would warm them as soon as it peeked its head over the horizon.

"I didn't realize Neverland was so close to a port!" Wendy called over the wind. "Or the coast!" Indeed, the coast was so close that they might have reached it in less than an hour, had they been sailing straight for it.

Jay, who was at the ship's wheel several feet away from where Wendy clung to the railing, just smiled. "I, too, was surprised the first time I ventured out with my uncle. I knew where Neverland's general vicinity was, but I hadn't known it was so close to civilization." He looked thoughtful for a moment. "I think it's part of the star's power. Neverland takes up very little space in the real world. But within the star's domain, your perception expands."

Wendy thought for a moment that perhaps it wouldn't have taken so long to hunt down King Everard yesterday, had she tried to do so immediately. But they were here now, and the king was surely on his way home, probably bolting home at inhuman speeds once again. Besides, she wasn't exactly in a position to argue. So she asked something else instead. "What happens when other ships try to sail through the barrier?" Wendy looked back at where Neverland had been only moments ago. Instead of a large island, there was only water.

"Peter has it rigged so that strong gales and heavy rain will drive them away if they try coming too close. And he did a good job of it. I knew a man once who refused to go around and ended up destroying his entire boat in the process. He was the only part of that ship to survive."

"What do the sailors think of it?" Wendy asked.

Jay smirked. "Most are superstitious and don't go near the thing. The more scientific-minded have all sorts of theories about how the currents and winds interact, but it's all just to cover up the fact that they haven't a clue."

Despite her determination not to spare him much thought, Wendy almost smiled. Leave it to Peter to ruin the boat but leave its sailor alive. He valued even the lives of those who would intrude on his paradise.

"What exactly are we getting at this market?" Wendy asked, squinting at the shore, which had only just appeared on the horizon.

"My men need to be well-supplied in casum balls and other weapons in the case that Tiger Lily attacks."

"I hope not." Wendy shuddered. "Do you think she'll really take the bait?" When she'd awakened that morning, Wendy had found that Jay was already hard at work, as he announced that he'd figured out how to distract Tiger Lily as they tried to make their escape.

"If we time it carefully, yes. I can rig the casum balls to explode at a particular time."

Wendy frowned. "How?"

"Casum balls are made up of two kinds of clay. The outside is merely a protective coating for the inside, which explodes when it meets the air. All I have to do is make sure the mud is peeling off the casum balls at a proper rate, and it will explode when I want it to. And they won't all explode at once. We'll have one going off every half minute or so in and near the canyon. That should draw them away from the tree."

"I'm still not sure I'll be fast enough to beat Peter to the ship. Flying isn't exactly predictable right now." Wendy frowned.

"If you go unnoticed, it won't matter how fast or slow you are," Jay said, rubbing a splinter off one of the decorative wheel knobs. "Once you have the star, I'll get Peter's attention. My men and I will trap him while you rush in and take the boys."

Wendy drew her shawl more tightly around her.

"Remember," Jay said gently, "we're doing this *for* Peter."

Wendy huffed. "I know. It just feels...traitorous." She recalled that warm, clear night when he'd taken her to see the Neverstar as though it had been hours ago, rather than months. She also remembered how excited he'd seemed when he'd informed her that she was the only other person who had ever been allowed in the Neverstar's cave.

And now she was going to use that privilege to steal the star and end his way of life forever. Wendy shuddered. This was for her brothers. And the Lost Boys. And Jay was right when he said that it was for Peter as well. She might not have been able to have him, but that didn't mean the fae got to keep him either.

"Chin up, though," Jay laughed. "You look like someone threw water on your kitten. I have a feeling you're going to enjoy this day immensely."

Wendy laughed. "I'm allergic to cats, but a wonderful day would be very welcome right now." She glanced back once more, though she knew she would see nothing but ocean. "It feels wrong to leave them."

"You're leaving to come back." Jay held up his hook and rubbed a smudge off of it.

"Is that really useful?" Wendy asked, watching the shiny hook with fascination. Then she caught herself. "I don't mean to be rude, of course—"

"It can be very useful." Jay grinned and stretched his arm toward her. With expert aim, he put the hook through the strap of the bag Wendy was wearing and used it to draw her forward. Wendy shrieked and laughed as he pulled her up against him, so close that their sides were touching. Her laughter probably sounded a bit ridiculous, like that of a saucy girl not old enough to be out of braids, but it was about more than she could handle to stand pressed against his warm side as he wrapped his arm around her and pulled her close. Then he turned them to face the east.

"There," he said, pointing with his good hand, "you'll see a sunrise like you've never seen it before. Right about...now."

As he spoke, golden light spilled over the ocean, making Wendy's eyes hurt as everything reflected back with enough grandeur to put the richest king's dreams to shame. Wendy had to squint terribly to see through the reflections that gleamed on every wave, but when she finally did, she was able to make out what Jay was pointing at.

A little city sat nestled against the gentle rolling hills that met the ocean. Dozens of boats bobbed up and down at the long dock, greeting the newcomers merrily. The houses that lined and filled the hilltops and their gentle slopes were painted varying shades of blue. Their wooden roofs had possibly once been another color, but they were so bleached by the sun there was little telling what color they had once been.

"It's riveting!" Wendy ran to the opposite railing to see better. Or perhaps it was to keep herself from getting too comfortable at Jay's side. She'd already dealt with two men in the last two months. The last thing she needed was a third. At least...at the moment.

"I thought you'd like it." Jay beamed. "This is Lispon, one of Ashland's best hidden treasures."

If Lispon was a hidden treasure, there must have been many people in on the secret, for by the time the ship was in the harbor, the streets were so crowded Wendy had to take care not to run into someone.

"Many cities have a central marketplace," Jay called over the noise of the crowd, offering her his arm. Wendy accepted, hoping not to be run over by some enthusiastic member of the throng. "Lispon was built on the coast, so they weren't able to create a marketplace the way most towns have."

"What do they have then?" Wendy asked, looking around at the hundreds of strangers bustling around her.

"That." Jay pointed up the hill, and Wendy gasped as she realized what he was pointing at. The street they were standing in stretched up the entire length of the hillside with shops on each side and houses behind them.

"It's so long!"

"It is," he said, nodding as though this satisfied him. "It also gets you devilish hungry."

Wendy laughed. "We can't have that happen now, can we?"

"I can show you exactly where to fix it." He placed his hand on the small of her back and turned her toward a bustling inn. Wendy nearly jumped off the ground at the touch. Not because it was unpleasant, exactly, but more because it was so intimate, as though they were already the oldest of friends.

If he noticed her surprise, he didn't give any sign of it. Instead, he moved her gently toward the inn, and as they came near the door, Wendy could see why he wanted to come. Even before they were through the door, the rich smells of onion, garlic, basil, bread, and several scents she couldn't name wafted out to them. Her stomach growled as though she'd gone all day without eating, even though they'd eaten only an hour earlier.

Men and women filled the small, round tables that covered the room, and Wendy was relieved to see that this place was far different from the inns and taverns she'd seen while in Solwhind. Instead of raucous, drunk men sloshing ale all over the floor and one another, these patrons, men and women alike, were neat and orderly, chatting as they breakfasted.

"Captain," a man called from the corner of the room. He had darker skin than Wendy had ever seen, and his hair ran down his back in countless long, skinny braids, which were decorated with brightly colored glass beads. He came to Jay, and Jay leaned forward and embraced him, slapping him on the back as he did. The man returned the gesture but seemed slightly confused.

"It's been a long time," the man said, stepping back with an uncertain smile. "I nearly forgot what you looked like."

"I've been busy with some unfortunate circumstances, but I'm glad to be back." Jay motioned to Wendy. "May I introduce you to Miss Wendy Darling? Wendy, this is Milo."

Milo raised his eyebrows. "Not too unfortunate, I see."

Wendy blushed. "It's good to meet you."

"My guest is hungry," Jay said. "Would there be any way to find a table?"

Milo blinked at him then seemed to straighten. "Of course. I'll have my men bring out an extra table and put it..." He looked around. "In that corner. Would that suit you?"

"I can wait very well," Wendy said. "I really don't mind."

"We'll take that table," Jay said, ignoring her.

Milo called over two young men in aprons and spoke with them. They ran out the back door and returned with a new table and two chairs. Milo led Wendy and Jay to the table, grabbed a rag from his belt, and began to scrub it vigorously.

The space was a little tight, and the patrons in the nearby chairs frowned a little as Milo help Wendy and Jay squeeze into the corner, but once she was sitting down, Wendy decided the view was very much like a painting. Unlike most establishments, this inn seemed to have enough money for the finer things in life, as three sides of the room were lined with windows with real glass panes. Morning light streamed in through those windows, and the harbor with its blue water and colorful boats was in full view.

"I'll make sure your food is ready in a moment," Milo assured them.

"He seems a little nervous," Wendy said in a low voice as he hurried away.

"Milo and I go way back," Jay said, taking tea from a tray brought to them by one of the serving boys.

Wendy nearly enquired more, but Milo returned, and with him, he brought a mountain of food large enough to make Wendy forget her question. Their plates were heaped with steaming rolls with butter, apple slices, orange slices of steaming pumpkin sprinkled with nuts and what looked like real sugar crystals, and crisp, salty bacon.

"I can't believe I've never heard of this port before!" Wendy peered out into the harbor once again to see the colorful ships bob up and down.

"As I said, Lipson's a hidden gem. Small enough that many of the larger traders will pass it up to head straight to Solwhind. But those who do come find an unusually diverse company here. And some incredibly rich trading resources, as a large number of the people here are supplied by their families, artisans who still live in the deep south and the far east."

"Solwhind is also made up of people from all over the world, is it not?" Wendy asked as she sipped at her cider.

"I suppose you could say this little port is much like Solwhind. Only, they're not having a civil war, as you can tell." He gestured through the window at the dozens of people passing by.

"I like Milo, by the way." Wendy stirred her tea. "You still haven't told me, though, why he's obviously terrified of you."

Jay gave her a wry smile. "He's a decent fellow and runs one of the best businesses I've ever seen."

"But?"

"He made the mistake of stealing from me a few years ago."

"Oh?" Wendy asked. For some reason, the sudden hard edge in Jay's voice took her by surprise.

Jay smiled and sat back. "But we're not here to talk about Milo. Tell me, Wendy. What would *you* like to do today?"

Wendy pulled a small bit of bread off and buttered it. "Aren't you here to restock?"

"My men can do that. You, however, have never been here, and I believe you will find it quite to your liking."

"Perhaps then," Wendy said, "you should show me."

Inside, she cringed at what her proper mother might say to the thought of her spending a day alone with a man who was almost but not quite a stranger in a market her parents probably didn't know existed. But she had come for her brothers, and sitting on the ship in her room as the sailors restocked supplies would do them no good. So as soon as they were done with breakfast, Wendy allowed Jay to lead her up and down the long market hill all day long, taking her from shop to shop to see and taste more trinkets and treats than Wendy had known all the world to hold. By the time they returned to the ship that evening, she was so tired she could hardly walk.

The next day was different but no less enjoyable. She watched in awe as the men made repairs to the ship. She felt much like a senseless ninny when Jay removed his outer clothes and wore only his trousers and his white shirt, which was buttoned halfway up his chest as he and the other men climbed up and down the ship to check sails and rigging. And it took more than a little self-control for Wendy not to stare like a nincompoop every time the wind whipped his shirt around his work-hardened shoulders and trim waist.

That night, there was a celebration on the ship's deck. The sailors dragged up tables and stools, and the cook created the best dish of parsnips, potatoes, roasted carrots, and beef Wendy had ever tasted. Everyone sat down to an evening of laughter and merriment. Wendy tried to soak it all in, reveling in the fact that, if only just for a moment, she could smile. They were on their way to saving not only her brothers, but the Lost Boys, too. And soon, even if he didn't want her, Peter would be free.

"You look thoughtful tonight," Jay said after they'd finished most of their meal. The two musician sailors were playing tunes again in the corner, and several of the sailors were even dancing. "What has you so thoughtful?"

Wendy smiled. "You seem so much freer now. Has your mother improved? Or have you found any sort of possible cure?"

His smile faltered slightly, and his eyes tightened as he looked at the table. "I have actually found a...a possible remedy."

"Jay, that's wonderful!"

"It is." He stared at a knot in the wood of the table, tracing it with his fingers. "But it shall be a costly one."

"You mean expensive?" Wendy asked.

He took a deep breath and paused. "In a way." Then his smile widened again as he drew his eyes back up to hers. "But only time shall tell."

"Will this distraction cost you precious days?" Wendy asked, guilt balling up in her stomach even as she did.

He smiled again as he reached out and squeezed her hand. "My mother would have beat me senseless, and properly so, if she knew the fate of young boys was resting in my hands, and I ignored them. Also," his cheeks reddened slightly, "I may or may not have told her about you. And she earnestly hopes to meet with you when this is all over."

Wendy looked down, hoping he didn't see the stupid way that made her smile. "I'm not sure what's going to happen when this is all over. But that is most kind of her, of course." Wendy looked up at the sky. Stars were just beginning to peek out of the darkening blue above. She sucked in a deep breath of heavy, salty sea air. "No matter where I go, I hope I can remember all of this when it's said and done. It's got the perfect makings of a story." She laughed a little.

Jay said nothing to this, but his gaze grew thoughtful, and he said little for the rest of the evening.

As for Wendy, she excused herself soon after that. Her legs were sore from walking all day, but in a good way, the kind of sore that made her curl up in her little bed and pull the covers up and sigh into them as the boat rocked her gently like a cradle. Everything was falling into place. Tomorrow, they would sail back to Neverland under cover of darkness. Jay and his men would spend the night preparing the casum balls on the shore. Then the next morning, she would sneak onto the island before dawn. Jay would begin his distractions. As the fae went out to stop the explosions, she would steal the star, and Jay and his men would take Peter. Then they would sail out of Neverland. She would give Jay the star, and she and the boys would fly back to Ashland, to where King Everard's guards were waiting. If they could get out without the fae realizing they were gone, they might be able to get to the mainland fast enough to go into hiding and make their way unnoticed to the farm. Jay said Neverland wasn't far from the mainland, so returning would be easy.

Jay's ship would sail east with the star, in hopes of drawing the fae apart, so they were less likely to focus all their efforts on finding one party. Wendy had already told Jay all that the king had told her about fighting fae, which had led him to purchase a fair number of boxes of something called fireworks while in port. Wendy had never seen one, but Jay said they were from the east, and he promised they would be magnificent.

And then...

And then what? She'd have to find a place for the Lost Boys, of course. Which meant she would be staying at home for a while longer. Her father might complain about the cost of extra mouths to feed, but Wendy knew he would never turn out hungry children. She could get them all placed in the homes of her friends, perhaps. That would take a while. Months at least.

Then she would be in the same place she was when she began. Because she most certainly wouldn't be welcome in her hometown anymore. Beddington had a long memory, and if she hadn't ruined all chances of matrimony with her public shaming of Reuben, she'd surely done so by running away for seven weeks.

She could always move away, the way she'd been planning to do. Now that she had met him, she was sure King Everard would happily help her find somewhere to settle down in Destin. She could start over. Jay could help his mother, and Peter could...Well, Peter would have to find his own way. At least he would be free to choose which way that was.

Even if her heart wasn't clear, her conscience could be.

THE NEXT DAY seemed to take longer to pass than the two before it put together. Everyone was quieter. There was no singing from the sailors as they scurried up and down the ship. Jay wore a pondering, faraway look as he guided the ship on her course west toward the invisible barrier. And Wendy spent most of her day wandering up and down the ship's stairs as her mind circled endlessly. Her brothers, the fae, Peter, and even Jay seemed continually before her as though they were all, more or less, the same person. Such thoughts tired her so much that she did what she hadn't done since she was a small child, and took a long nap in the middle of the afternoon. But even there, her thoughts were churned into choppy, foamy, restless dreams.

Several hours later, long enough that the dark of evening was close, Wendy was awakened by a knock at the door. The cabin boy called out that supper was ready, and the captain was asking her to dine in his quarters tonight.

This shook all drowsiness from Wendy's senses as she hurried to wash her face and rebrush her hair in an attempt to look presentable for supper. The nap had made her look what she thought was rather haggard, but when she was shown into Jay's quarters, his first exclamation was how lovely she looked.

"I hardly feel it," she laughed a little as he pulled a chair out for her. "I don't think I've slept that hard since I was three years."

"It's a good thing you rested," Jay said, pouring a cup of tea for her and then for himself. Tonight, he wore a gray coat with black silk embroidered in subtle, delicate coils at the wrists and around the buttons, and his dark hair was gathered at the nape of his neck. "Tonight will be a long one."

"Forgive me if I'm being too forward," Wendy said as she took her tea, "but I can't help being incredibly impressed by your skill with your...your hook." Her face reddened as she said the word, but he only smiled.

"My uncle made me train with weapons before he would allow me onto a boat. Said a captain isn't worth his title if he can't fight off a few pirates. So I simply applied the same principle of study and found it wasn't nearly as difficult if one was motivated."

"Well, I applaud you," she said as their food was brought in by several sailors. "It seems to have paid off."

"Having an unusual limb can actually work in one's favor." His smile widened slightly. "If nothing else, it terrifies those who might be noncompliant."

Wendy wondered how he could have had time for such training and chances to threaten people in the short while that he had been gone, but she decided not to question his claim.

"Wendy," he said abruptly. "I have something to ask of you, but I'm afraid it will be quite impertinent and untimely."

Wendy laughed. "If you knew the people of my hometown, they'd tell you that impertinent is part of my being."

"Well, I'm glad to hear that, because this is going to be highly impertinent." He frowned slightly and hesitantly reached for her hand. He didn't grasp it the way Peter always did.

Why did Peter have to continue creeping into her thoughts?

Instead, Jay merely laid his hand on top of hers, and Wendy realized it was going to be difficult to swallow the bit of beef she'd just placed in her mouth.

"Having you on the ship has been a true joy. Not only to myself, but to the crew, too. There's...something about having a woman present that reminds everyone to do a little better and be his very best."

"I thought having a woman aboard a ship was bad luck." Wendy grinned from behind her teacup.

"If you're a pirate, perhaps." He chuckled and ran his hook down his coat as though he didn't know what to do with it. "But what I mean to say is that you keep talking of seeing the world and putting it in your stories. And while, of course, I don't know all about your current situation at home, it seems very unlikely that life will afford you much chance to travel like this again. At least, in the near future." His eyes searched hers carefully. "Am I wrong?"

Wendy sighed and gave him a sad smile. "I'm afraid you're not."

He nodded. "Then, I was wondering...I know I have no right to ask this, but as you would so like to see the world, and I so enjoy having you..." His voice trailed off, and he had to clear his throat twice before speaking again. Wendy thought her heart might fall into her stomach if it kept beating this fast.

"Would you like to stay with me? Here on the ship, I mean?"

Wendy stared at him. "Are you...Are you proposing marriage?"

"I know it wouldn't be the same as what you had with Peter," he said in a rush. "And I couldn't expect it to be. Not at first, at least. I would give you all the time in the world to feel comfortable with me, and I would never pressure you to be or do more than you wanted." He paused, seeming to need to catch his breath. "But the world is a big place. And I think you'll find that the ocean air is healing to the soul. You could write your stories and go on adventures, and maybe one day," his face seemed to redden slightly in the light from his fireplace, "when my uncle gives the company to me, we could settle down and raise a family. If that's what you wanted, of course."

Wendy felt unable to breathe, much less move. Captain Jay, after knowing her for all of two months, had proposed to her. And he'd offered her everything she'd been searching for.

That he valued her company, she had no doubt. In their time at the port and even back on Neverland, he always looked at her with a warmth Reuben had lacked. When they conversed, it was on various topics from various angles, and as a result, his intellect had impressed her greatly. He wanted to take her on adventures and let her write, and, unlike her idiotic former suitor, knew children should be raised by their parents at home.

It was everything she'd wanted. It was the answer to her prayers. She could go home, get the Lost Boys settled, say goodbye to her parents, and see the world. She could travel home to visit them now and then without worry about the cost, and her old neighbors at home could wag their heads all they wanted without the satisfaction of seeing her ruined. For no matter what happened, she couldn't go back to being the square peg in the round hole that living in Beddington required.

And as for Jay himself, he was educated, sensible, caring, and (if she was being honest) ridiculously handsome. Not in the boyish promising way Peter was, but rather, with all the trappings of a full man. And though she hadn't known him long, he had been Peter's best friend, which had to count for something, as Peter didn't choose his intimate friends carelessly. She would be a fool not to accept. And yet, when she examined her heart...

She did not love him.

"I'm so very honored," Wendy said, meeting his gaze with the best smile she could offer. "And I think your offer is far from impertinent."

Jay's face fell slightly. "But?"

"Not but, but rather...might I have some time to consider it?" She looked through the window, which was useless now, for the fog. They must have crossed back into Neverland while she'd been asleep. "There's so much going on right now that I can't seem to remember which way is up."

He relaxed slightly, and his smile seemed more genuine again. "I would want nothing more."

Wendy thanked him, and soon after, retired back to her room

to try to steal a few more hours of sleep before she set off in search of the star in the wee hours of the morning.

Unfortunately, now that her body was at rest, her mind was determined not to be.

Wendy wasn't in love with Jay. She knew it, and Jay knew it. He was even kind about it. And yet, for some reason, he still wanted her. Nothing had been hidden. So why shouldn't she accept? Perhaps she wasn't in love with Jay. Not in love, at least, the way she'd thought she loved Peter. Her heart didn't feel like it was being stretched thin when he was gone, and he wasn't...

Well, he wasn't Peter.

Still, Jay was a good man. He had a few rough spots, of course. His drunken, desperate kidnapping of Tiger Lily had proven that. But his passion was endearing, as was his affection for his mother. He was offering Wendy the world and all the time she needed to go with it. She liked him well enough already. She was sure that in time, she could learn to love him as well.

That thought brought a thrill to Wendy's bones while simultaneously breaking her heart.

CHAPTER 22
ALSO...

Though Wendy had gone to bed earlier than usual, sleep did not come to her in the first hour she laid down. Nor the second. Every time she was nearly asleep, some new thought would assail her, and her problems would present themselves all over again, each passing thought awakening new strands of anxiety to further complicate her concerns.

Finally, during what was probably the ninth hour of the evening, she threw her covers back and dressed once more.

She would go to Jay.

She would tell him that she was accepting his offer.

Once the fae were dealt with, and she had found new homes for the boys, he could come to her farm and fetch her. Her family could join her, and they could perhaps have a wedding in the city where he lived, surrounded by his friends and people who didn't look down at her as the town's greatest disappointment. She would go on adventures with him and see the world. In time, she would come to love him as she did Peter. They would have children, and life would become something new and exciting like she'd never imagined before.

It would be different, of course, she thought to herself as she silently closed her door behind her and padded toward the stairs that led up to the deck. Never in her life had she imagined marrying...

Well, if she was truly honest with herself now, more honest than she'd ever been, she'd never imagined herself marrying anyone but Peter. He had always been there in the back of her mind, even before she'd come to Neverland. He had been the ideal partner. Fun and loyal and brave and new, everything she'd ever heard in the stories and then seen in the moonlight with her fourteen-year-old eyes. But that Peter, Wendy was realizing now, had never existed. Sure, the real Peter was fun, and he had a bigger imagination than she'd known humanly possible. But he wasn't brave. At least, not brave enough to stand up for those who needed him. He was capable of defeating the fae. She knew he was. But his inability to rouse himself to action had led him to choose the fae over her. And that had been his decision, not hers. So who was to blame her for finding a new future?

"...bit of a surprise."

Wendy paused at the sound of Jay's voice at the end of the hall. It was coming from the main storeroom on the right, just beside the stairs. Thinking him to be addressing one of the sailors about the night's plans, Wendy stood just outside the door and waited for him to come out. She would speak to him as soon as he was finished. But when she heard the second voice, familiar in its low, smooth tones, the blood in her veins froze, and she couldn't have taken another step if she'd tried.

"What do you want, Jay?"

What was *she* doing with Jay in the ship storeroom?

"I missed you, too, Tiger Lily."

"You fairly ruined the island last time you were here," Tiger Lily hissed. "Now that it's little more than a floating piece of rot, you come back?"

"I—"

"And don't even think of asking Peter for any favors. He's spent the last few days scrambling to find food for his little brats, so you'll get no sympathy from him."

Wendy's chest ached with guilt so strong it left a metallic taste in her mouth. What would have happened to the boys if they'd come a day later? Or if they hadn't left the food before they'd gone? Her face burned as she imagined her brothers, hungry and scared.

"If you'd let me get in a word now and then, you might learn what you came to find out," Jay said in a soothing tone.

"Don't patronize me, Jay. I—"

"I came for the star, Tiger Lily."

Wendy's heart, which had been beating in an erratic rhythm, all but stopped. What was he doing? Was he really going to tell the fae about their plans?

Was he going to betray her? Had that been his plan all along? Wendy gripped the railing that ran along the wall for strength. For though the ship was perfectly still, Wendy felt like the world was spinning all around her.

"Jay, if you think I'm going to let you sail out of here with the very lifeblood of Neverland—"

"Neverland's dying as it is," Jay said in that same calm voice. In fact, he sounded almost bored, like he was soothing an overexcited child. "I knew that when I left. And since then, I've found some very interesting information on stars and their healing powers. You can't blame me for trying, really."

"Stars don't heal people," Tiger Lily snapped. "At least, not the way you're hoping. Besides, the star will die violently because of the very power it holds. You'll die if you're anywhere near it when it goes. And then what good will you be to your mother?"

"See, and you've always said that, but I'm convinced it's just another ploy to keep Peter and everyone else in line."

"Then you're a fool."

"My mother is dying, Tiger Lily. I'm beyond the stage of doing nothing."

"Our star is dying, too! Why would you take something that can't save her?"

"You see," Jay said, his voice still silky smooth. "That's the thing. I don't need the star to be alive when I use it. In fact, I need quite the opposite."

Wendy had to remind herself to breathe. He was lying, of course. He must be trying to throw Tiger Lily off his trail. But then, why would he tell her all of this in the first place? It would only make Wendy's job harder. Wendy kept her ear near the door and prayed no sailors would walk down the hall to find her.

"So, you don't need the star to be...alive?" Tiger Lily asked.

"No. I just need the star."

There was a long silence before Tiger Lily spoke again, more slowly this time. "In the east, there are men and women who sell fallen stars. They collect them after the life has gone out of them, and they break them into hundreds of pieces and sell portions of them to those who wish to use them for herbal remedies and such."

"I have also heard that," Jay said. "But they charge more gold than I have resources for. Kings purchase their wares."

More silence. "If I were able to bring you such resources, would you leave Neverland and promise not to return?"

Despite her confusion, Wendy had to shake her head. Neverland was practically dead, and for some reason, Tiger Lily still spoke as though they would be able to revive it and live just as they had been before. How delusional had she become? Perhaps it was the lack of food.

"I would be open to hearing your proposal," Jay replied. "If it can get me a star within the next two weeks."

Wendy strained to hear his answer, but a thump sounded on the stairs. She flew back to her room as fast as she could, praying no one had seen her. Then she threw herself against the door and tried to control her breathing, should someone come to check on her.

He was trying to distract Tiger Lily from the work his men were doing on the island. That had to be it. Surely, he wasn't planning on killing the Neverstar. She assured herself of this repeatedly as she pulled on her cloak from King Everard. She grabbed her reticule, with the rest of her gifts, and tied it on as well. If anyone asked, she was going out to survey the mountain.

But what she really needed was to clear her head.

Thankfully, most of the sailors were on the island by now, preparing the casum balls. None of them noticed her take to the sky and set off in the direction of the island. Despite the unusual chilly breeze, Wendy welcomed the stark reminder of reality. She just hoped reality wouldn't include the stardust failing and dumping her in the ocean as she made her way across it.

Doubting Jay felt wrong, especially since she had been moments from accepting him as her intended. And really, she had convinced herself at first that he was only distracting Tiger Lily. Doing so would make perfect sense, keeping her away from the island and her attention off Wendy. After all, he'd never betrayed Wendy's name, so it was likely he'd made it all up.

And yet...

He had also mentioned to Wendy that he'd recently discovered a possible new cure. And when Wendy had suggested he take the star, he'd readily accepted. There wasn't even a question as to what he might do with her or how he hoped the healing might work. He'd just seemed confident that it would.

With more questions than ever, Wendy found herself flying toward the treehouse. The trip up the mountainside should have been quick, but flying felt even less stable than it had been before. Wendy stayed just a few feet above the ground, so if the stardust failed, she wouldn't have very far to fall. The very thought of flying far out over the ocean through Neverland's barrier with small children in tow was so nerve-wracking that she pushed the idea to the back of her mind.

By the time she landed, there were less than two hours until midnight, and the boys would most likely be asleep. But Wendy needed to see them. Perhaps being near her brothers and all the other boys would help her make a decision. They were her goal, after all. Jay's offer had seemed a promise of escape from the mess she was in. But now...The boys were all that mattered. Everything else took second place to getting them home.

Thankfully, the fae seemed to have abandoned their posts near the boys. Probably thanks to the ship's arrival, which Tiger Lily obviously knew about by now, so it was easy to get to the tree without being spotted. When Wendy landed on the mountain, what should have been soft, silent grasses and pine needles crunched loudly under her feet. She hoped they would all be out of Neverland by the time the sun rose the next morning because she didn't think she could stand to see how far it had fallen since leaving. She went up to the entrance stump and then paused.

She couldn't very well just waltz in when Peter was there. The plan had been for her not to visit the tree until she had the star, and the casum balls had pulled Peter and all the fae away. What other entrance...

Wendy stole up the tree and into the branches. She peeked through the window of Tinkerbell's room. Empty. Wendy thanked the Maker silently as she pushed the window open until it was wide enough for her to fit through.

She landed in a pink room that was covered in what had probably until very recently been fresh flowers. Roses, zinnias, hyacinths, lilac, daisies, and a dozen more Wendy couldn't name, dusted the messy bed, which was covered in pillows. A vanity, which was covered in what looked like gems, stood beside the bed, and on the floor were rugs and a pile of clothes.

But it wouldn't do to be caught in here if Tinkerbell returned. That would mess everything up. Wendy hurried down the tunnel that led from Tinkerbell's room to the main room underground, praying the whole time that no one would appear in front of or behind her.

She reached the end of the tunnel and gingerly pushed the flap open an inch, just enough to see the general activity level of the room. The room was mostly dark, with the exception of a dying fire in the hearth. The crates that Jay had dropped off at the edge of the island were stacked in one corner, mostly empty already. Most of the boys were asleep. Wendy pushed the flap open a little more to see if they were all asleep. Then she froze. Two souls were still awake.

Peter was sitting in her rocking chair, the one he'd made for her when she'd arrived in Neverland. In his arms was little Slightly. The little boy was crying softly, but he was turned into Peter's chest and clung to his shirt. Peter stared down at the small boy, dark circles under his eyes, looking years older than she'd left him. His shoulders drooped, and his eyes were half-closed, but he continued to hold Slightly in the crook of his right arm and caressed the little boy's face with his left hand. He hummed a tune that Wendy had taught them, even as his eyes tried time and time again to close. Each time he dozed off, his head would nod. Then he would jerk himself awake and start comforting the little boy again.

The wall Wendy had built up around her heart, the one that hadn't wanted to talk to her father and the one that had thought she might be able to love Jay one day after all, the wall that had kicked every thought of Peter out as soon as it had surfaced, shattered.

Jay was an impressive match to be sure. From his finely tailored coats to his muscular chest and arms to his smooth words and larger-than-life promises, he was more than any girl could ever ask for. But now that she saw Peter and remembered the gentleness that had first drawn her to him, she couldn't help but see the truth. There was an edge to Jay that Wendy had noticed enough to hear the faint warning bells in her heart. She'd wanted to deny it at first, but now that she was faced with the juxtaposition between the two men, she could no longer forget.

Drunk or not, Jay had used his men and his resources to abduct Tiger Lily to get to Peter, not a scheme an inebriated fool could have thought up and carried out all while under the influence of drink. She'd excused it as such at first because that was how he'd explained it, but she could see now that that was also wishful thinking on her part. Then there was the way he'd been so silent about his acceptance of the star, and the fear in Milo's eyes back at the restaurant. Jay had said the man had tried stealing from him once, but Wendy had never asked Milo for his side of the story, either. As much as she hated to acknowledge it, she would never know for sure.

Jay wasn't Peter. Jay went on adventures, but Peter rocked crying babies to sleep at night. Jay used the world as his personal breadbasket. Peter gave more than he ever took. Jay talked of having children one day when it fit his plans, but Peter couldn't seem to live without them.

Also, Wendy loved Peter.

She nearly groaned aloud. These revelations, of course, meant that plans would need to change yet again. This time, there was no Jay to fall back on, no one to call for help. Every bit of help she would receive would come from King Everard and his men back in the Old World. And she would just have to get everyone there herself.

But first, she had to get that star.

CHAPTER 23
BEGINNING OF THE END

Peter stared down at the empty crates of food. Whoever had left them had left exactly enough for four days. Of course, Tiger Lily had demanded some for the fae after catching Peter during his fourth trip to the beach to retrieve the rest of the food. So Peter had directed the boys to hide their crates and given most of the apples to the fae, threatening Tink with utter banishment if she dared breathe a word of the remaining food to Tiger Lily. To his surprise, she hadn't, and three days had passed.

They would be out of food in less than twenty-four hours.

He had watched his young charges. They slept now, but their behavior during the day had frightened him. They no longer ran and played and screamed and laughed. Instead, they huddled in little groups around the room and whispered or cried. It was painful to see them frightened and hungry, and Peter felt as though someone was twisting a knife in his stomach every time one of them lifted his sad eyes to Peter's.

Peter made very little attempt to fix the island these days. At least once a day, he headed out and did something obscure, such as trying to resuscitate an apple tree, so Tiger Lily would see his efforts. They were useless, of course, but the fae woman was ruthless in her determination that they would make it. The power of the star would fix everything.

The fae chieftess had gone mad.

If only he'd taken Wendy's advice sooner and gotten the boys out when he could. The fae would have allowed, even welcomed it at one point. But how was he to know everything would unravel as quickly as it had? He'd thought he would get decades, or at least years if they played their cards right. Then he would send the boys off with Wendy when the time came, and face it all with the fae until the end. He hadn't known how fast Neverland would crumble or that it even could crumble in just days. And he guessed the fae hadn't known either. Otherwise, they would have used the boys as a tool to control him far sooner than they had.

But it was too late. The fae knew he would do anything to save the boys, and they were using that against him by keeping them hostage in Neverland. If he could have gotten the boys out the way he did Wendy, he would have. But on the day he'd returned Wendy to her home, when he'd seen the fae floating like sentinels around the forest, he'd known then and there that Tiger Lily would do everything in her power to maintain what they had left of Neverland. Even if it meant threatening the boys so she could control him.

Slightly finally slept, so he slipped him into his crib. Then he called out quietly, "John. Nibs."

The boys must not have been sleeping because they scrambled out of bed immediately and came to stand at his side. Peter tried to ignore the accusations in their eyes. Not that those accusations weren't justified. Peter had brought them here. And now Peter had let them all down.

"I'm going to go a little farther tonight to try to find food," he said, giving them the best smile he could muster. "Care for the boys, will you?"

"Like we have any other choice," John said under his breath.

"Be on your watch," Peter said, glancing up at the little boys. He lowered his voice. "I'm going to do my best to come up with a distraction." He glanced up at the room. He couldn't see their guards outside the tree, but he was sure they were there just the same. "I want you to take turns keeping watch. Wake the boys after I've been gone for a few minutes. If you see your fae guards disappear, I want you to take everyone and fly away from here as fast as you can."

Nibs's eyes grew wide. "Without you?"

"Flying's getting harder." John frowned.

Peter nodded. "That's why we have to try tonight." He paused, his throat swelling painfully. "And if you can get out...don't look back."

"But where would we go?" Nibs whispered.

"Fly to the west, in the direction of the setting sun. Fly as far as you can, and don't stop until you make it to a place called Maricanta. Find the king or queen and tell them where you've come from." He paused. "Tell them about the fae and ask for protection."

For the first time since Wendy left, John looked at him directly with something other than scorn. He studied Peter a moment before quietly answering, "We will."

Nibs looked around. "Where's Tink? Is she coming with us?"

"Tiger Lily needed her for something tonight. And, no. She's not coming. In fact, if she shows up, I don't even want you to tell her about this. Understand?" That should make him feel bad. After five hundred years, his little friend was gone, and he would most likely never see her again. But Tinkerbell's loyalty was divided. And he couldn't afford that any longer.

Peter wanted to kiss them all goodbye. But he knew that would only wake them, and then they would cry, as they always did now when he left. And they couldn't afford tears tonight.

223

Today was their last day of food. The star was drawing closer to death by the second, and fae guards or no fae guards, Peter would have to figure out a way to get them out. But he couldn't do that in the confines of the tree. So he gave them one last longing glance and went to stand below the entrance stump.

If he was able to come up with a distraction the way he hoped, this would be the last time he'd ever see them.

Just as he was about to go up the stump, however, he heard a whining below him. Looking down, he found Nana, staring at him through large, mournful eyes.

Even the dog was broken, too.

Then he had an idea. "Come on, girl," he said, softly scratching behind her ears as he met her soulful gaze. "Let's go see Wendy."

Peter flew inches above the ground with Nana following him. If he'd been flying high like he had done two weeks ago, they could have made it to the gemstones in minutes, but as flying was no longer stable the way it used to be, they took longer to reach their destination. By the time they got there, Nana was tired. She perked right up, however, when Peter gestured for her to join him in front of Wendy's gem.

The purple was gone from the stones, leaving them more varying shades of gray and brown. The faces inside of them were also beginning to fade. Nana, however, didn't seem to mind. She barked and barked at the moving image of Wendy. Only after several minutes of the Wendy in the gem not responding, did the dog finally lie down and sigh, her chin delicately on her white paws as she stared up at the image of her master.

Peter settled himself on a smaller, unused gem, leaned back, and closed his eyes. He had to save the boys. He needed to think of a distraction. Tonight.

Tiger Lily was in denial. Only yesterday, she had assured him for the hundredth time that he could save the island if he would actually *try* purging Wendy from his mind. She'd even offered to help, an offer which had been more unsettling than any of her prior threats. She still seemed to be under the impression that things could go back to the way they were. But Peter knew it was fruitless. There was nothing in the world that could make Neverland go back to the way it had been. It would be like cutting his feet off to lose the two inches he'd grown in the last two months.

The star was dying. And while he didn't know exactly what a star's death entailed, he could feel through the bond they shared that the star's end would be powerful and violent. He could feel the instability in the air all around him. He could see it in the way the fae were flickering all over the island. The very ground they walked on was compromised. And once the star reached her end, there wouldn't be a thing he could do for them. He had to think of something now.

But how?

He had tried a million times to think of a way to sneak them out without the fae seeing them. Unfortunately, Tiger Lily had stationed fae everywhere on the island. There was no way in the world he could sneak out eight young boys without alerting the fae somehow.

If he still had the power he'd possessed even a month ago, he might have been able to create an invisible bridge between worlds to get them out. As the star's power waned, though, so did his, and that was no longer an option. That kind of power would be dangerous, coming from a star that hovered near death.

And what if they did get out? Where would they go from there?

Ideally, he would cause a distraction and still escape with the boys and the star. Escape would be the difficult part. Peter had already worked out what he might do if they could actually get out unseen. As much as he longed to run straight to Wendy, he knew the fae would be less than understanding. They would set out to find him the second Neverland disappeared. And no matter how much he wanted to protect Wendy, he knew he would need someone with more power than he had to do so. But he couldn't tow eight boys around with him all over the continent.

He didn't know the Sea Crown, Queen Arianna of the merfolk, well. But he knew where to find her and that she was known as kind and fair, as was her husband, King Michaelangelo of Maricanta. He also knew that the merfolk could create charms to temporarily allow humans to stay underwater. He didn't know if the fae were capable of living underwater, even in their forms of choice, but either way, if he could give his boys over to Queen Arianna, she would be powerful enough to keep them safe while he went to find King Everard. If they knew the magnitude of the destruction the fae were capable of, the queen and her husband might even help him get to Destin faster. Then the powerful King Everard could take care of the fae. And if the star didn't have to support Neverland, she might last long enough for him to get the king's help. Once the fae were taken care of, everything else would fall into place, and he wouldn't have to worry about the boys' fates anymore.

It wouldn't be easy, but he could do it. He had to. And even if he couldn't make it with them, surely he could at least give them their best fighting chance. They might not be able to fly all the way to Maricanta, but they could at least try. It was better than watching them fall.

"I miss her, too." Peter reached out and rubbed the dog's head.

Nana sighed before moving her head to his lap. For some reason, this made Peter's heart break all over again.

He looked up at the faces in the gems around them. Each one had a name, each voice and personality etched in his memory. Most of them were dead now. They'd left Neverland long ago and had lived out their lives in the Old World. But they were still all boys to him. What would happen to their memories after he was gone? It would be as though they'd never existed, all memory of them gone with him.

Peter cleared his throat as he stood to survey the island once again. There had to be a way—

An explosion rocked the island. Then another. And another. Fae flew overhead to the east side of the island.

Peter's heart nearly stopped in his chest. Had it begun? Was this the beginning of the end? He leaped to his feet and followed the sounds, Nana close behind.

CHAPTER 24
A CHOICE

Wendy had stolen out of Tinkerbell's room before Peter noticed her, and none too soon, as she nearly flew within sight of the little fae on her way up the mountain.

She needed to get the star and then get Peter and the boys to follow her. She had only a few hours. Jay wouldn't know she was missing immediately. At least, she hoped he wouldn't. She hadn't noticed him check on her any of the previous nights. If all went as it should, she just had to get the star and fly everyone out of Neverland. It would be dangerous, of course, especially if the fae noticed them flying away. But if all went well, her little band wouldn't have to fight or defeat the fae. They just had to beat them to her parents' farm.

Peter wouldn't go easily. As she could no longer count on sending him with Jay, however, she would have to find a way to convince him.

Wendy slowed her thoughts and her flight as she neared the cave at the top of the mountain. Flying was growing more diffi-cult, which was probably due, she guessed, to the ever-dying star. She glanced up at the moon, which was muted by a thin layer of clouds, making everything look a dull brown against the black of the night. This would have to be fast.

Hopefully, getting Peter and the star away from Neverland and the strain of keeping it in existence would free up the star's efforts. And perhaps, as it had been strengthened the first time they'd bonded, the star could be healed by simply being with Peter. Not that Wendy had any proof of this, of course. But it was a better hope than nothing.

She stole into the cave with guilt so sharp in her gut it was nearly painful. Even worse was when she rounded the corner to find the star.

The star no longer floated in the air. Instead, she lay on the floor, her light barely flickering in the darkness. Her many arms stuck out, putting her at what looked like a painful angle, even if she wasn't human.

Wendy ran to her side and picked her up, cradling her as well as she could.

"Neverstar," she breathed. "What happened?" It was a silly question, of course. The star didn't talk. At least, not the way humans did. Peter could speak with her, but Wendy had never been able to. Wendy looked around, trying to think of something she might do to keep the star alive. Perhaps the star would revive some if she was reunited with Peter. After all, he had said she was on the cusp of death when he'd first met her. Binding herself to his heart had saved her the first time. Perhaps being near to each other would work again.

Wendy half stood to leave, but before she could take a step, the world around her disappeared in an explosion that rippled out to the edges of Wendy's vision. And instead of the little cavern, Wendy found herself in a green valley. She didn't recognize it, but she did recognize the boy in the middle of the valley. Instead of seventeen or eighteen years, however, he looked far younger, much closer to Michael's age than John's. He was surrounded by the fae, and Tiger Lily stood in front of him.

Wendy couldn't hear what Tiger Lily said to him, but she did see her lips move. Peter the boy frowned up at her then shook his head. He tried to dart off, but she caught him by the shirt. Peter fought her again, and Wendy's heart broke as Tiger Lily held him tight. If only he'd fight like that now, he might stand a chance.

The scene changed again, and though the valley was still there, it was night. The boy Peter was bound with a rope, and he was sleeping on the grass next to a log. Tiger Lily and the other fae were watching him. And slowly, each fae began to disappear.

And reappeared as green whorls of light.

Wendy trembled as she watched them. They were all around her but didn't seem to see her at all. They were transfixed on the boy. Tiger Lily, whose shape was more or less something like a human, but had also taken on an unearthly glow, threw her head back and screamed.

The scream was like that of the panthers that sometimes wandered onto her father's farm when they were unusually hungry and tried to hunt the cattle. Wendy could still feel the star's sharp points in her hands, but her mind seemed imprisoned in whatever valley the fae had taken the boy Peter to. At the sound of Tiger Lily's scream, the boy had screamed as well, bolting upright from where he slept. Then one by one, the whorls began to fly up into the air and then descend upon him.

Wendy felt tears running down her cheeks, and she sobbed uncontrollably as they came at him again and again, his young wail echoing in her ears. She wanted nothing more than to hold him, to draw him close and to protect him. But there was nothing she could do.

Then the valley was gone, and Wendy was back in the dark cave.

"I thought they gave him a choice," Wendy whispered.

Once again, she was transported away. But instead of the angry whorls, the fae were once again in their human forms. The boy Peter was no longer curled up in a ball. He was standing before Tiger Lily.

"Are you ready?" Tiger Lily asked. Her voice was gentler. If Wendy hadn't seen what had happened before, she might have thought Tiger Lily a kind motherly figure as she removed the star from the bag at her side and placed it in Peter's shaking hands.

For a moment, nothing happened. Peter studied the star with a wary gaze, and the fae watched him, unmoving. Then Peter's eyes grew wide, and his mouth fell open, and the world around them began to change once again. The moonlit valley faded away. Instead, Peter, the star, and the fae stood in what looked like the night sky. Stars flickered around them, and the sky echoed with songs no human could have conceived. The sun burned fiercely to their right, and to their left, the moon and other heavenly bodies Wendy had only heard of floated in the vast, black expanse. An energy moved through the space around them that made Wendy's whole body pulse in a rhythm, like something grand was about to happen.

Then it was gone. Young Peter stared down at the star in his hands, but he no longer held it at a distance. Tiger Lily's smile was wild, nearly terrifying in its joy.

"So," Tiger Lily said as the fae whispered amongst themselves. "What do you think about our proposition?"

Peter looked back down at the star and touched it gently. The star, nearly as dull as it had been in the cave with Wendy, flickered.

"I'll do it," he said in a small but determined voice.

The fae flew with Peter to an assortment of places. They didn't stop, however, until they found a small, barren island in what looked like the Sharyn Sea. Peter pointed to the island, and that was where the fae put him down. He walked around in a circle a few times. Then he closed his eyes. And though his hands were still trembling, he smiled. Opening his eyes, he said, "This is it." He raised his hands, the barren island exploded with color.

And then, once again, the vision was gone. Wendy was back in the cave with the star. She took a long, shuddering breath. "I can't leave Peter to Jay or Tiger Lily. Can I?"

The star didn't speak, but Wendy knew the answer. If she wasn't going to trust Jay to take him away, she would have to do everything herself. She tried to think fast. Peter might be tied to the star in some weird way she still couldn't understand, but he was bigger and stronger than she was, and probably wouldn't come willingly. This would complicate things greatly. Unless...

"I know you're weak right now," Wendy said. "But would you be able to give me a Wasaaca flower? If I'm to take Peter with me, I'll need to keep him unconscious." Her mind was already racing. The fae's attention would no longer be split between herself and Jay if she had the star and the boys and Peter all to herself. There wouldn't be enough time to get them all back to the farm. And even if they were able to get to the farm, she doubted the two guards, skilled as they were, would be able to fight off the entire fae clan. No, she would have to go to the source of that help.

"I could send the boys with John," she said slowly, as though the star might respond. "And if I didn't have to worry about them, I could go faster, even if I was carrying Peter. They won't chase the boys if they know Peter's not with them. And I could take Peter straight to Destin. We should be able to make it there if you're actually with us..." She frowned down at the dull star. "Hopefully."

A small scratching sound came from her right. But when Wendy looked, expecting a mouse or large beetle, she found that a small flower had pushed its way up out of the damp ground.

"Thank you," she told the star, plucking the Wasaaca flower

and carefully tucking it into her reticule. Then she paused. "I'm going to have to take you with me."

The star flickered, and though there weren't words shared, Wendy felt a sense of peace come over her. Peter had said that the star loved him, rather like a mother. No mother would wish to see her son treated the way Peter was. Wendy had no doubt about that.

Gently, she tucked the star into her reticule. Then she fastened her cloak securely and stepped out of the cave. She hesitated, though. Where should she go? But before she could make a decision, an explosion blasted the air above and around her, and Wendy was thrown to the ground. Another moment of explosions, however, revealed that it was only Jay's casum balls going off. This brought her a moment of relief until...

It was far too early for the casum balls. He must have realized she was gone. Wendy leaped up and began to run. She had to get to the boys.

CHAPTER 25
SMOKE

Wendy arrived breathless at the treehouse what felt like hours later, though it couldn't have been above thirty minutes. She'd nearly crossed paths with three fae on the way, but they were so distracted as they'd zipped toward the harbor where the casum balls were planted, that none had even seemed to notice her. Flying would have been faster, but Wendy knew that every ounce of the Neverstar's power must be spared. The fae were using too much as it was.

She could only pray that there would be enough stardust left for the boys to make one final flight away from the mountain.

This time, when she arrived at the treehouse, she went straight down the entrance stump. To her relief, all the boys seemed to be there, and to her great surprise, they were even awake. Best of all, Tinkerbell was gone. Unfortunately, so was Peter.

"Wendy!" the boys screamed, practically throwing themselves at her as she tried to count them. The room was an eruption of talking and joy and crying.

"Where did you go?"

"Wendy, there was a big explosion outside!"

"Peter went somewhere without telling us!"

"Wendy!"

Wendy looked up from the little boys to see John. She threw her arms around him, not caring whether or not he welcomed the display of affection. Michael clung to her, and she pulled him into her arms and held them both close.

"John," she called over the hullabaloo. "You have to go now!"

"We all have to go!" John cried. "You're not staying here!"

"I have to find Peter!"

John glared at her. "We're not starting with that again. Remember what happened last time?"

Wendy put Michael down and dragged John over to a corner. Nibs followed.

"I've had help from King Everard."

John's eyes bugged. "King Everard? But now?"

"No time to explain! But if I don't fly with Peter and the star to Destin, you and the boys will never make it back to the farm alive."

"Then we should all go to Destin," Nibs said.

Wendy shook her head. "It'll take too long with the little ones. I can go faster if it's just me, Peter, and the star. Besides, they'll be more likely to follow us, so if you can get the boys to the farm, the king's guards will protect them." She removed the Wasaaca flower from her reticule. "I'm going to put Peter to sleep and take him as soon as you're all off."

John and Nibs looked at one another. Wendy braced herself for Nibs's objections. If anyone loved Neverland the most, it was him. But to her surprise, he nodded and sighed. "Neverland's not Neverland if we can't eat. Let's tell the boys." They turned to the little boys, but as they did, a scratching sound came from above. Wendy came to a horrible realization.

There wasn't time to look for Peter. They would simply have

to hope they could make it out of Neverland undetected. Time to find the next best bad choice. Maybe they would have to attempt flying to Destin after all.

"We need to hurry," she said, and John and Nibs nodded.

"Boys," she said, turning to the little boys with her best smile. "We're going on an adventure!" Then she paused. "Where's Nana?"

"She's with Peter," Michael said.

Of course she was. Wendy wanted to groan.

"What about Peter?" Tootles asked, looking back and forth between John and Nibs.

"We can't leave Peter!" Pop cried, and his brother echoed him.

As much as Wendy's chest hurt at the thought of leaving without Nana, she knew from the growing explosions outside that she couldn't wait to get everyone out the way she had hoped, nor could she send them on their own. It was too dangerous. The stardust was dying, and she had no doubt Jay and the fae would be looking for them soon. And though she felt traitorous for even considering such a plan, she knew Peter would agree with her.

New plan. She would get the boys out of Neverland. She had the star, which she hoped meant they would all fly better over the open water and speed their escape should one of the fae spot them. Then if she still could, she would come back for the dog and Peter after the boys were safe.

She hoped.

Wendy, John, and Nibs did their best to calm the boys with promises of fun, but it wasn't easy. Wendy would have just taken them all out, crying or calm, but she was afraid the fae would hear them if Tootles continued to wail. Desperate to go, Wendy finally promised there would be all sorts of treats in Destin, and she would return to them as soon as she could, with Peter in tow. Michael, to his credit, told the twins, Tootles, and Curly about all the good things his mother could cook, and he promised Slightly that he could have a cat. Though Wendy knew this promise would have to be revisited later, she was just relieved that the boys stopped crying.

"We'll need to be quiet, though," Wendy said when they were all holding hands in a line. She held her finger up to her lips. "We don't want the fae to hear us. So everyone needs to be as silent as stone."

Slightly wasn't exactly silent, but his quiet chattering to himself was as close as Wendy guessed they would get. So she sent the boys up the stump one by one. Then, just before she went up as well, she took one more glance about the room.

So many dreams had been born here. So many happy memories of love and laughter and fun. The star might have wished for Peter to have something different, but no one could deny that he had done an incredible amount of good in this room. And though they must leave, it was with bittersweet feelings that for the last time, Wendy touched the edge of her rocking chair and said goodbye.

Then she went up the stump one last time.

At the top, she expected to find the boys in a line as she'd instructed them to stand. Instead, waiting to greet her were a dozen men. The boys cried and whimpered all around her as the men held them in place.

Wendy whipped her father's knife from her reticule. There was a movement to her right, and though Wendy could hardly see, she slashed her knife at it. Someone cursed, and Wendy turned, ready to strike again.

She would fight her way out of Neverland, even if it meant bleeding everyone else to death. She would keep her boys safe.

But before she could reach anyone else, two strong hands reached out and grabbed her by the shoulders. The pressure was so strong that she dropped her knife, where it hit the ground with a useless thud.

"Get your—"

Her words were cut off by a rag being wrapped around her mouth. Her hands were bound behind her back, and she was blindfolded.

All Wendy's plans went up in smoke.

CHAPTER 26
TINK

Whoever was carrying Wendy, thrown over his shoulder like a sack of grain, bumped her around enough that her stomach began to turn. And judging from the way he was flying, he must not have been an expert flyer. At first, she tried to fight her way free. She could fly up if she was able to get out of his grasp...

And do what? She couldn't very well help the boys or even fly anywhere else bound, gagged, and blindfolded. So she was forced to wait as they continued their strange journey down the mountain. Instead of fighting, she tried to think of who might have taken them.

Her first instinct had been to blame the fae. But the fae were good at flying, and they certainly weren't this obvious. If Tiger Lily had wanted to take them, she would have done it neatly and swiftly, the way she did everything.

That left only one person.

Wendy's heart fell into her stomach as she and the boys, who were whimpering through their gags, were tossed into what felt like a boat. The water sloshed over the bottom of the boat as they bobbed up and down, oars splashing in the water in a rhythm, almost as if to a dance. Wendy tried to orient herself with the timed splashings, anything to keep the panic at bay. Slightly was so little. If he tried to get up and slipped out without anyone noticing...

Count the splashes. Breathe in time with them. Count the splashes.

Between praying to the Maker and focusing on the sounds of the water, Wendy made it through the ride without bursting into angry tears. When the boat stopped, she was hauled over someone's shoulder yet again and balanced there precariously as he began to climb. She did her best to hold herself in place, praying desperately that they'd be more careful with the boys than they were with her.

Once they were more or less level, she was carried unceremoniously down more steps and across flat ground again until she was placed on the floor, where her binds were tied to a column of some sort behind her, and her feet were stretched out in front. She could hear the whimpers and muffled yells of the boys as they were brought in as well. Boots stomped around, seeming to rearrange everyone several times before they all stomped out and locked the door behind them.

Only then did Wendy become aware of yet another kind of presence in the room. Desperate to check on the boys and see who else was there, Wendy tried to get her blindfold off with her shoulder. But her shoulder couldn't reach high enough, especially with her hands tied behind her back. So instead, she brought her knees up and began rubbing them against her face until she was able to get the blindfold to slip down over her neck.

The room was so dark that having the blindfold off barely made a difference. But Wendy wasn't about to let a lack of light stop her from checking on her boys. She used her knees to work the cloth off of her mouth.

"John?" she called when she was free.

She got a muffled answer in response. Her heart surged with hope as she began to call others. "Michael? Slightly?"

Michael growled, a sound she knew well, and Slightly began to wail. The sound of his fear filled Wendy's heart with a rage unlike she'd ever known before. But knowing the little boy was all right, she swallowed her rage for later until everyone had answered, relieved beyond words that they were safe. Wet and angry and scared. But safe.

Now she just had to figure out what to do with them.

"We must be on Jay's ship," Wendy said as loudly as she dared. She knew John and Nibs would want to hear even if they couldn't speak. What she didn't expect, though, was to hear a woman's voice in reply.

"You're on his ship all right."

Wendy nearly shrieked at the sound of the voice to her left. She looked over to see the slightest flickering of green light.

"No need to panic." A dry chuckle. "It's hard to do much when you're in a cage."

"Wait..." Wendy squinted as the green light flickered again, this time, revealing part of a face. "Moon Flower?" she gasped.

"And about twenty more of us."

"But...how?" Wendy asked. "Is Tiger Lily here, too? And Tink?" Had Jay somehow lured them all in? But that was never part of the plan. At least, not any part he'd revealed to her.

"No." The old woman let out a long breath, flickering again as she did.

"What happened?"

"After you left, Peter pleaded with us to let the island go. He said it was past saving, and everyone here was being endangered by staying. After he left, some of us decided we agreed with him. We'd taken him as a boy and kept him here for five centuries. With the star dying," her voice softened, "it only seemed right to let Peter spend the rest of his life as he wished."

"What do you mean the rest of his life?" Wendy asked.

Moon Flower shifted. "It didn't matter because Tiger Lily was not impressed."

"But how did Jay get you?" Then Wendy remembered something. "Wait. Before I went back to the island, Tiger Lily was meeting with Jay. She said something about giving him a way to make money to buy part of a star with. Lots of money."

"We're dangerous creatures unleashed. But if one can manage to get a fae confined, there are few monarchs in the world who wouldn't pay great sums of money to have one of us in his collection."

"But...can't you just...change into your light form?" Probably a stupid way to describe their other state of being, but Wendy didn't know what other words to use.

"The star is too weak for us to keep control over our forms one way or the other. Tiger Lily knows this, so she and her followers captured us in our human forms. They bound us so tightly that we can't escape unless we regain complete control over our ability to shift. That won't happen as long as we're in Neverland. And by the time we leave the barrier, Jay will have put us in bindings from which not even our fae forms can escape."

"Peter always said Jay had carefully laid plans." Wendy frowned into the darkness. "I didn't think he could have schemed this, though, considering that he couldn't have known if and when I would call him back."

"But he left you the summoning object, did he not? He wouldn't have left you any way to call him back if he didn't expect you to use it."

Wendy closed her eyes. She felt dirty. Not because they had been abducted and thrown into a ship's hold, but because Jay had used her. And she had let him. Not only had she played into his little scheme, but she had very nearly agreed to marry him. She shuddered. What she wouldn't give to have Nana bite him right about now.

"What do you think he wants with us?" she asked.

"Miss Darling, I'm afraid you know perfectly well what I want."

Wendy whirled around to find Jay silhouetted in the doorway, the light at his back, making his face as impossible to see as the hold around her. In the hall light that spilled in behind him, she could see the boys bunched together, huddling in the corner, and her blood pulsed hot again.

He walked in, his boots tapping softly on the wooden floor, until he came and knelt in front of her. He reached out to touch her face, but she jerked away. He paused and then withdrew his hand.

"Why didn't you wait for me?" he whispered. His voice was pained and gentle the way it had been when they'd discussed how much he missed Peter.

"Why did you follow me?"

He hesitated. "I know how much Peter means to you. I was afraid you might decide he was worth one more try after all." Then he stood. "Unfortunately, it seems I was right."

"I wouldn't have gone anywhere if it hadn't been for your conversation with Tiger Lily."

"And that's an unfortunate coincidence I hadn't meant for you to hear. Tiger Lily approached me after you had gone to bed."

"You never said anything about killing the star." Wendy glared up at him from the floor. "That was never part of the deal."

"You want to kill the star?" Moon Flower cried.

He turned his head to the fae then back to Wendy. "An unhappy sacrifice that must be made. But it will yield more results than drawing out the death of the island. A woman's life will be saved. Peter's suffering will come to an end." He nudged

Moon Flower's leg with his boot. "The fae will be under far more control than they would have been otherwise."

"But Tiger Lily was going to pay you!" Wendy cried. "So you could buy your own star somewhere else!"

"Oh, I certainly plan to. You see, I'll use this star now, but you never know when you'll need another." Jay looked back down at Moon Flower. "And these here will fetch a pretty price all over the world so I can do just that. But you don't think I'd actually let Tiger Lily have her way, do you? After all she's done to you and me and Peter?"

"You don't understand!" Moon Flower struggled against her bindings, flickering harder than ever. "Peter's heart is bound to the star."

Wendy froze. "What do you mean?"

"If the star dies," Moon Flower shouted, "so does Peter!"

Wendy looked up at Jay in horror. "You knew this?"

"To die a free man is an honor, Wendy."

"But he doesn't have to die!" Wendy sought desperately for some way to awaken the tenderness she'd heard in him before. "What would your mother say if she knew how many lives you were sacrificing to save hers?"

"That is a heartbreak I plan to spare her from. She's fragile, and the doctor says anxiety will only make her palsy worse."

"He's your best friend!" Wendy cried. "He saved your life, and you speak of avenging him! And yet you'd kill him in cold blood?"

Jay's face contorted into a sneer of anger, a shape Wendy hadn't believed his friendly features to be capable of. "She's my mother!" he roared. "So, yes, I would!"

"No mother would want that from her child."

"It's funny." Jay gave her a strange, sideways look. "You always speak as though you've had the privilege of being one yourself. Now, if you'll please forgive my impropriety." With one large hand, he grasped her ankles to keep her legs still, and with his hook, he pulled back the corner of her cloak.

Wendy landed a kick to his face. She watched with satisfaction as he fell back and blood dripped from his nose onto his starched white shirt.

"Tink," he snapped loudly. "You said she has it. Now get in here and find it."

The little fae flew in from the hall. Jay held Wendy's legs down as Tinkerbell fished around in Wendy's skirts until she found the reticule. She squinted as she rummaged through the bag. Wendy prayed she would leave the little clay balls alone without understanding what they were. And to Wendy's relief, she did. Unfortunately, however, the Wasaaca flower, already slightly wilted, was thrown to the ground. Then Tinkerbell's eyes grew wide and flashed with green as she reverently pulled out the star.

"I should have known *you* were involved," Wendy grumbled.

Tinkerbell curled her lip up at Wendy, but Jay took the star.

"When we realized you had gone, Tiger Lily suggested sending Tink after you."

As he spoke, Wendy remembered the sound they'd heard while in the treehouse.

"I'm glad to know the man who offered for my heart trusted me so implicitly," she snapped.

"You were the one who betrayed me, Wendy! Do not forget that!"

Tinkerbell's mouth fell open as she stared up at him. "You, too?" she cried. Then she huffed and stomped back out into the hall.

An idea came to Wendy as the little fae left. "Tink! Jay isn't going to give the star back! He's going to kill Peter!" she screamed as fast as she could, praying her voice carried down the hall.

Jay clapped his hand tightly over her mouth.

"Best to leave politics between myself and the fae." He pulled Wendy's gag back over her mouth. Then he slowly stood and looked down at her with a pained expression. "For what it's worth, I'm doing Peter a favor. Death will free him from the fae's grasp, and his sacrifice will save a sick woman." Then he paused, and this time, his voice was nearly a whisper. "I'm only saddened that it came to this. Truly. I meant it when I said I've never met a woman like you."

"As if you expect me to believe that," Wendy muffled through the cloth.

"I really did want to marry you, Wendy Darling." Then he tucked the star into the pocket of his coat and left, locking Wendy, the fae, and the boys in the dark once more.

CHAPTER 27
ONE LAST, LARGE SUPPER

Explosions rocked the island as Peter darted to the pinnacle, Nana at his heels. He knew better than to try flying while carrying something so heavy, so they took off at a run.

As he ran, Peter argued with himself that he should go back to the boys to check on them. Hopefully, they didn't think the explosions were his diversion and fly straight into danger. He was already mostly up the mountain, though. If it was the star dying, he might be able to lower its range of destruction. Perhaps he could bend the destruction so that it moved away from the boys. But as he got closer, he realized that the light and noise wasn't coming from the star's cave at all. Exhausted relief threatened to slow his feet and pull him to the ground, but he pushed himself on.

He passed the Neverstar's cave and stopped at the tip of the island. There, on the other side, near the bay where Jay had once docked his ship, was the source. Explosion after explosion lit the night sky. Fae were hurrying down by the dozen, flying low and shouting to one another as they tried to figure out how to stop them. Many of them froze as soon as they crested the mountain, their eyes glazing over as they focused on the fireworks. And for those who weren't transfixed, it was evident that their flight was being impeded, too. But there wasn't, that Peter could tell, any reason or rhyme to the cause of the explosions. They would shoot up from the beach to the right, then from the forest to the north. All within the same radius of about two miles, but there seemed to be no end to them.

First the food, then the explosions. Two completely unforeseen, mysterious instances. And why?

A particularly strong explosion knocked Peter to the ground. He scraped his hand on a rock, and as a trickle of blood ran down his wrist, it occurred to him.

The *why* wasn't really important. What was important was that for once, the fae weren't watching.

Peter tore down the mountainside again. He did his best to fly, but after crashing painfully three times, gave up and continued running. Nana would just have to keep up. He had to get to the boys. As he panted, doing his best to avoid trees and boulders and ledges, he cursed himself silently for making the mountain so blasted high.

Nana, faithful dog, stayed at his heels, never once slowing or stopping to catch her breath. As she ran beside him, Peter, for the first time, really began to appreciate the dog for who she was. The dog was just as good at keeping up as Tink had ever been, and she complained a lot less. But there was no time for reminiscing or even for appreciation. They had boys to save.

The run, which slowed into a climb down the mountain, lasted twenty minutes. Peter was forced to exercise caution in certain places and lower himself down ledges and ravines he'd hardly known existed, deep cuts in the land he had always soared right over.

By the time he was at the tree, half of him was sure this was their chance. No matter who had provided the distraction, this was his chance to get the boys to Maricanta. Or at least, to escape Neverland. The other half was full of misgivings he refused to listen to, thoughts of all the things that might go wrong. Who might see them. Whether or not Slightly would cry. How many fae would leave the explosions behind to make chase. What they would do with Nana.

All these fears were silenced, though, when he finally threw himself down the stump and landed in a heap on the treehouse's floor, only to find that all the boys were gone.

PETER FELT as though the world had lost all sense. He scrambled back up to the surface and began yelling for the boys. Perhaps they'd gone looking for something to eat. Or looking for him. He'd given John and Nibs directions before leaving, but given the circumstances, perhaps they'd thought they needed to find him. Or, as he'd instructed them to do, they'd found a chance to escape.

Or, he thought as his stomach churned, the fae had taken them somewhere on the island. Tink had been angry following their last conversation. It would have been easy, perhaps, for Tiger Lily to talk the little fae into betraying their secret entrance to the tree. She could have taken all the boys to a new location in an attempt to strong-arm him into fixing the world the way Tiger Lily was still sure it could be fixed.

For a moment, he did what he had never done before, and stood still, frozen in fear about what to do next. Nana, however, was not afraid. Instead, she began to sniff the ground. And with each sniff she became more and more excited until she was barking and practically leaping with joy. Peter had only ever seen the dog that excited about one person.

She couldn't be back. Could she? He hadn't left her with any extra stardust, not enough to get back, at least. But then, there had been the food and the explosions. He hadn't the first idea as to how she could have managed all of that, but Wendy was resourceful if nothing else. And as she'd already been to Neverland before, she could easily have brought others with her, just as Jay had.

Peter followed the dog, who was busy sniffing the ground. But all too soon, her enthusiastic wagging became stiff, and she began to growl.

Something shifted to Peter's left. A shadow moved in the trees. At first, he thought it was someone hiding. One of the boys, perhaps, too scared to come out. But as he got closer, he realized that there was no body, only a shadow.

Only one other person knew how to separate body from shadow.

The shadow darted away, and Peter followed, hoping beyond hope as he crashed through the forest behind it. Hoping was foolish, of course. It couldn't be Wendy. It would be too good to be true. And yet...

Who else could it be? Peter picked up his pace as the shadow wove its way through trees. He couldn't really tell what shape or height the shadow was at all. But then, he'd only ever taught Wendy how to cast her shadow. And though it was strange of her to run away, he had banished her after all. It only made sense that she wouldn't be thrilled to meet him.

"Wendy!" he shouted breathlessly as he chased the shadow. "Please stop! I just want to talk!"

The shadow was making its way down the mountain, and Peter and Nana followed. It paused on the outcropping of a little ledge and looked out at the sea. The trees had kept him from getting a good look at the shadow, but just when he was nearly close enough to see it in full form, a body slammed into him so hard it knocked him to the ground. Nana barked as Peter landed hard on his back.

"Tink!" he cried from underneath her. "What are you doing?"

Tink scrambled to her knees. "Saving you! You need to get out of here now!"

"I'm following Wendy's shadow!" He pointed at the shadow through the trees. Tink squinted at it for a moment before her eyes grew wide.

"That's not Wendy!"

Peter jumped to his feet. "Of course it is! She's the only person I ever taught to separate her shadow." As he spoke, though, he grabbed Nana's collar before she could take off toward the ledge after the shadow she was growling ferociously at.

"I don't know who that is, but it's not Wendy! Now we don't have time for this! You need to listen to me!"

For the first time since giving chase, Peter stopped trying to look at the shadow and looked at Tink. "How do you know that?" He glanced down at her person. "And why are you all wet?"

"Because I fell in the ocean three times on my way over here."

"And why were you over the ocean?"

Tink, who had been wiping the mud off her legs and arms, froze briefly then resumed drying off.

"How do you know it's not Wendy?" Peter shouted.

"Because Wendy is a prisoner on Jay's ship," Tinkerbell snapped. "She's tied up in the hold right now."

"You know that how?"

She jutted her little chin out. "Because I helped put her there."

Any shred of affection that had remained in Peter's heart went up in smoke as Peter swallowed Tink's story.

"Why..." He glanced back at the trees where the figure had been. It was gone now. "Why would you—"

A deafening boom sounded where the shadow had been. The ground heaved beneath them. Explosions like those Peter had seen in the air on the other side of the island flashed with blinding light, and Peter and Tink were knocked to the ground. Peter hit his head on a rock, and his body throbbed all over. His ears rang as though someone had hit his head with a stick. It took him three tries to sit up straight. Tink groaned as well and pushed herself into a sitting position beside him. Peter regained his senses enough to roll away from the cracks in the ground, and Tink followed.

Before either of them could get to their feet, though, a cracking sound ripped through the air. They watched as the ledge the shadow had been standing on crumbled and disappeared below. And though Peter couldn't see it, he knew that the pieces were slamming down on the rocks beneath.

"Don't you see?" Tink coughed. "It was trying to kill you."

Peter's body felt like someone had beat him senseless, but he pushed himself to his feet anyway. Then he went over to Tink and pulled her up, too. Instead of letting go, though, he put his hands on her shoulders and gave her his most baleful glare.

"Details. All of them. Now."

"Why should I?"

"Because it sounds like you just aided whatever tried to kill me."

Several emotions flicked across her face.

"Whether or not you help me," Peter said, keeping hold of her shoulders, "I'll be paying a visit to Jay either way."

She glowered up at him for another few seconds before scoffing. "Fine. Jay came back, and he must have had Wendy with him."

"Why didn't we see them?" Peter asked.

"They've been hiding in the fog. Once Tiger Lily saw the ship, she called me to come with her. When we got there, we didn't know Wendy was there at first. Jay told Tiger Lily he'd come back alone for the star."

"Why?"

Tink rolled her eyes. "If you'd stop interrupting, I'd tell you. He found some sort of cure for his mother, but to use it, the star has to be dead. So Tiger Lily cut him a deal. She would give him... the means to buy another star from the traders in the east, and he would leave. He agreed, but as we were getting ready to leave, one of his men reported that Wendy was missing."

Peter's head swam as he tried to make sense of it all. Why was Wendy with Jay? How had they found one another? And was she part of the scheme to steal the star?

At least now he knew who had left the food.

"Tiger Lily told me to go after Wendy and to try to find her, and Jay sent some of his men over after us. I found her at the star cave and then followed her to the treehouse. Jay's men met me there. I'm pretty sure he has the star now." Tink looked at the ground. "His men took them all back to the ship."

Peter nearly fell over. "All of them? Even the baby?"

Tink nodded.

Peter stared at her as she studied the ground. He knew he should say something, but words wouldn't come.

Tink continued in a rush. "I saw Wendy and the boys. They're all alive. He's got them in the hold of the ship. Along with..." She stopped and bit her lip. "On my way out, I heard Wendy shout that Jay was going to kill you. So I came to warn you. In case he'd changed his mind and broken his deal with Tiger Lily." She paused. "It seems he did."

Peter had to search for his voice before he could speak. "Did it ever occur to you to say no?"

Tink frowned. "And allow them to steal our star?" She gave him a defiant look. "Besides. You never told them no, either."

Peter felt as though someone had stabbed him in the heart. Remorse and memories made his vision bleed. Because Tinkerbell was right. Wendy had begged him to stand up to the fae, but fear for all that the fae could do to the boys and to Wendy had held him back. He could have gone for help sooner, but fear had kept him captive. For five hundred years, he'd allowed himself and his boys to stay hidden in Neverland because he had been afraid, chasing away all his choices and chances until he had nowhere left to turn.

Or rather, it seemed that way.

"I might not have said no before," he said, studying the ocean. "But I'm doing it now." He turned and sought to lift off the ground. Nana would just have to wait. When his feet failed to leave the ground, though, he knew he would have to run for it. So he began to search for the best way down. "Come on, Nana." Nana gave another indignant snort at the broken cliff and turned to follow him.

"Peter?" Tink ran up behind him. "Before you go, I have to ask you one question."

He ignored her.

"What did she ever do for you that I didn't?"

He paused and turned. "She believed I could be free." With those words, he began to run.

"What are you doing?" Tink called after him.

"Ending this!" One way or another, this game was coming to an end.

By the time Peter reached the beach, he felt ready to pass out. He would have made the island smaller if he'd ever thought he would have to actually traverse the thing. Faithful Nana, however, seemed barely winded as she came to a stop beside him.

"I can't fly anymore," he told the dog as he stared out at the horizon. The fog was too thick to make out anything beyond a few hundred yards. "And it doesn't seem like I can see well either." Panic threatened to consume him as he realized he hadn't the slightest idea as to where the boat would be.

He needed to save everyone he loved and didn't even know where to find them. Then his blood ran cold as a thought crossed his mind.

What if Jay had already left Neverland?

Nana barked, and Peter turned to see her staring out into the fog as well. But after several seconds of searching, he found what looked like the dimmest of lights.

"Good girl!" he said, reaching down to rub the dog's head. "Now, how do you feel about boats?"

Ten minutes later, Peter was dragging one of the boys' hollowed out log boats to the edge of the water. He whistled for Nana to jump in, and as soon as he'd shoved the boat out into the water, he climbed in and began to paddle as well.

Just after a minute of rowing, something splashed behind him. Peter turned in time to see a dark figure fly over the water at him. It wrapped its hands around his neck and began to squeeze. Nana barked and growled and did her best to bite the thing, but it stayed high enough she couldn't reach it without falling out of the boat. It was the same shadow. Peter couldn't see any defining features, but he was sure of it.

The boat was rocking hard, and Peter knew from experience that water wouldn't stop the shadow. He'd used his own shadow to tease the boys countless times when they were swimming. If he tipped the boat, the shadow could continue choking him, and he would be out of the little air he was getting now.

Now that he was within its clutches, he could tell for certain that it wasn't Wendy's shadow. It was too big. But how did one kill a shadow? He'd always known what he could do with his, but he'd never tried to fight anyone else's.

Spots and lights began to fill his vision, but just as real fear crept in, so did a thought. The lights in his vision gave him an idea. Putting his hands together, he summoned all the stardust around him. At first, there didn't seem enough, for nothing happened. So he swept his hands through Nana's fur. This time, he could feel the store of dust that had collected all in her thick fur, and he thanked the Maker as he pulled his hands away from the dog and put them together once again.

This time, with a spark and a snap, a little tongue of flame appeared in his hands. Peter groaned as he pressed with all his strength into the fire. Then he split the flame into two, one for each hand, grabbed the shadow by the wrists, and squeezed.

At the touch of the flame, the shadow gave a silent scream and dissolved into nothingness. Peter and the dog were alone. Nana gave an offended *ruff* before settling back into her spot in the back.

"I can see why Wendy puts up with you," he croaked as he rubbed her head and his own neck at the same time. Then he picked up the oar once again and began to paddle.

Pain and panic threatened to take him. He'd never gotten a good look at the shadow without trees obscuring his view, though he had a strong conviction that Jay was to blame. Jay had been around him enough as a boy to probably have figured out how to separate his shadow as well. And where did Wendy fit into all of this? But he didn't have time to wonder what Wendy was doing in Neverland with Jay, or why she was helping him. He could only go faster to find out.

"I don't have much longer," he told Nana as they moved into the fog. "But we're in this together now. You up for one last adventure?"

Nana barked, though it sounded more like a reminder to focus than a word of solidarity, and Peter chuckled.

"Sounds good to me." He began to row but then paused. A

familiar shape appeared ahead of their canoe, like a log just peeking over the surface of the water.

"Hello, old fellow," Peter called softly, dangling his fingers in the water. "I have a job for you, if you're up for it."

The crocodile grunted.

"Considering that I didn't let them skin you, yes, I think you ought to help me." Peter gave the crocodile a grim smile. "That, and I get the feeling you might get one last, very large supper tonight."

CHAPTER 28
JUST IN CASE

Wendy huffed and let her shoulders droop. An hour and a half had passed since they'd been brought to the hold, and she hadn't been able to get the ropes even remotely loose. Slightly was crying, and Pop and Tootles were whimpering as well. If only she hadn't dropped the knife her father had given her. This would have been exactly what she needed it for.

When she got free, Wendy was going to deliver a swift kick to Jay's shins for each cry the little boys let loose.

"You're not going to get those ropes loose," Moon Flower said. Her voice was breathy. Each flickering episode left her struggling for air, and as the episodes increased, Wendy grew more worried.

"What happens when the star dies?" Wendy asked as she started fighting with her bindings again.

"We don't know for sure." Moon Flower gave what could have been a sob. "But whatever it is, it will be bad for anyone who's too close. There's too much power in the thing for it to be anything less than violent."

One of the boys moaned. Wendy looked over, but she couldn't

make out who it had been. She could only see the outlines of their shadows in the dark.

Their shadows.

Wendy closed her eyes and did her best to focus on her body, just as Peter had taught her. She'd failed miserably the first time, when she'd sent her shadow to explore the fae camp, and it ended up destroying the camp instead. The fae had nearly kicked her out of Neverland then and there. What had Peter said again? It was all about knowing what you wanted. No distractions. No split desires.

Well, right now, Wendy needed to get the boys out of Neverland. She needed to save Peter. If they could take back the star, perhaps the star could get them out of Neverland, especially if she no longer had to uphold the entire island.

In short, Wendy needed to get the star.

Slowly, so slowly, Wendy imagined peeling her shadow away from her skin. The first few times, nothing happened, and the fourth time, she nearly gave up. Her skin was clammy and hot, and she was more tired than she could describe. But her fifth try brought victory. Her shadow stood before her, and without opening her eyes, Wendy smiled.

"Go find Jay."

The shadow ran to the door and studied it from several angles before sliding through the keyhole. It was a strange sensation, feeling both the wood floor and pole beneath and behind her, while also feeling the shadow's surroundings as well. Up the stairs the shadow went, slowly so as not to attract attention. Several times a sailor passed it in the hall, but the shadow was unbelievably quick, faster than Wendy could have ever been. It melted back against the wall wherever it was and waited for the human to pass before resuming its search.

The shadow didn't find the captain on the deck or in the little room where he'd met with Tiger Lily. It finally found him in his quarters, arguing with his first mate.

"I don't know when they'll be back, Captain." The first mate held up his hands. "They were supposed to return as soon as they'd laid the casum balls."

"The fae must have gotten to them." Jay ran his hand through his shiny black hair, which was far less groomed than Wendy had ever seen it. His bloodshot eyes had bags beneath them. "Look, I'll give them another quarter-hour. If they're not back by then, we've got no choice but to go."

"And leave our men?" The first mate sounded horrified.

"It seems as though the fae can no longer fly over the water, which has saved us. But if Tiger Lily knows we've crossed her, and she somehow manages to get her people to this ship, there won't be a ship left for any of us to sail home on."

The first mate stared at him a second longer before slowly nodding. "Aye, Captain." He saluted and left the room, shutting the door behind him, leaving Jay, the cabin boy, and Wendy's shadow.

Jay collapsed on his bed and rubbed his eyes as the cabin boy began to straighten up, and Wendy's shadow looked about the room. There was no sign of the star on the table, the shelf above the fireplace, or on a chair. Which meant it was most likely still in his pocket.

If Wendy's shadow could have frowned, it would have. This mission was growing more dangerous by the minute. Not only was she under the time constraint to have the boys and fae freed in the next quarter-hour, but the cabin boy was also nearby to witness her doings. If he spotted her and reported her to the captain, there was no telling what Jay might do when he realized what she was now capable of.

Wendy's shadow crept up to the side of the bed and watched Jay's breath rise and fall several times until she was sure it was in some sort of pattern. Then she reached slowly, slowly until the tips of her fingers were actually in his pocket. She could feel the heat radiating out from the star. But just as her fingers brushed the star's highest tip, Jay rolled over, and her shadow had to dash back down under the bed.

She spent a good minute mulling over what to do before she remembered that she was, in fact, using her shadow, which meant she could climb to the other side of the bed without getting stuck underneath it. Slipping up through the crack between the bed and the window, she tried again. Unfortunately, he had rolled too far over, and the star would not come out without bumping its sharp edges on the leg against which it was wedged.

Wendy's shadow looked all around the room until she spotted a little bowl of pepper on the table, along with Jay's supper scraps that the cabin boy hadn't yet cleaned up. Darting over him when the cabin boy wasn't looking, she grabbed a pinch of pepper and positioned herself between Jay's head and his hip. She reached her hand back into his pocket as far as she dared before slowly, very slowly, dribbling the pepper over his nostrils.

At first, nothing happened. But just as she was about to give up and look for something else to make him move, Jay sneezed. Wendy didn't even wait to see if he woke up or not. The moment he moved, she snatched the star from his pocket and darted out through the window. Then she climbed up the edge of the ship, and avoided the sailors, hopping between shadows as she made her way back down to the hold. When she got there, though, her heart sank. The door was still locked. And unlike the first time, she couldn't go back through the keyhole. Not with the star, at least.

"I know you're tired," she called softly to the star, hoping it could hear her real voice through the door. "But could you open the door? Just this once?"

For a moment, there was no response. Then the door clicked open. The shadow rushed inside, closing the door behind, and ran to Wendy's side.

"Loosen my ropes then unlock the cages!" Wendy hissed. Obediently, the shadow freed the fae as Wendy untied the boys. When everyone was standing, the shadow joined itself to Wendy once more.

Wendy tore a strip off King Everard's cloak and wrapped the star inside of it. Then, unwilling to have it snatched from her reticule twice, she tied it inside her skirts, concealing it in a special knot that she hoped the fae wouldn't sense.

"Wendy!" Slightly cried. Wendy grabbed the little boy up in her arms and hugged him close as the other boys crowded around her, throwing their arms around her waist and legs and clinging to her for dear life.

"Now, boys," she whispered as loudly as she dared. "We need to get off this ship and out of Neverland."

"We don't have much time," Moon Flower said. "The star is weakening."

"What about Peter?" Top asked. "We can't leave him here!"

Wendy drew in a deep breath and closed her eyes. *What do I do?* she prayed silently. She didn't want to leave Peter at the hands of the fae any more than the boys did. If nothing else, he deserved to be free, even if he and the star only had a few...

No. It didn't signify even thinking about. She didn't have the first idea as to where Peter might be, much less how she would get him to leave with her.

"Perhaps he'll join us," she told the boys in the most courageous voice she could muster, praying they wouldn't hear the tears behind her words. "But I know that no matter what, Peter wants you all to be safe. I know that for sure. So we'll honor him by keeping one another safe, yes?"

The boys' murmuring made them sound doubtful, but Wendy

didn't have time to worry about their misgivings. So she turned to the star. "Do you think you can help us fly out? Just until we're out of Neverland?"

The star flickered several times. Wendy took that as a yes, but her dying light didn't inspire confidence. She turned to Moon Flower. "Could you fly us out, perhaps?"

"I'm afraid not." Moon Flower sighed. "We can fly somewhat up and down in our fae form, but not over long distances. Besides, until we gain back one form or the other, as long as we're tied to Neverland, our forms won't be predictable enough to carry anyone safely." Even as she spoke, her eyes glowed green several times, sputtering out only a second later each time.

"John. Nibs." Wendy turned to the older boys to discuss taking one of the rafts. But before she could say anything more, the door burst open, and Jay and several of his men filled the frame.

"Wendy," Jay said, his voice cracking. "Why?"

"Why what?" Wendy asked, playing the fool.

Jay glanced around at the boys and fae all standing together. "I was going to take you all home," he said softly. "I didn't actually wish to hurt anyone."

"Except Peter?" Wendy glared. "Forgive me if I don't trust you implicitly."

"I told you I was going to free him!" Jay growled.

"By killing him?"

"Jay!" a woman's voice screeched from far away.

Jay's eyes closed and he sucked a sharp breath through his nose.

"We have much to discuss, it seems," came Tiger Lily's call from above.

"Don't let them out," Jay told one of his guards as he turned and strode down the hall. "Keep them here and hidden until I come back."

Wendy stared at the light streaming through the door. If only she knew how to fight. Her shadow could take down one of the guards simply because of its speed, but not both. They stared at Wendy's odd crew, holding their swords up, knees bent as if ready to spring forward. Maybe if she could use her shadow to distract them—

Before Wendy could put any of her plans into action, one of them let out a cry as three of the fae, including Moon Flower, flew at his leg and one came down on his head. The other guard was attacked similarly. The attacks were neither neat nor safe. Two of the fae screamed as the guards' swords bit flesh, their bodies flickering as they seemed frozen, unable to move from where they had fallen, but Moon Flower hurried Wendy and the boys out before Wendy could make sense of it all. When they reached the end of the hall and stood in the room with the stairs that led up to the deck, one of Moon Flower's fae, who must have slipped out without Wendy noticing, was already on his way back. He whispered something in Moon Flower's ear before joining the others.

"Jay just received a new batch of sailors," Moon Flower said. "Their boats are being pulled up now."

"They must have returned from planting the casum balls." Wendy frowned. Then she realized something. "We could use their boats!" Rowing out of Neverland was far from ideal, but she was willing to try anything at this point.

"We'll have to lower them as well," Moon Flower said, glancing up at the top of the stairs. "As soon as you and the boys are in one, we'll find a way to let you down. Then I want you to row as though your lives depend on it." She put a hand on Wendy's shoulder. "Because they do."

"If Tiger Lily is here, you'll need help," Wendy said. "King Everard gave me several items to distract the fae."

Moon Flower stopped. "King Who?"

"Everard Fortier of Destin."

Moon Flower's eyes bulged. "You got help from a *Destinian* king?"

Wendy nodded, realizing why Moon Flower might find that offensive. But they didn't have time to care. "He says power will distract them...you. If you all know that I'm going to throw them up, can you ignore them?"

Moon Flower pursed her lips and looked back at her comrades before nodding. "It won't be easy. But Wendy?"

"What?"

Moon Flower's eyes flashed green several times as she squeezed Wendy's shoulder. "We have lived our lives. And they were not well-spent. So if you break free, don't wait for us."

"But—"

"Don't wait." She stepped back and raised her chin defiantly. "Let us try to make up for the evil we've put in the world by taking some out."

"Why are you doing this?" Wendy asked. It still felt strange to trust the fae...even if they now shared a common enemy. "I've ruined everything here."

Moon Flower gave her a dry smile. "At one time, the fae did not only seek power and ease. As much of a pain as you've been, you've reminded some of us that we were made to give as well as take. I suppose it's high time we returned our share. So please. I want you to escape and not to look back. Give us whatever honor we can scrape from the dregs of our existence."

Wendy swallowed. She understood, of course, but it went against everything inside her to agree to leave a friend behind. Because that's what Moon Flower had become. A friend.

A friend who had one last request.

"Very well," Wendy said, nodding. "We'll go."

"There are many of them," one of the other fae said. She was peeking over the edge of the deck. "Tiger Lily hasn't left any behind."

"And there will be Jay's men, too." Wendy climbed up the stairs just enough to peek over the edge of the deck as well.

It was even worse than she thought. Tiger Lily and Jay were arguing. Tiger Lily must have realized Jay's little trick. The remaining fae, of which there were probably about three dozen, stood behind her. Jay's men stood in a semicircle around him. The only signs of vulnerability in their ranks were the way the fae flickered and the way Jay's men kept glancing back at their leader.

"Go," Moon Flower whispered to Wendy, nodding toward the closest boat, which hung over the water. Wendy nodded and ushered her boys up and pointed them toward it.

"Get the boys into the boat," she whispered to John.

"What about you?" he whispered back, his eyes large as walnuts.

"She's going, too," Moon Flower said, giving Wendy a hard stare.

"But just in case they separate me," Wendy said quickly. "You're in charge. You're not allowed to come back or to wait. I want you to get out of Neverland as fast as you can."

"But—"

"For the boys, John." She grabbed him in a fierce hug. And for once, he hugged her back just as tightly. She felt him nod against her shoulder as his silent tears wet her sleeve. But there wasn't time to reminisce or cry about the fact that this might be the last time they saw one another. Instead, Wendy somehow managed to pull away and led the excursion up onto the deck. They stayed low and darted from hiding place to hiding place to the nearest rowboat, which hung over the water on the right side of the ship. Nibs slipped in first, and John handed him the smaller boys, one by one. They were almost all inside by the time Tiger Lily's voice cut through the night.

"They're getting away!"

CHAPTER 29
FALLING

Both sailors and fae made a rush at them. Wendy tried to jump into the boat with the boys, but someone grabbed her arms and dragged her back. She was thrown against the deck, and far too many hands held her down as Tiger Lily knelt before her and began to feel up and down her clothes.

"No need to be crude," Jay snapped from his place beside Tiger Lily.

Tiger Lily paused to give him a disdainful glare. "And would you allow a few extra ruffles to keep you from the star?"

"You could just ask her."

Was he suddenly feeling gallant now, after locking her and a bunch of little boys in the hold of a ship? Wendy nearly said as much, but held her tongue to keep the attention away from the boys.

Tiger Lily sneered. "Very well. Wendy, will you *please* give up the star?"

"Neither of you are getting it," she said, trying to back away. If she could just keep their attention away from the boys. But she didn't get far, as her captors kept her where she was. Jay advanced another step. And Wendy knew if she didn't think of something fast, it would all be for naught.

"Wendy!" Michael jumped out of the boat, his arms outstretched toward her, but one of Tiger Lily's fae, who had been standing quietly to the side, grabbed him and held a knife to Michael's chest. John tried to throw himself at the offender, but another fae grabbed him from behind and held him as well.

Tiger Lily looked from the boys back at Wendy, a smile on her face. "Have we made ourselves clear?"

"Fine!" Wendy cried, her voice shaking and her hands trembling. "Fine. You can have it, just...wait." She reached down into her skirts and pulled out the star. Her heart pounded faintly in her chest as she unwrapped it and held it up with shaking hands. She wished she could grab her little casum balls from the king, but she didn't dare reach inside her reticule now just to have them taken away, too.

Where was Peter now? a stupid, frightened voice inside her cried. So many times, he'd rescued her. But now, he was nowhere to be found. He probably couldn't even fly over the ocean even if he wanted to come to their aid. No one was coming to rescue them. And as much as she had hoped to have it all—the star, the boys...Peter—it just wasn't going to happen.

Tiger Lily grabbed the star, but before she could snatch it away, Jay's large hand closed over the star as well.

"It's mine!" Tiger Lily hissed, but Jay's eyes stayed on Wendy's, pleading.

"Come now, Wendy," he said softly. "You might as well give it up. The star is aging. Peter will be dead soon. I'll bring you and the boys to freedom either way, but we have to do it before he dies and Neverland goes with him."

Then Tiger Lily's hand was no longer on the star. Instead, she was in Jay's face, grabbing his lapels with her hands and yanking him down to face her. "Dead soon? What did you do to him?"

"I sent my shadow to end him several hours ago." Jay's jaw tightened. "I thought it was a more fitting ending than having you all draw his suffering out until you'd bled him dry of every last drop of life." He turned back to Wendy, pulling on the star even as he spoke. "We will be in grave danger if you don't give me the star now and let me sail out of Neverland. I told the shadow to wait before killing him so we could get out, but when he dies, there's no telling what will happen to anyone still here!"

Wendy stared at Jay in horror. He'd sent his shadow after Peter? But how...

Then she remembered what Peter had said about Jay on more than one occasion. Jay was always prepared. It was possible that he had watched Peter enough over the years to have figured out how to separate from his own shadow. But Peter still thought Wendy was the only one who knew how to do it. So if Peter saw Jay's shadow trying to kill him, he could very well believe it to be Wendy's shadow until the shadow grew too close, and it was too late.

Wendy's heart dropped into her stomach, and she resisted the urge to vomit. Peter would think that she was trying to kill him.

Tiger Lily let out a shriek of anger and threw herself at Jay, who fell back onto the deck. Wendy clutched the star to her chest as pandemonium erupted, fae and sailors clashing. Jay's men fought with their swords, while Tiger Lily's fae were armed with an assortment of unusual weapons, from bows and arrows to knives to crude swords. Sailors screamed and fae fell.

"Wendy! Wendy!"

Wendy blinked, trying to free her focus from Jay's horrific revelation. Moon Flower was screaming her name as John and Nibs shoved the distracted fae out of the boat and into the water below. Wendy looked at her brothers, trying to focus enough to remember what they needed her to do. Yes, it was good they were getting the fae out. Something was missing, though...

When another sailor jumped into the boat and took a swing at John, Wendy's memory snapped back into place. John and Nibs had gotten the boys back into the boat as they needed to be, but that wouldn't be enough. They needed to get the boat down, too. Wendy looked around wildly to find the lever to lower the boat. But before she could locate it, the rowboat began to drop.

A movement to her left caught her eye, and she found Moon Flower and several of her fae turning a crank.

"Go!" Moon Flower shouted. "We'll catch up!" Wendy turned to run to the boat as well, but even as she ran toward it, she saw several of Tiger Lily's fae eye the boat, too. It wasn't going to be enough. The boat might reach the water, but the boys weren't professional sailors. Jay's men would be on them in minutes, even if they rowed out toward the barrier unassaulted. Likewise, the fae seemed to be capable of short bursts of flight, not because of the stardust, but because of the nonhuman forms they were quickly taking more and more.

If the sailors didn't get the boys, the fae would. Even now, Tiger Lily's fae were thrashing the sailors, the instability of their forms being the only reason they hadn't killed them all already. Just as King Everard had said, they were fast and deadly. The only times the sailors seemed able to kill them were when they had to pause in their fighting to flicker back and forth between forms. That's when she remembered.

King Everard. He'd said the fae were drawn to power of any kind. The casum balls he'd given her wouldn't be enough to draw off the entire fae army, but a larger explosion...

Wendy ran back to Moon Flower. "Get the fireworks from below! They're in crates, just below the stairs!" she shouted over the noise of the battle. Two of Tiger Lily's fae spotted her and ran straight for her, but Moon Flower's fae intercepted them so Wendy could finish. "Then light them on the other side of the boat by setting the little tails on fire. Tell your people to do their best to ignore them and escape!"

Moon Flower grimaced. "It will be difficult," she said, looking out at the battle. "Small bits of power are easier to ignore if we know ahead of time, but fireworks—"

"You must!" Wendy cried. "I'll draw their attention first. Then you draw it after. The boys should be able to get away, and then you can go as well! Protect them as well as you can."

Moon Flower frowned. "And you?"

Wendy gave her a hard smile. "I'm finishing this."

Moon Flower shook her head. "I don't know what to make of you, Wendy Darling. You seemed destined to turn everything upside down."

"As long as you get the fireworks!" Wendy called over her shoulder as she dashed off. By this time, the boys were low enough that they were nearly invisible over the edge of the deck as Moon Flower's fae continued to lower them into the water. Wendy paused only to pray that they would make it out safely before running and jumping into one of the escape boats on the other side of the ship, where she swung precariously over the water. She not only had to capture the attention of Tiger Lily and Jay's men but then to hold it as the boys got as far away as they could. She reached into her reticule and grabbed one of King Everard's little casum balls.

"I'm sorry," she whispered to the star. In return, she felt what she was sure was a flicker of peace. And somehow, she knew that the star knew what had to be done. Then Wendy threw the king's little casum ball into the air, where it burst into a pillar of blue light that shot up into the night.

The fae turned toward it like moths to a flame, and the sailors did almost the same.

"Here's the star!" Wendy shouted, holding the star up in the air. She held on to the ropes with her left hand as the boat swung back and forth beneath her. "I demand that the Lost Boys and Moon Flower's fae go free."

"Or you'll do what?" Tiger Lily called. The blue pillar of light had begun to dissipate, and Wendy could see their eyes beginning to focus again. "Kill the star, and you kill Peter."

"The star isn't human." Wendy watched her audience carefully, not daring to tip them off by peeking in the direction of her brothers. "She doesn't need air to live." She held the star closer to the edge of the boat.

Tiger Lily's harsh smile froze.

"I'll drop her," Wendy continued, "and none of you will find her. Peter will live every last breath he and the star can muster, doing whatever he pleases, and you will have lost it all."

"For what?" Tiger Lily spat. "So the mermaids can find her and control Peter that way?"

Wendy gave Tiger Lily a cold smile. "The mermaids would be better masters than you."

Tiger Lily turned a strange shade of gray.

"Can't you just send one of your heathen creatures after it?" Jay yelled at the ashen Tiger Lily.

"Oh." She turned her wrathful gaze upon him. "So you care whether or not we get it now?"

"If we don't do *something*, neither one of us will have it," Jay spat back.

"It wouldn't matter if I turned myself into a manatee!" Tiger Lily screamed. "The water's so murky we could be searching down there for years. Neverland will be gone before anyone finds it!"

"I'm telling the truth!" Wendy shouted, holding the star inches from the edge. "I'll drop her."

"And if we give you what you want?" Jay called, turning back to Wendy. "What then?"

Wendy hesitated. What then? The last thing she wanted to do

was surrender the star. And yet, she knew that both Peter and the star would want the boys to live.

"If you can prove to me that the boys and Moon Flower's fae will be allowed to go freely, I will—"

Something small and hard plowed into Wendy. Wendy lost her grip on the rope and fell into the rowboat. The star was knocked from her hands and bounced several feet away. Wendy scrambled onto her knees to grab it, but the small form got there first, and Wendy found herself staring up into Tinkerbell's glittering eyes.

"You were so close," Tinkerbell said, picking up the star and examining it closely.

"Tinkerbell!" Tiger Lily shrieked. "Give me the star!"

But Tinkerbell's eyes had widened, and she seemed to be frozen in a trance as she stared into the star's pulsing crystal depths. "Peter's heart," she whispered. "It's finally mine."

Wendy swung her arm around into the backs of Tinkerbell's knees. Tinkerbell's legs gave out, and her form began to flicker, wavering between human and the green whorl Wendy had come to loathe.

Wendy jumped up and snatched the star back. She'd only gotten to the edge of the boat, though, when she felt Tinkerbell grab the back of her dress and yank her down. Wendy tried to jump to the side, but her feet slipped. She grabbed the first thing she could find. It was the rope that she'd held on to before, only now she was dangling over the water. As if that weren't bad enough, she heard an all-too-familiar snap. Glancing down, she let loose a word her mother would have been appalled to hear.

Why in the world had Peter insisted on creating that stupid crocodile? And why was it all the way out here in the water now?

"Give me the star, and I'll pull you up!" Tinkerbell reached over the edge, her hand outstretched.

Wendy met the little fae's eyes. "No, you won't," she said.

Tinkerbell smiled. "You're right. I won't." Then she lunged at Wendy's other hand. Wendy jerked back, her legs swinging over the crocodile's head. Tinkerbell brushed Wendy's body as the little fae plunged into the depths with a scream that was cut short by the crocodile's snapping jaws. When Wendy looked down again, the only sign of Tinkerbell left was the foamy water, which was slightly tinged red.

But before Wendy could feel relief, the taut rope slipped from her sweaty hand, and she was falling, too.

CHAPTER 30
FROZEN

Wendy shrieked as she fell, but instead of landing in outstretched jaws of the crocodile, Wendy found herself in a strong set of arms instead. She opened her eyes to see Peter's face inches from her own.

"You came," she whispered.

Instead of answering her, Peter pressed himself against the bottom of the ship, barely keeping his balance with his feet on the canoe and one arm holding the rope ladder that went up the side of the ship. He put Wendy down beside him so she could help keep the canoe hidden, but he kept his arm around her shoulders.

"Where is it?" Tiger Lily's voice was shrill above them.

"I don't see any sign of her," was Jay's reply.

"We can't just leave it below!" Tiger Lily's voice began to fade, as if they were moving farther away. "This is all your fault! If you had just let things be and taken the fae I gave you—"

Before Wendy could hear another word, something white, brown, and blurry shot out from beneath a blanket on the bottom of the canoe, and they were both nearly knocked in the water by a large, wet ball of fur.

"Nana!" she whispered, laughing as loudly as she dared. Nana threw herself into Wendy's arms, trembling as she barked and licked and barked and licked some more.

Peter squeezed her shoulders. "I wasn't about to let you have all the fun without me," he whispered with a tired grin. "And, apparently, neither was she." Nana had stopped kissing Wendy and was now sniffing every square inch of her, as though sure Wendy had been harmed in some way while they were apart.

"But why now..." Then she remembered what Jay had told her. "Peter, about the shadow! That wasn't mine! Jay must have—"

"Figured out how to use his own." Peter nodded. "He always was a resourceful bugger." He sighed, and his smile disappeared briefly before returning. "Shall we finish this?"

"How much longer does the star have?" Wendy asked, studying the star's dim light, her voice wavering treacherously.

He gave her a sad smile. "If we play our cards right, long enough to get you and the boys out safely."

Wendy stared into the depths of his green eyes. She wanted to scream and rant that it wasn't fair. He deserved to live, too. Not as a hostage in a world he'd created, but as a real...

Well, a real man.

Instead of screaming, she nodded and put the star back in her reticule. "Let's save the boys."

Peter began to climb the rope ladder, but halfway up, he realized she wasn't following him. "You ready?" he called back down.

"We can't leave her," Wendy said, wrapping an arm around her dog. Peter rolled his eyes, an expression Wendy was only too glad to see again, and came back down the rope ladder. Then he wrapped one arm under the dog and pulled himself up with his other arm. Wendy followed him. It was a slow, painstaking process, thanks to Nana, but eventually, they did reach the deck. Peter set Nana loose and then leaned down to pull Wendy up.

Everyone, fae and sailors included, stopped fighting for a long moment to stare at them. And, to Wendy's dismay, John and Nibs.

What on earth were they doing on the deck? They should have been in the water, rowing away by now.

"Get the star!" Tiger Lily shouted.

Immediately, Peter was in front of Wendy, machete drawn. And so the melee began. Two seconds later, Moon Flower's fae were with him, and the boys squeezed and shoved their way to the front as well, as an army of angry fae and sailors descended upon them. For once, Wendy was glad the boys had practiced fighting the fae back in the forest, before everything had fallen to pieces. The boys had gathered a surprising number of weapons, and were expertly slashing at calves and legs as Moon Flower's fae attacked from above. All but Michael and Slightly, who Wendy spotted hiding in one of the boats. Thank goodness John had had the sense not to release them all into the fight. Nana's teeth drew more cries from the sailors and fae than all the Lost Boys put together, an expression of fierce glee on her furry face. One at a time, Wendy threw her casum balls from King Everard into the air, distracting Tiger Lily's fae enough for Wendy's defenders to push them back.

Most impressive of them all, however, were Peter and his shadow as they moved like dancers in the night, slashing and stabbing with expert aim, turning and dodging without flying but moving almost as if they could. Someone set off the fireworks from the back deck, which Wendy could see Moon Flower's fae trying to ignore as their counterparts on Tiger Lily's side struggled to maintain focus.

The effort seemed to be working, as more of the fae and sailors fell, but the victory came at a cost. Moon Flower's fae were falling as well, and Wendy doubted they could keep fighting this hard for much longer. Jay was cutting fae down right and left, leaving a path of carnage as he moved straight through the line that was protecting Wendy. Wendy could only pray the younger boys were somewhere safe.

It couldn't go on like this for much longer. Something had to give.

Someone grabbed Wendy's hair from the back and slammed her head down against the wooden deck. The world spun for a moment, and Wendy felt the reticule being ripped from her body. She tried to blink away the blur in her vision. Her eyes cleared just in time to see Tiger Lily snatch the star out of the reticule.

"No!" Wendy screamed, but it was too late. Tiger Lily's eyes glowed green as she held the star reverently next to her heart. She closed her eyes and breathed in deeply, as though she felt perfectly at peace amidst the bloody battle.

Wendy awkwardly got to her feet, but she didn't have the slightest idea as to how she would get the star back.

"That's Peter's!" she cried weakly. "It belongs to him."

"No, we gave it to Peter for safekeeping." Tiger Lily took a step back. "He chose to squander it. But the star was weak before, and he healed it. It can be healed again."

"No. Not if he doesn't want it," Wendy said, taking another slow step forward. "It's his decision to make."

"Stay back!" Tiger Lily reached out and snatched Curly from the crowd. He shrieked as she held the pointed edges of the star to his throat. "I'll—"

Her threat was cut off by her scream. She let go of Curly, and with her free hand, she reached behind her and tried desperately to swat something away. Wendy looked behind her to see Nana, her jaws clamped down on Tiger Lily's backside. Tiger Lily stumbled forward when the dog released her, and the star flew out of her grasp. Her hand shot out, and she caught the star as she fell, landing on it with a heavy thud. Wendy waited for her to get up, but when she didn't, Wendy took her by the shoulder and turned her just enough to see a small pool of blood spill out from where the star had impaled the fae just below her heart.

The thing Tiger Lily had revered as her savior had been the very thing to bring her death.

Wendy did her best to pick up the star by one of its clean arms. Then she wiped the blood off the best she could with her skirts and looked around.

"Peter!" she cried as he shoved one of the sailors into the water.

He looked back, and his eyes widened when he took in Tiger Lily's still form. Until that moment, the other fae hadn't seemed to notice. But when they did, a cry went up, and many cowered back, leaving Jay and his men facing Wendy, Peter, John, Nana, and the seven or eight that were left of Moon Flower's fae. Thankfully, it seemed Nibs had had sense enough to herd the younger boys back to the boat yet again.

"Come on, Jay," Peter said, holding his machete up. "Tiger Lily's gone. Let's put an end to sacrificing other lives and have this out honorably."

Jay studied Peter. He breathed heavily, and sweat ran down his brow and made lines in the dirt on his face, but his shoulders did not droop, and a strange gleam came into his eyes. "What if I choose to simply wait it out?" he asked. "The star can't live much longer. I could just let you die and then take it from you."

"You could. But you would most likely die, along with everyone here, and there would be no one to take the star to your mother." Peter grinned. "Besides, where would the adventure be in that?"

Jay studied Peter for a moment and shrugged. "Where indeed?" he repeated softly, almost as if to himself. He glanced at Wendy, then looked back at his first mate and gave him a nod.

"No interfering with the captain's duel," the first mate cried as he motioned for the sailors, who seemed more dumbstruck than disobedient, to step back.

"Winner takes all," Peter said. "But whoever wins must bring

Wendy and the boys back to the other side before Neverland falls."

"And what of us?" Moon Flower shouted.

Peter nodded. "You too, of course."

"And if I kill you," Jay asked, "how will I get the star without it killing me in your death? I still am skeptical, you know. I think the fae made that up to scare everyone away."

Peter shrugged. "Then you have nothing to worry about when I die. Now, what of my terms?"

What was he doing? If Jay killed him, they'd all die. Peter was usually confident, but this was ludicrous.

Jay began to take off his coat. "They sound reasonable enough."

"John," Wendy whispered to her brother, who had come to stand by her side. "Get in the boats. We're leaving now."

"Belay that order," Jay called out. He looked at Wendy. "I'm sorry, ma'am, but I'm the only one who gives orders around here." Then he looked back at Peter. "No cheating. No tricks."

Peter held his hands out. "As you can see, there's not enough dust for flying. As for cheating," his smile hardened slightly, "I never cheated."

Jay gave him a look as he handed his coat to his first mate. "Really? Creating weapons out of thin air wasn't cheating?"

Peter's smile widened. "Not when the world is yours. And the world was never yours." He stood taller for a moment, and Wendy realized that even in the days since she had left, he seemed to have grown another inch closer to Jay's height. "Now, before we begin, I'm giving you one last chance to let go." His voice softened. "Go to your mother. Tell her goodbye. She deserves that much."

Jay's face, which had been the picture of calm, contorted. "She deserves to *live*!" He smacked a railing with the butt of his sword, cracking the wood with his force. "She would have lived if you hadn't been so selfish! And now look at Neverland. Was it worth it? All that righteousness about saving the world, only to sacrifice it for your own personal pleasure? Curse it all, Peter. That woman gave up everything for me. The reason she contracted this horrid disease is because she went searching for me in the darkest underbelly of all of Ashland and exposed herself to—" He closed his eyes and drew in a deep breath through his nose. "No. This ends tonight."

Peter bowed his head slightly. "If that is what you wish, then so be it." He held up his machete as Jay brought his sword crashing down over Peter's head.

Wendy wanted to scream. What kind of game was Peter playing? Was he really so confident as to gamble with the boys' lives?

Peter dodged the attack effortlessly and darted to the side. Jay attacked the same way two more times before Peter moved in for his own attack. Instead of keeping Jay at a distance, however, the way Jay had kept him back, Peter moved in close. It made Jay's formerly liquid, graceful movements awkward as he sought to push Peter back with his sword while Peter attacked from close range, twisting and turning the machete in a way that was difficult for Jay to counter.

Several times, Wendy was sure Peter would end Jay. And several times, she was sure Jay would end Peter. But Peter never went for the kill, nor did he allow Jay to either. Instead, he kept Jay dangling, always close enough for hope, but never close enough to kill.

"Confound you, Peter!" Jay cried, stepping back and mopping his brow with his sleeve. "Why are you toying with me? Every moment, my mother slips closer to death, and you play like a child. Why not just give me the star and die in peace as I sail back to my mother in Ashland?"

"Because you've betrayed my trust. Now I'm giving you every

last chance I can," Peter said, lowering his weapon slightly. "Once again, will you forfeit?"

"Never!" Jay shouted, lunging at Peter, sword outstretched. Peter stepped aside just enough to let Jay's momentum carry him so he hit the railing. Peter then grabbed his hook in one hand and shoved his forearm against Jay's body so that the top half of Jay's body was dangling over the railing.

"You brought the crocodile?" Jay spat. "I never understood why you insisted on creating that blasted thing to begin with." He shoved Peter off, and they began to circle again.

"I like crocodiles." Peter gave him a hard smile.

Jay shook his head, all signs of humor gone from his face. "You always took things a step too far, Peter."

"No." Peter swallowed, also breathing heavily as they continued to circle. "That was your job."

Jay let out a shout and lunged again. Rage fueled his steps, slashes, and parries, each attack seeming more violent than the last.

Wendy began to shake, praying silently as they dueled. Despite Peter's recent growth spurt, Jay was still bigger and stronger than Peter. Peter's evasion techniques began to slow, and as they did, Jay's attacks created longer points of contact.

Then Peter tripped on a hole in the deck. Wendy cried out as he fell back against the ground, his head cracking loudly as it did.

Jay was immediately on top of him. He pressed his hook against Peter's throat.

"Give it up, Peter," he said through gritted teeth. "Surrender now, and I'll let you ride with Wendy and the boys out of Neverland before I kill you."

"You're too generous." Even on the ground, Peter managed to give Jay a mocking smile. Wendy was afraid to breathe.

"Please, Jay," she cried. "Don't do this here and now."

"Woman, you lost your right to beg when you betrayed me,"

he hissed without looking away from Peter. "Now, Peter. Do you surrender, or will you force me to kill you right in front of Wendy and the boys?"

"I really did want you to change your mind," Peter said in a quiet voice. Then his foot, which he'd been slowly moving out from beneath Jay's kneeling form, came round and kicked Jay in the temple. Jay lost his balance and fell over the edge of the boat. He grabbed the bottom of one of the railings with his hook and struggled to grab it with his good hand as well. But his fingers seemed slick, and he moaned when the crocodile let out an audible snap beneath him. Instead of going after him, though, either to finish or to help, Peter jumped to his feet.

"Wendy!" he shouted. "The star!"

Wendy ran to his side to hand him the star, too terrified to toss it. To her surprise, though, instead of taking the star and turning to look for Jay, Peter grabbed her up in his arms and rose slowly into the air.

Wendy gasped. "We're flying! But how?" She looked wildly around before something else dawned on her as well. "Everything...everything's frozen."

Indeed, the world around them had come to a halt. The boys, all but John, were still in the rowboat. Slightly's mouth was open, as though he were demanding something, but instead of shrieking, he was silent and still. Likewise, none of the boys moved, though most of them looked as though they had been caught in the middle of some great struggle. John had been frozen mid-run, one foot in the air. Two boatfuls of Tiger Lily's fae were stuck in the water, where they must have escaped after their chieftess's death. Jay's men sat and stood motionless, and Moon Flower's fae were the same, several even seeming frozen in their state of flickering. Wendy looked up into Peter's face.

"What's happening?"

CHAPTER 31
DON'T LET GO

Peter traced Wendy's face with the backs of his fingers, yearning with every fiber in his being to have more. To further his agony, she shuddered as he touched her and brought her hand up to cover his. He trembled, doing his best to memorize every line, every contour of the beautiful creature in his arms.

The beautiful creature he would have to give up in just a few moments if he hoped to protect her one more time. He could feel the star's power growing more erratic by the second, pressure building as its stability began to crumble like dry sand on the shore.

"The star has just enough power left," he said softly.

"Power for what?" Her eyes searched his.

He gave her a sad smile. "I wish I had time to explain." He swallowed hard. "But it's time. And I have only just enough control left to keep you safe."

Wendy's eyes widened as she seemed to realize his meaning. "Peter, you can't die! Not after all..." Her voice faded as her eyes filled with tears. "There has to be a way." She reached up and caressed his face, her fingers leaving trails of blazing heat wherever they touched. Heat that he wished he could bask in forever. Then she gasped and reached into her reticule. She pulled out something small and silver. Then she pressed it into his hand. He opened it to see the thimble. Why did that make him want to cry?

"Look. I saved it for you." She smiled through her tears. "It's yours, just like I am." She pulled in a shuddering sob. "Please don't throw this away." And he knew she wasn't talking about the thimble.

"Everyone has a first love." He did his best to smile through the tears that were rolling down his own face. "So don't you dare decide you're done with marriage after this little adventure."

Wendy glared at him through red-rimmed eyes, but he only shook his head and put his finger to her lips.

"I want you to find someone who appreciates your stories. Get married. Take care of my Lost Boys." The smile he was trying so hard to keep crumbled as he choked back a sob. "Have beautiful babies and live your adventures and find your happy ending."

Wendy let out a broken cry that threatened to break Peter's already battered heart into two.

"Whatever you're going to do," she whispered, "don't do it. We'll race to Destin. I'm sure King Everard can sever you from the star if we get there in—"

"Wendy." He kissed her tear-stained cheeks, letting the salt linger on his tongue and his lips against her skin. Then, though it nearly killed him, he pulled back to look down at her face once more. "It's time for this story to come to an end." He kissed her temple. "It's time for me to grow up."

"Peter—"

"You gave me hope for a future I never thought I'd have."

"Peter, please—"

He moved his lips to her ear. "You were the future I always dreamed of." Then he closed his eyes and drew back and let them fall to the ground. As soon as their feet touched the deck, he called for Moon Flower and John.

"Come get her," he said as all feeling drained from his chest, time charging forward around them once again. "And don't let go."

"No!" Wendy screamed. She tried to rush back to him, but Peter summoned what little power was left in the star and rose high above the ship once more as John and Moon Flower wrestled Wendy back. Peter watched their shrinking figures for as long as he could in the gray light of pre-dawn. But eventually, he was in the clouds. He could feel the top of the barrier above him, pressing down as the star threatened to loosen its grip.

"Keep them safe," he prayed softly to the Maker as he turned to face the horizon. "And let them find their happily ever afters."

Five hundred years. Centuries of seeking without finding. Endless pranks and games and a continuous changing of his little world in an attempt to fill the void inside of him. And just when he'd been sure he couldn't stand another day in the wretched, perfect life he lived, Peter had found the beginning of his end in a pair of big blue eyes.

Wendy had brought all of his worst fears to life. She'd broken Neverland beyond repair and brought death to both him and the star. But the sacrifice had been worth it. She had been worth it. Because what she'd broken was a lie, a facade he'd created to make life liveable as he bowed to Tiger Lily's wishes.

Once more, as the star began to bubble and gurgle inside, Peter held it to his chest.

He could save them. And that thought brought him peace. The blast which the fae had feared would kill everyone and everything in Neverland would indeed be strong.

But his love was stronger.

After all, it had been his heart that had ruined everything. The damage done to Neverland had never been Wendy's or Jay's doing at all. Peter's feelings had grown in potency, and as his desire for more had intensified, the power the fae had held over him had begun to unravel. And now that he knew where it came from, he knew he could use that potency now. He could make sure those he loved stayed safe, and their enemies would never touch them again.

"Thank you," he murmured to the star.

No, thank you.

He gripped the star more tightly. "I'm sorry it's ending like this. I never wanted you to die."

Death is only the beginning when eternity is at hand, Peter.

Peter smiled wryly to himself.

But Peter?

"What?"

May your next adventure be grand.

The heat that radiated from the star began to burn Peter's hands, heating the thimble and making it burn his palms even more. But he held both the thimble and the star tightly against his chest. Hotter and hotter they grew until Peter let out a cry. And as the fire of the morning broke the horizon, the star began to disintegrate against him, and everything was engulfed in white-hot light. And for one brief moment, he felt the pain of every unrealized hope crashing down on him.

But no, Peter thought as the world around him began to break apart. Growing up had been grand. It had given him a chance to set the ones he loved free. And though it broke his heart to do so, that was enough for him.

Then Peter breathed in and out once. Twice. Then he let go, welcoming death's embrace.

CHAPTER 32
ADVENTURE IS HERE

When the noise and the pressure and the feeling of white, hot death was gone, Wendy sat up and looked around blankly as Moon Flower and her fae and the boys picked themselves up off the ground. Neverland was gone. The island they sat on now was more a large sandbar than anything else, and the mainland was only several hundred yards to their south. Jay, the crocodile, his men, and Tiger Lily's remaining fae were nowhere to be seen, as were the bodies of the dead that had scattered Jay's deck.

Peter was gone, too. The morning sky was filled with scattered wispy clouds as the sun painted everything in its yellow light. The star was dead. Which meant Peter was, too.

Wendy's breath came in and out too fast, and the world around her threatened to spin.

Peter was gone.

The thought circled in her head like the dry, dusty whirlwinds that sometimes moved through her father's wheat fields. She squeezed the dry ground beneath her until her fingers hurt, hoping desperately to be awakened from this nightmare. The only sensation of familiarity was the feeling of Nana's frantic tongue as she kissed and fussed over Wendy from head to foot.

"Wendy?" Michael cried. Wendy had to push Nana out of the way to see Michael and Slightly clinging to one another in a small ditch some yards away. The panic in his voice snapped Wendy out of her daze, and she stumbled to her feet and ran to their side. Collapsing beside them, she wrapped both boys in her arms and hugged them close.

"Wendy!" John was at her side. Curly, Pop, and Top joined them as well. Wendy pulled them all in as close as she could, paying no heed to their protests. If Peter was gone, at least she could honor him by loving his boys. Their boys.

"I wonder where we are," Nibs said, looking around.

"This is what Neverland was before Peter changed it."

Wendy looked up to see Moon Flower standing at their side.

"So..." Wendy swallowed and looked around again at the lonely waves crashing against the barren beach. "How did we get here?"

"When Peter destroyed the star, everything went back to the way it had been. Or rather, the way it always was deep down."

"But it's so small," Nibs said.

Moon Flower nodded, a strange, sad smile on her lips. "Peter was larger than life, so everything he touched became that way, too, thanks to the star."

"But where's the ship?" Michael asked.

"Gone," Moon Flower said. "Everything that was in Neverland is gone."

Wendy frowned. "Then how are we here?"

Moon Flower's voice was quieter this time. "Because Peter and the star gave their very last bit of strength to protect us while everything else faded into the wind." She looked up and put her hands above her eyes to block the sun. "We're also not far from your farm."

John's mouth fell open. "How do you know that?"

"Tiger Lily had Peter followed once so we would all know where to go in case Neverland fell, and we had to get revenge."

"Do you think the others will come after us?" Wendy looked around anxiously as she remembered that some of Tiger Lily's fae had fled in boats after the fall of their leader.

But Moon Flower shook her head as she began to unbraid her hair. "They weren't able to make it to the barrier in time."

Wendy frowned as she stood, Nana still sniffing her all over as though she might be broken. "How do you know?"

"The boats they were rowing wouldn't have been fast enough to make it." Moon Flower began to rebraid her hair. The only sign of anxiety Wendy could make out was the way her eyes tightened, and tears gathered in the corner of her eyes as she wrapped her hair up around her head.

Though Wendy harbored no fond feelings for the fae who had stayed loyal to Tiger Lily, her heart went out to her friend. Moon Flower had been forced to kill a great number of her own people. Wendy wouldn't have wished that kind of pain on anyone.

"I'm sorry," she said softly, touching Moon Flower's arm.

Moon Flower drew in a deep breath through her nose. "It was our own doing. We chose to push Peter and the star until they broke." She paused and gave Wendy a sideways look. "We need to get you home. That star died violently. Peter must have labored hard in his last moments to keep all of us safe." She gave Wendy a wry smile. "Let's not let that death be in vain."

"Peter's dead?" Top asked, his voice breaking.

"He can't be dead!" Pop cried.

"But where is he?" Curly ran to one edge of the little island and then the other.

"Peter," Wendy said, doing her best to smile, "is with the Maker. And he is happier and freer than he's ever been. And," she had to raise her voice over the boys' wails, "he wants you all to be safe and fed and warm, and made sure I could keep you thus when he was gone." She hugged each one in turn and kissed their heads. "So let's go and make sure Peter gets what he wants, shall we?"

The boys weren't convinced, and Wendy knew they would be grieving for a long time. But the sandbar was getting hot, and they all needed food and water. So the fae, who could now change forms as they pleased once again, took their green spirit-like forms and flew over the water to the mainland. There, they fashioned a raft of driftwood and rowed it back, where Wendy coaxed the boys on with the promise of food as soon as they could reach the farm.

Once they reached the mainland, Wendy realized that she recognized their surroundings. Another pang of anger struck her when she remembered how Jay had made her home seem so far that they wouldn't be able to chase down King Everard. Perhaps they wouldn't have been, but he hadn't bothered to tell her how close to her home they really were.

Then she sighed. Not that such revelations would change much now.

They needed to head south. One of the fae flew up higher and spotted the main road, and it wasn't long before they were making their way home. John and Nibs were helpful in encouraging the younger boys to keep walking, and some of the fae temporarily took human form again to carry the littlest ones. Nana ran from one person to another then always back to Wendy, sniffing everyone as though she were very pleased with herself that she was finally able to do her job. Wendy worried, though, as they went. She had no doubt her parents would feed and shelter them upon arrival. Her father could be stubborn and loud, but he couldn't bear to turn out a stray cat, let alone homeless children.

How would they care for them, though? Their poor shoes and tattered clothes hadn't mattered much in Neverland because they flew so often or simply went barefoot. And the weather had always been perfect so that no one was hot or cold. But now, as they walked the dusty road, she could see that their leather shoes, which Peter had constructed by tying leather strips together with cord, were falling apart, and those that weren't were filled with holes. And how were they to feed them all? Winter was close enough that they should have ample room in the sleeping barn, as most of their hired hands would be gone by now. But clothes and shoes were hard enough to come by for the Darlings alone. John had grown through two pairs this year already, and her parents had spent several nights each time trying to figure out where the money would come from to get him new ones.

How were they supposed to find the resources to care for six more?

When the children grew too tired to walk, Wendy taught them to pick the heads from the wild wheat that grew on the side of the road and eat them as they went. They found a cold stream to drink from and a long line of wild grapes growing on some old fencing nearby as well. And as they walked, Wendy did her best to regale them with stories of the farm and of her parents, hoping to see some sort of relief in their eyes. But the task was very near pointless. Peter was dead, and they all felt it as strongly as she did, even if not in the same way. Peter had been a friend and guardian. He'd rescued them and given them a new world. He'd made them feel safe and loved. But now all of that was gone.

Still, as much as she hated seeing the sorrow and shock on their little faces, Wendy actually considered their need for her as something precious. As long as she had a duty to the boys, she could focus on them, and she could ignore the gaping, bleeding wound inside her own chest. The thought of rising the next morning to get up and dressed and go about her day made her nauseous. Going on in a world without Peter Pan seemed wrong, as though the sun was rising from the west, and no one but her was aware. Rising for the boys, however, was something she could do. She could go on for them. And she could even smile.

They arrived at her farm that night, just as dusk was setting. Silas was the first to spot them, and Michael and John ran ahead of the rest to greet their parents, who came tearing out of the house with arms wide open. Before she joined her family, though, Moon Flower pulled Wendy aside.

"We will leave you now," she said. "You should be safe since all the other fae are gone."

"Where will you go?" Wendy asked.

Moon Flower took a deep breath and looked at the mountains, which lay to the south. "We'll go to Destin."

Wendy's mouth fell open. "Destin?"

"Strange, isn't it?" Moon Flower gave her a dry smile. "Going back to the place from which we fled." Then she sighed, and her proud shoulders drooped slightly. "I've spoken with the others, and we're tired of running. Perhaps this Fortier will have mercy. I assume he can open the bridge his ancestor closed between his world and our own."

"And if he doesn't?" Wendy asked, remembering the ease with which the Destinian king had killed Tiger Lily's spies.

"That is what I wish to ask you." Moon Flower surprised Wendy by taking her hands. She furrowed her brows and pursed her lips as she studied Wendy's hands. "I know we don't have the right to ask it of you, but I wish you would write down our story."

"Like in a book?" Wendy asked.

Moon Flower nodded, still studying Wendy's hands. "You are a gifted storyteller." She snorted. "Gifted enough that it made Tiger Lily ripe with jealousy. But if you wrote down our story, there would be some sort of record in the world to prove that we were not all bloodthirsty beasts. Not that we deserve to have any such thing recorded, particularly after what we attempted at Destin's Fortress and the life we forced upon Peter. Still..." She finally looked into Wendy's eyes. "Then, if the Destinian king doesn't have mercy, we will still exist, even if only in the minds of those who read it and remember."

Wendy hadn't the slightest idea as to where she would get enough parchment for such a venture, but she found herself nodding slowly. Then she remembered something.

"You might not have to beg the king after all!" She told one of the boys to call King Everard's guards to her.

The guards were more than slightly shocked at the sight of the fae at first, but once she explained the situation, it was soon decided that they would accompany the fae to Destin. Hopefully, the king would have mercy on them with the witness of his men.

"Thank you." Moon Flower gave Wendy one last long look then nodded to the rest of the fae, who were waiting on the road. As she backed away, she called Wendy's name once more.

"Yes?" Wendy asked.

"You have a strange talent for turning the world on its head."

"I'm not sure how." Wendy shrugged. "I'm just being me."

"Exactly." Moon Flower flashed her a white smile. "Don't stop."

Wendy watched as the fae began to shift into their green light form, and she didn't stop until every bit of light was gone. Then she took a deep breath and looked up at the stars.

"I'm going to do this, Peter," she said softly. "Taking care of the boys and all. I just wish you could be here to do it, too." Then she turned and walked slowly back to the farm. And for the first time in a long time, she had no intention of leaving.

As Wendy had expected, her parents welcomed the boys. And not only her parents, but the whole village as well. The citizens even asked the magistrate to purchase shoes for the boys from the town funds. Unsurprisingly to Wendy, Reuben refused, citing the need to purchase other resources, such as paying to have a ditch dug and several plots of land cleared to plant flower gardens next spring. What was surprising, however, was that this put him on less than friendly terms with many of his constituents. Reuben's popularity seemed to have been doused just as quickly as it had sprung up.

Wendy's parents gave up fashioning any rational explanation for their children's reappearances and the gaggle of boys who had come with them. They simply told those who asked that their children had found other children in need and brought them home. And generously, the town shared with them what they could.

"It's you, Wendy." Moira gave Wendy a sly smile when Wendy explained it all to her friend. "The town might shake its head at you, but you're full of spirit, and no one can grudge you enthusiasm or care."

"Or it's probably more that they've washed their hands of my untamed ways," Wendy laughed.

"Possibly." Moira smiled. "But no matter what you or Reuben or anyone else says, your family is the reason so many in this town have survived these last few years. We're not about to forget that."

And Moira's words proved true. When Reuben refused to help, the villagers did their best to provide for the boys. Second and third-hand shoes were passed down. Shirts and trousers were taken in, and even the milliner had enough extra material to make all the boys hats for the winter. Wendy's mother set to work quickly to sew each of the boys a coat from the wool and leather their animals provided, and in spite of Wendy's father's worries, thanks to the efficient, hard work of the hired hands that harvest, there was enough food to keep them all through the winter.

Their six Lost Boys turned to seven when Wendy's mother decided that it was high time Amos stop getting drunk in the town square and should earn his keep like any decent man. So into the sleeping barn he went as well, assisting Wendy's mother during the day with easier chores such as drying food and spinning wool. And at night, he told the boys tales of their beloved Peter Pan, something even Wendy's parents came to look forward to.

Halfway through the winter, they had a pleasant surprise that brought their Lost Boy count back down to six, when a man and woman arrived at the farm and enquired about the fate of a young boy named Frederick.

"Our son was only a year old when we lost him," the woman said, her voice catching as she did. "But that was nearly half a year ago."

"We were going to visit the beach with our family," the man continued, his arm wrapped tightly around his wife's shoulder. "He would have been in the wagon with us, but he wanted to go with my wife's sister and her husband instead."

The woman let out a choked sob. "I never should have let him. But we thought there would be no harm done, as we would all meet in the same place."

Wendy frowned, trying to place why this story sounded so familiar.

The husband continued. "When we came to the carriage, we found it had overturned in a ravine. My wife's sister and her husband were dead. They'd broken their necks in the fall. But Frederick was nowhere to be found."

"We scoured the countryside everywhere." The wife let out a shuddering breath. "We even checked the creek bottoms. But we couldn't find him anywhere."

"I'm afraid we don't have a boy named Frederick." Wendy's mother smiled sadly. "At least, not that we're aware of. The boys all took nicknames before they came to us. I'm afraid we don't even know their given names."

But as she spoke, Wendy was thinking. The ravine. Wendy felt her heart jump into her throat. "Wait!" She turned and ran upstairs, where Slightly was sleeping. He had refused to sleep anywhere but with Wendy, so while the other boys had all moved into the barn, he had stayed inside. With trepidation and hope, Wendy gathered the little boy into her arms and studied him one more time. His perfect little face was peaceful, and he tucked his hands beneath his cheek as he rearranged himself in the crook of her arm.

Though her heart brimmed with hope, Wendy wiped a tear from her eye. "I hope you've found your family," she whispered. "But I'll miss you dreadfully."

Slowly, she came downstairs. When she entered the kitchen, she opened her mouth to tell the couple about Slightly's story, but before she could speak, the woman let out a shriek. This shriek woke Slightly, who began to wail until he laid eyes on the woman, to whom he held his arms out and clearly uttered the word, "Mama!"

Slightly, or Frederick, apparently, came from a family who lived in the town just south of Beddington. Actually, it was the same town in which Wendy and King Everard had found Amos. His family had given up hope of ever getting him back until they heard that there was a farm nearby that was housing lost children. Their friends had told them it was a fool's errand, sure to bring heartache, but now that they had him back safely, his parents swore that they would bring him to visit often out of thanks for all the Darlings had done.

And then, just as the world was beginning to thaw the next spring, there was another unexpected visit.

"Wendy!" Pop shouted as he tore through the barnyard. "Mr. Darling! Come quick!" He grabbed a pitchfork and looked as though he was ready to run back to wherever he had come from when Wendy's father took the pitchfork out of his hands.

"How about you tell me what's going on before you declare war?"

"He's on the way!" Pop could barely speak, he was so excited. "He's on the road to the house, and he's coming now!"

Wendy, who had been milking a cow, and her father exchanged a glance as she got up and looked out the barn window. A tall figure was making its way down the road toward the house, just as Pop had said.

"I don't recognize him." Her father squinted.

Wendy was about to say she didn't either until he came close enough for her to make out the golden hook where his left hand should have been. About that time, Nana began to bark ferociously.

"It's Jay," she whispered, unable to tear her eyes from the man's approaching form.

Her father straightened, and the end of the pitchfork came down on the floor with a crack. "The one that tied you and the boys up?"

Wendy nodded and frowned. It was Jay all right. But he wasn't carrying a sword, and he was alone.

"But I thought he was dead."

"He was."

"What does *he* want?" Nibs came to stand between them, glaring.

"I'd better go out and see," Wendy said slowly, taking a step toward the door. Her father caught her arm, though, before she could leave. She turned and met his gaze. "Father, please get Nana."

"You can't be serious," he said. "Let me go out there and tell him what happens when he dares tie *my* children up." Wendy wasn't exactly sure when, but her father had begun calling the Lost Boys *his* boys, something that pleased them to no end.

"I don't think he's here to fight," Wendy said, studying their visitor as he paused between the barns and the house, as if not sure where to begin. "He hasn't even got a weapon."

"I still don't trust him," her father growled.

"Let me go see what he wants," Wendy said, taking her father's hand from her arm and squeezing it. "You can stand behind me. And if he gets bold, you can let Nana eat him." She gave him a little saucy smile.

Her father didn't smile back, but after a long moment, he finally gave her a little nod and followed her to the courtyard, where he took hold of a very unhappy Nana.

"Miss Darling," Jay said, removing his hat quickly when he saw her. The boys had mostly gathered round them by now, though they all stayed in the shadows of the buildings.

"Jay," Wendy answered in an even tone. She could barely hear herself over Nana's deafening barks.

"I came..." he looked around and squeezed his hat before turning his gaze back on her. "I came to speak with you. Do you think we might have a word in private?"

"I think this is private enough." Wendy glanced back at her father. "Besides, if you tried to get me any more private, my father would probably run you through with that pitchfork. Not that I can blame him." As she spoke, the anger came flooding back. Rage Wendy thought she'd buried and left with the vestiges of Neverland on that barren sandbar filled her body until she thought it might burst into flames. Four months, and she could still see him flailing away at Peter as if it had happened yesterday.

"That's fair," Jay said, bowing his head at Wendy's father. "I only came to apologize."

"You tried to kill him," Wendy said, unable to raise her voice above a whisper. Tears threatened to spill down her face, which

supposed to be with the people who needed her. And she wouldn't have it any other way.

The months continued to pass until it was late summer, nearly the time for harvest again. This year, her father didn't need to hire quite as many hands, as the boys were surprisingly industrious little workers. The war in Solwhind had also begun to wane, meaning the young men who had previously been fighting were now in search of work. This led to a better selection of workers than they had seen in several seasons, and in less than a week, they had as many workers as they needed. Life on the farm was finally starting to look up.

Two weeks after all the positions had been filled, Wendy was in the middle barn, examining Silas's estimates for their harvest revenue when she heard Michael call her name. She looked up to see him running toward her.

"Goodness, Michael." She coughed as he came to a screeching halt in front of her, bringing a cloud of dust with him. "Do you have to bring in the entire outdoors?"

"There's a man here." He climbed up on her work table and sat on it. "He's asking for a job."

"We're all filled up now," Wendy said, going back to her figures.

"Yes, I know. But there's something funny about him."

"Oh?"

"He's all dirty, and he's unshaven."

Wendy laughed. "Michael, you've described half our workers."

"I know. But I mean it, Wendy! There's something strange about this one. And I think you ought to see him."

Wendy sighed and put her pen down. "Very well. Lead the way."

Michael trotted out to the road, where Wendy could see a tall, lean figure staring up at the house.

"Can I help you?" Wendy asked. "I hear you're looking for..."

The words died on her tongue as she drew closer, and Wendy came to a halt.

It couldn't be.

Wendy and the man stared at one another for a long time. There was so much dirt on his face and arms that Wendy suspected it had darkened his skin and hair color considerably from whatever they were beneath. His eyes were wary, and any boyish glint that had once lit them was now gone. Unfamiliar lines crossed his young face, like lines of a man who had seen too much. He was several inches taller than she remembered, and there was a set to his shoulders that hadn't been there before. His face looked as though he hadn't shaved in days, and the golden-brown hair on his head was long, pulled back at the nape of his neck, stretching down past his shoulders. But beneath it all were eyes of blazing green.

Wendy tried to say something, to form a coherent sentence of some sort. But words wouldn't come. Instead, she could only stand there staring into the face she knew she would never see again.

The young man, who looked to be in his twenties, looked down at his ill-fitted boots, which were filled with holes. "I heard you have work here," he said in a voice so soft she could barely hear. "I was hoping to find an honest job."

Wendy tried to swallow three times before she could actually do it. "Um...we don't have anything available, but I could talk to my father..." This wasn't possible. He was dead, and no amount of wishing could bring him back. Unless, of course, this was all a figment of her tortured imagination, the one that made up stories of her forever lost happily ever after while she hovered on the cusp of sanity.

"No." He gave her the ghost of a smile before looking back

down at his hands. "That's all right. I'll look farther down the road."

Wendy stood stupidly and watched him for about ten seconds before she was unable to hold it in any longer. She turned and ran, ducking behind the first building she could find.

Behind the barn, Wendy sucked in long, deep breaths through her nose. It was only a coincidence. There were lots of young men with green eyes and golden hair. Falling apart every time she laid eyes on any who looked remotely like Peter Pan was useless and idiotic.

Despite her brave chidings, however, the tears began to come. She slid down the side of the barn until she was sitting on the ground. Burying her face in her arms, Wendy let them fall. Yes, there had been tears when Jay had come, but those had been only a drop in the ocean of all she'd bottled up every day since coming home. But this...This was as though the floodgates had opened, and Wendy's soul was in her hands for all the world to see.

"Wendy?"

When she met his eyes, he took a hesitant step toward her.

"You're not him," she whispered, shaking her head. "He's dead."

"You're right," he said, kneeling beside her. "The boy is dead." He met her gaze, the sorrow in his eyes haunting and shadowed.

"I don't understand."

He lifted her hand and traced her knuckles with the tips of his fingers. Wendy was too terrified to even think about pulling away. Finally, he spoke.

"The fae were right when they thought that the death of the star would kill me."

"Then how are you here?" Had she gone mad? Was this her mind's way of telling her she couldn't handle it anymore, acting as if everything would be all right when it clearly wasn't?

He gave a sad smile. "That boy you fell for? He's gone. When the star died, he died, too." His brows furrowed as he stared at her hand. "When I woke up after the star died, I found myself in the field where my heart had bonded to hers." Then he shook his head. "I don't know how else to explain it."

"The boy died," Wendy said slowly. "But the man lived."

"I'm sorry," he said softly as he ran the backs of his fingers gently down the side of her face.

"What for?"

"I tried to stay away," he said, leaning back on his heels and running a hand through his hair. "I knew the boys were probably getting all settled and didn't need anything new upsetting them. And I knew your father was likely to set the dogs on me if I ever showed my face around here again."

When he laid his hand on the side of her face, she could feel his fingers tremble. "I also wanted you to have a chance at a normal life. Not to feel like you had to stay with me out of loyalty. You deserve a good man. Someone who's whole and confident and can provide for you. Someone who earned your love without half-abducting you and calling it an adventure. But..." He looked back up at her helplessly. "But I couldn't find my place in the world. I tried. So many places I tried. I'm afraid I'm a terrible failure."

Wendy watched him in a daze. He felt real enough as he clasped her hands in his, seeming unsure of what else to do with them. And what he said...it actually made sense. That the Never-star would take the boy within her—the boy to which she had bonded, made sense as well. The star had never seemed to fear death for herself, but knowing how much she loved Peter, Wendy now realized that the star hadn't ever seemed afraid for him. She couldn't imagine the star being careless about Peter's death. So... maybe the star had known. Maybe that's why she wanted to die. She knew it would free him from the life the fae were determined to enslave him to.

"I need you to know," Peter said now, his eyes pleading with hers. "I'm not the person you fell in love with. I'm broken and lost and..." He shrugged. "Without Neverland, I don't even know who I am anymore or what I'm supposed to do."

"I can answer that for you." Wendy rose to her feet and pulled him with her. "You are Peter. You are the soul that sacrificed for five hundred years so that others might live. You took in children no one else saw, and you honored your word, even when it hurt. And let me tell you something else." Her voice grew fierce, and she shook with excitement as she stretched up on her tiptoes, her face inches from his. "I didn't fall in love with Neverland. I fell in love with the boy with the beautiful mind that created it. And as for what you can do, you can do this." She took his hands and placed them on her hips. Then she put her hands on his neck and pressed her lips against his.

For an eternal second, Peter froze. Then something changed. His hands tightened their hold on her hips, and he pulled her closer to him. His mouth was like fire against hers, no longer hesitant and careful as it had been in Neverland, but very much alive and insatiable, as though he might never have enough. Wendy sighed into his kiss and let him hold her, aware in every muscle and bone of her body that she had found the one she'd been searching for. She didn't need someone to take her on adventures. He was her adventure.

"Ewww!"

Wendy and Peter turned to see Michael staring at them, open-mouthed.

"Wendy, that's disgusting."

"What's disgusting?" Nibs walked out from behind the barn. He followed Michael's horrified gaze to Wendy and Peter. He stared blankly for another second before his eyes lit up and he broke into a sprint. "Peter!"

This cry brought the rest of the boys running, and a moment

later, Wendy and Peter and the boys were laughing and crying and hugging and tackling, and Wendy felt her tears change from fear to joy as she watched it all. Nana, who had been in the field with Pop, threw herself into the mix as well, barking joyfully as she pushed her way into the brawl. Between them all, even the dog, it seemed, there were countless scars and wounds on all their hearts. But it only made their love that much sweeter.

Peter caught her eye as he sat up from where the boys had wrestled him to the ground, and smiled. And in that smile, for the most fleeting of seconds, Wendy was sure she might have seen the shine of a crystal rainbow. Or maybe it was the blinding reflection of boulder-sized gems. Or perhaps even the glow of a star, and she knew her instinct had been right.

Her adventure was here, and it would be the greatest story imaginable.

EPILOGUE

O nce Wendy cut his hair and made him shave, Peter looked much more like himself. And while many in the community had not forgotten his little game at Moira's wedding, and viewed him with great suspicion at first, the old ladies decided that rake or not, he needed to be fattened up a bit. Whether they succeeded was another story, but with a steady diet of food and a regular place to sleep, it was with great satisfaction that Wendy watched him grow stronger over the next few weeks.

Wendy's father was harder to impress than the little old ladies. In his eyes, Peter was the reason his children had disappeared for two months and been put in terrible danger. But the recent months with the Lost Boys had softened him. That, and Wendy's insistence that if he didn't accept Peter into the family, she was going to run away again. But in the end, three weeks after their betrothal was announced, her father surprised them by telling them to take a walk down by the creek on a corner of his land about ten minutes from the main house. Peter and Wendy set off right away, Nana close on their heels, and when they had walked a little ways up the creek, Wendy let out a little cry.

"Peter! Do you see it?"

Peter was so dumbfounded that he couldn't even find the words to reply. A plot had been cleared and leveled, and a pile of lumber was already stacked neatly beside it.

"Mister Darling says you'll need some privacy, so he's building you a house."

Wendy and Peter turned to see Top trailing them. Wendy laughed. "I wonder why that would be."

Top, who had his hand buried in Nana's fur, shrugged. "No idea."

The beautiful little cottage, made out of oak and whitewashed with blue trim, was finished two days before the ceremony. The house was more beautiful than anything Wendy had ever hoped for, with a kitchen and sitting room and two bedrooms. Peter, who had acclimated to farm life so quickly it surprised even him, managed, with Wendy's father's help, to build them a bed, small table, and two chairs so they could be ready to move in. And, of course, a rocking chair as well. And Wendy's father even topped the gift off by admitting that he wasn't sure how he'd managed the farm without Peter before.

The wedding was held that fall, almost exactly a year after Moira's had taken place. There were even more people present for the wedding than there had been for Moira's. Wendy wasn't sure how much of that had to do with their devotion to her as opposed to their curiosity about the strange young man with a veiled past and a puppy-like adoration for his bride. Not that it mattered in the end.

Wendy was living the life of her dreams. Unfortunately, however, those dreams didn't come cheaply. The war ended, and the economy finally began to turn. More workers were available, and more people had money to actually pay for their grain again. But Wendy's father found soon after that his equipment was in sore need of replacement. Even harder was keeping a farmful of boys fed and clothed, something that got more and more expensive as word spread. Once it was known that the Darlings took in orphaned boys, more dirty little faces began to show up at their front door.

And Peter knew it, too. Wendy could see the stress in his eyes and mouth when he watched the boys, fear mixing with love. How she wished she could take that fear away. He had proven to be an adoring husband and continued to be the boys' guiding hand. But the spark never returned to his eyes, and he seemed unsure of himself more often than not. There were days when Wendy wondered if he believed anything he did would ever be good enough for those around him.

Even if the fae were gone, they had left their mark on his heart, and the scar was a deep one. A scar Wendy wasn't sure she would be able to heal no matter how hard she tried.

Six months after the wedding, Wendy's father called Wendy, Peter, Silas, John, Nibs, and Wendy's mother in for a meeting late one night at the main house's kitchen table.

"I've gone through the numbers again and again," he said, rubbing his hands over his eyes and down his beard. "And for the life of me, I can't come up with a way to make it through this year. At least, not without selling some of the horses."

"But we need the horses," John said, frowning. The shadow on his upper lip became more pronounced as he glared darkly at the parchment his father had tossed on the table. "We can't plow the fields fast enough without them."

Silas shook his head. "We won't be plowing any fields if we can't get our equipment fixed or replaced."

"I can make the boys' shirts this year," Wendy's mother said. "The only reason I didn't last year was because they arrived so fast that I didn't have time to make clothes for all of them. That should help, shouldn't it?"

Wendy's father gave her a sad smile. "It will." Then he

scrubbed his face with his hands. "Just not enough. We'll make a fortune next year if we can get all the fields plowed. But for the life of me, I'm just not sure how we'll do it."

Wendy and Peter shared a long look. The boys, who numbered nine now, were a great help around the farm, but what no one in the room was mentioning was how they all ate more than a small army. Feeding them during harvest was never a question, of course, but the shortfall in money was becoming a real problem. And while Wendy's parents had never once complained about the responsibility that had been thrust into their laps in an already strained economy, it didn't seem fair that they should be the ones to shoulder the burden.

Wendy's stomach fluttered, and she was hit with another wave of anxiety as Peter made a suggestion to her father. She put a hand on her belly and inwardly sighed. Today was supposed to be a good day. She'd awakened with news of her own to tell Peter. The solemn turn of conversation, however, had her wondering if she ought to just wait until later. He would rejoice, of course, but there might be that little whisper in his heart that said this was just one more responsibility that they couldn't afford. So she swallowed her nausea and tried to focus on what her mother was saying.

Before she could refocus, though, a knock sounded at the door. Everyone at the table froze and exchanged confused looks. Nana, who was nursing a bone, let out a warning bark. Dusk had fallen, and all the little boys were in bed. Not that any of them ever bothered knocking. Peter excused himself to answer it, and Wendy's father stood and went to the door as well. When Peter opened the door, his eyes widened slightly.

"Can I help you?" he asked in a tone that was slightly awed.

A woman stood on the other side. Her hair shone copper in the light from the fireplace, and she wore rich blue capes over a handsome riding habit and polished boots. She was flanked by two soldiers, and Wendy could just make out the silhouette of a carriage in the courtyard.

"Is this the home of Peter and Wendy Pan?"

Nana growled, but Wendy's curiosity nearly ate her from the inside out. Peter hadn't ventured from Beddington since he'd arrived, and this woman certainly hadn't been to their wedding. Wendy grabbed Nana's collar to keep the dog under the table as she tried to puzzle it all out. How in the depths did such a refined person even know that they existed, let alone where to find them?

"I'm Peter," Peter said with a short bow. "And Wendy, my wife, is over there." His voice was calm, but Wendy could feel his nerves from across the room. And she could understand why. There was something familiar about this gentle, intimidating woman, but she couldn't understand why in the world the feeling struck her as such. That was, until the woman came closer, and Wendy could make out the rings of blue fire that burned in her eyes.

"Your Majesty!" Wendy breathed, and half-stood, half-fell into a curtsy. Wendy's family looked at her as though she'd lost her mind and then looked back at their guest with awe that bordered on fear.

"I'm afraid we're at a disadvantage." Wendy's mother gave a nervous laugh. "It appears our daughter knows something we don't."

"Please don't trouble yourselves." The woman's smile was warm and kind. "I'm afraid I didn't exactly give you ample warning of our arrival. But I was close to your southern border, and as I've wished to visit you for some time, I excused my rudeness in hopes that you would as well."

"Of course," Wendy's father said. "Um, please take a seat. And...how is it that we should address you?"

"I am Isabelle Fortier," the woman said as she sat. "I believe you've already met my husband, Everard Fortier of Destin."

The queen of Destin was in their kitchen.

For a moment, Wendy wondered if her mother might faint. The rest of the family seemed not far behind. Even Nana had ceased barking. Having the most powerful king in the western realm show up in their barn had been enough of a surprise, but the stress of their missing boys had affected Wendy's parents enough that they'd simply been grateful for any help they could get. Receiving Destin's queen, however, who was infamous for her own unusual gift, was something they had been far from prepared for.

"Your Highness!" Wendy's father dipped a low bow. "Can we get you anything? Tea, perhaps?"

"I'm afraid we don't have anything befitting someone of your position..." Wendy's mother hopped up and began rummaging nervously through the cabinets.

"You needn't worry about feeding us, as we ate along the way. Though...I wouldn't object to a cup of tea." The queen smiled again. Then she settled her gaze back on Wendy and Peter, who had shut the door and pulled a chair up for the queen. "I understand you both have had extensive experience with a group of beings called the fae."

Peter came back to the table and stood behind Wendy, putting his hands on her shoulders. It was a protective gesture, but Wendy could feel his fingers tremble through her sleeves.

"I lived with them for five hundred years."

"And I met them when I went to Neverland for the first time," Wendy added, hoping desperately that this had nothing to do with any conflict that might have arisen when Moon Flower's people had returned to Destin. Suddenly, her already finicky stomach made her wish she could forget what little she had been able to eat at supper.

Queen Isabelle nodded, thanking Wendy's mother as she poured her a cup of tea. "My husband told me what you told him about the fae taking you captive." She looked at Peter. "He wanted nothing more than to follow your wife to Neverland to deal with them himself, but as there seemed to be no way for him to be transported there, he was left with the regretful decision of letting her go alone." The corner of her mouth twitched. "Then, not even two weeks later, we were given one of the most startling visits of our lives." This time, the smile escaped. "And I can assure you, startling us is no easy thing to do."

Based on what Wendy had seen of King Everard, she believed that with all her heart.

"Did Moon Flower come to you then?" Wendy ventured to ask.

The queen nodded. "She did. And if it hadn't been for my particular...gift, my husband would have ended them before they even reached the Fortress."

"But he didn't, did he?" Wendy asked, breathless.

The queen gave her a reassuring smile. "No, he didn't. In fact, once we knew that they were speaking the truth, he did just as they asked and sent them back to their home world, sealing up the veil behind them."

Wendy reached up and squeezed Peter's hand, breathing a sigh of relief. She'd often wondered what had become of their friends.

"They also," Queen Isabelle said, leaning forward and putting her tea on the table, "told us that they had charged you with an unusual request."

"They wanted me to write down their story." Wendy looked down at the ground. "I'm afraid I haven't been able to write it down yet. Not because I don't want to," she hurried to explain, "but money has been...tight. And parchment is expensive."

"I thought you might say that." The queen turned and nodded at one of the guards, who had taken up a station in the corner near the ice box. The soldier bowed his head, and he and his partner went outside. A minute later, they came back in carrying a chest large enough that a roasted turkey could have fit inside. The queen stood and went to the chest. When she opened it, everyone gasped.

Gold and silver coins were piled inside, topped with a thick stack of cream-colored parchment. Queen Isabelle took the stack of parchment and brought it to Wendy.

"Paper is quite costly. Hopefully, this will be enough to see you through not only this project but your next as well. I've included pens and ink in the chest, too."

Wendy somehow managed to pull her eyes from the paper to look back up at the queen. "My next, Your Highness?"

The queen smiled more broadly this time, her eyes twinkling. Wendy would almost call it mischievous.

"Wendy and Peter, if you wouldn't mind walking with me, I have a proposition for you. You're free to turn it down, of course, but I hope you'll hear me out first."

"Um...of course." Peter helped Wendy stand and then hurried to open the door. The three of them ventured out into the early night, Nana trotting behind them. She'd long ago ceased growling at their stranger. In fact, now she seemed to be following the queen as much as she was her master. A thin ribbon of blue light hovered on the western horizon, which was quickly turning to gray. All the windows in the boys' barn, as it had come to be called, were dark, and the only sound of animals came from Nana, who happily followed them.

"I would like for you to write down the history of the fae, just as they wished," the queen said, walking along the drive that circled the house. "Don't leave anything out. Mention Peter's bonding with the star, your introduction to and interaction with Neverland, everything up until now, so we have as complete a history as possible."

"So..." Peter said slowly. "You want a book?"

Wendy's heart leaped in her chest. Of course. The Fortress's great library. She nearly laughed as she recalled her father's prophecy, how she would never make a living on any such hopes as writing for the king and queen of Destin.

"My husband and I believe the past is too important to lose," the queen said. "We've begun collecting volumes of not only our histories in Destin, but also from the world around us. We wish to have as complete a picture as we can so we might not be doomed to repeat what follies our fathers suffered before us. We also wish to emulate them in their victories and successes. The fae, especially, have a particular significance to Destin."

"I would be honored to write for you," Wendy said, hoping she didn't sound like a pathetic little girl, drooling at the feet of a hero. "But I'm not sure what you meant by my next project?"

At this, the queen stopped walking and faced Peter. Her hair was lit like a halo in the light of the moon, but her eyes with their blue fire burned even brighter.

"Peter, how long were you in Neverland again?"

"Five hundred years, Your Majesty."

She nodded. "Then I want you to write down all your adventures in Neverland. The ones that did happen, and the ones that didn't." Her smile widened. "But put Wendy in it this time, as well as Michael and John with the Lost Boys. And..." She paused. "Make Jay a pirate."

Nana barked, and the queen laughed and reached down to rub her under the chin.

"And you too, Nana."

"But...we weren't there for all of his adventures," Wendy said. "Only the very last few."

Queen Isabelle laughed again. "Surely, Wendy, you of all people understand the power of escaping into stories that never were, but that you wished could be."

Wendy nodded faintly. "I...I do."

Peter spoke again, but to Wendy's surprise, there was an incredible amount of sorrow in his words.

"I wish I could, Your Highness. Truly. But..." He held his arms up and shrugged helplessly. "I can barely read. Let alone write an entire book."

"You may not be a gifted writer," the queen said, "but your wife is." Her chin lifted slightly, and the flames in her eyes danced. "And before you decide you can't, I want to know why you're so hesitant to visit that place again."

Peter looked startled, and Wendy understood his confusion. The queen seemed to have an uncanny ability to recognize even their secret emotions. How had she known what emotions mentioning Neverland would dredge up inside of him?

"Neverland was..." he said slowly, "a place I changed on a whim whenever I felt like it. I'm afraid it won't feel the same on a page. I can't go there anymore and write down all the little details. It's gone. I'm afraid I can't do it justice."

Queen Isabelle tilted her head and put a finger to her cheek and stood that way for a moment as she studied him. "Peter, do you know how my gift works?"

Peter shook his head.

"I see truth. I know when someone's lying to me, and I know when people are lying to themselves. The Maker even allows me to project the truth to others. Sometimes, he even lets me know a truth about another person before they do." She tilted her head thoughtfully. "I think you have a gift, too, but you've been lied to for so long that you've forgotten what a gift it is."

Peter blinked. "And what gift would that be, Your Majesty?"

Queen Isabelle grasped Peter's hand in her right and Wendy's in her left. "Neverland was never a place of its own. It was always a part of you. Neverland is within you, Peter. And, I would venture to guess, so are a good many other worlds. Now, close your eyes," she instructed, "and think about Neverland."

Wendy and Peter did as she said. For a moment, Wendy saw nothing, only darkness. But just as she was about to ask if she should keep them closed, a flash of color caught her mind's eye.

The rainbow.

Wendy stared in awe at the crystal rainbow, bowing out over the water as if it were directly below her. The water, which was dull at first, took up its usual shine and began to stretch out, as though filling in little bits of the dark world at a time. Then she saw the familiar shape of the island. Piece by piece, Neverland began to come back. She even heard Peter laugh when he wrapped a vine of edible flowers around the rainbow under the bright sky. Birds and deer and foxes and chipmunks and every sort of fruit imaginable popped up all over the surface of the mountainous island. In fact, it was more vibrant than ever. And this time, there were not one but two crocodiles.

"This is incredible," Wendy said as, in her mind, she flew over the island, which boasted bolder and brighter colors than it had even held in the best of days Wendy had lived there.

"I get the feeling," the queen said with a smile in her voice, "that this isn't the only world Peter's dreamed up."

"Well...no," Peter said, as though admitting to some petty crime. "I mean, I wanted to. But Tiger Lily said I had to keep it the way I made it the first time. She said it would be too much work acclimating to new worlds all the time."

The queen gave an unladylike snort. "Hypocrite. Well, now is your time, Peter. Imagine away."

Wendy let out a cry of girlish glee as the ground melted away from beneath them, and they were suspended, holding hands, in the heavens. Stars glittered near and far, and the sun burned to her left. All around them twirled planets of every shape and size and color. But before she could even ask about where they were, the scene changed again. This time, they were in a cave with the height and breadth of a castle. The floor was made of flat, polished lavender marble that matched the sparkling walls and stalactites above. Flowers of royal blue and silver bloomed all around the edge of the polished floor, hanging from the walls and ceilings, their bell-like petals opening delicately toward the center of the room. Out of the middle of the polished floor rose a winding staircase. It spiraled up, up, up to the ceiling, which Wendy realized rose up like a tower. Above was the sky, a soft blue glow in the distance.

Faster and faster, the scenes began to change, each more wonderful and vibrant than the last. Wendy looked over to see Peter, his eyes uplifted and a smile on his lips like she hadn't seen in a long time. And best of all, the light was in his eyes once again.

"All of this was in your head all this time?" Wendy asked when the queen let go of their hands, and they were back on her parents' drive once more.

He looked at her slowly, his face nearly glowing. "The fae didn't want to hear of them, so I kept them locked away inside." He chuckled slightly. "I thought no one else wanted to see them."

"You have been given a gift," Queen Isabelle said, the flames in her eyes continuing to leap wildly. "And with each gift comes a duty given to us by the Maker who gave us the gifts in the first place. I was able to show you and Wendy those worlds because it is my gift to show others the truth. Now it is your turn to share the new worlds you have dreamed up with our world."

"But why are imaginary places so important?" Peter asked. "It's not as though they can change anything."

The queen gave him a sad smile, and for the first time that night, Wendy caught a glimpse of the stress lines in her face. Wendy didn't know the queen's exact age, but upon reflection, it seemed probable that the queen had seen more than a few struggles of her own.

"This world is a strange, beautiful, hard place. The Maker gave people like you and your wife the ability to take us out of it, even if only for a few moments. Then, when we can see the world in a new light, we remember that even in all the darkness surrounding us, we were made for more than the misery that wearies us and makes lifting our heads difficult every dawn. We were made for more."

She turned and began walking back toward the house. "As much as I would love to stay, I must be going now." She stopped in front of her carriage. "But before I go, I hope that you and your daughter will all come see us at the Fortress. Just send us word, and we'll send a carriage to bring you so you don't have to pay for the travel on your own. Of course, you'll be compensated handsomely for your work. We'll show you all around the Fortress and hopefully, get to know you more." Her eyes twinkled. "As soon as your convalescence is over, and your daughter is ready to travel, of course."

And with that, she climbed into the carriage, which was accompanied by more soldiers Wendy hadn't seen before. And then they were gone.

For a long time, Peter and Wendy stared at one another. Wendy felt like she should say something, but she couldn't quite find the words. Peter seemed to feel at a loss as well.

In one swoop, their problems had been solved. The money in that chest would be more than enough to cover all the farm's expenses. It was almost like the queen had known exactly what their struggles were. And not only that, but they'd been promised future work as well, doing the very thing Wendy had dreamed of since she'd first picked up a pen.

"I'm...I'm going to be a writer," she finally said, half-laughing as she stared into the dark where the carriage had disappeared.

Peter's mind, however, seemed to be on another path. "So," he said, drawing her close and holding her against him. "A daughter, huh?"

Wendy laughed in earnest this time. "I suppose so."

He put his mouth to her ear and traced her jaw with his nose, making her shiver with delight. "It seems," he said in a low, throaty voice, "as though we'll need to make this daughter happen. Can't be disappointing a queen."

The butterflies hit again, and Wendy's face reddened, though why, she hadn't the slightest idea. She was married for goodness sakes.

"Actually," she said shyly, "I think we already have."

He froze briefly before pulling back to squint at her in the moonlight. "What?"

Wendy tried unsuccessfully to hide a grin. "You heard me."

He stared at her for a long moment before breaking into a peal of laughter. "Wendy, you trickster! When were you going to tell me?"

"Today," Wendy said. "Honest! But then we had the meeting with my father, and I didn't really want to talk about it with everyone so solemn, and then the queen came and...Peter, your spark is back!"

"What spark?"

Wendy stared at his eyes in joy. The queen was gone. Peter's strange worlds were nowhere to be seen. But sure enough, the spark was still in his eyes.

"The one you always had in your eyes when you were a boy. The mischievous one."

"Well." Peter pulled her more tightly against him. "Maybe I'm feeling a bit mischievous." Then he laughed and let go of her, putting his hands on his head and walking in a circle, staring up at the night sky. "I'm a father, Wendy." He turned and yelled into the open field. "I'm a father!" Then he turned and caught her up in his arms again, crushing her to his chest. "You don't under-stand," he said as he kissed her face over and over again, "what this means to me." He pressed his forehead against hers and closed his eyes.

"What do you mean?"

He laughed and shook his head but didn't open his eyes. "Wendy, for five centuries, I woke up with every day the same as the last. I've lived here over half a year, and I still wake up most days and don't remember where I am."

Wendy listened in awe. She knew he'd been toting fear with him everywhere he went. But she hadn't realized it was so bad.

"I've been dreaming of a family of my own for hundreds of years," he said, cupping her face gently in his hands. "It's going to take a long time before this feels like it's truly mine to keep."

Wendy grinned up at him. "We've got the rest of our lives."

He tapped her nose then leaned in for a soft, slow kiss, one hand on the small of her back, keeping her close, and the other buried in her hair. "Then," he whispered, "there's no better time to begin."

The Sentinel's Song

A Retelling of St. George and the Dragon

TWO GUARDS in white appeared from the shadows. Sabra swallowed when she recognized Shakirat.

He bowed his head and held out a hand toward the end of the hall. "Princess."

She regarded him for a long moment. One more soul she had trusted implicitly. That she had loved.

"I suppose you're here to escort me to my captor."

Shakirat flinched just as Nazan had. "Your intended," he whispered, keeping his eyes on the floor.

"We've known each other too long to tell such tales." She stared at him until he unwillingly met her eye. "Let's call it as it is, shall we?"

He closed his eyes and scrunched them tight. More emotion than she'd ever seen on his stoic face. "Princess, please--"

Sabra marched past him, unwilling to let him see the tears that were forming once again in her eyes. Was this penance for pushing away tears so often in recent weeks? Having them all spill at once?

The walk to the throne room seemed eternal. Images of her father, her mother, and George revolved in her mind with each step. And above all, the question of why.

Why had the Maker built everything up just to burn it all down?

"Princess."

She looked up to see Mahzar beside a holy man at the front of the throne room. Somehow, she'd walked to join them without even realizing it. The holy man kept glancing at the nearest doors, but Mahzar looked completely at ease.

Well, as at ease as one could look with an injured arm and a bandage wrapped around his rear end, its cloth so thick it made his rear twice its usual size.

If Sabra had been any less heartbroken, she would have found this quite funny.

Actually, he looked like he was in a great deal of pain. Good. Hopefully, it would haunt him until he died.

And yet, the pain didn't keep him from smiling as she joined him at the front of the room. Citizens filled all the extra spaces against the walls and in the balcony above, but from what Sabra could see, Mahzar was the only one who looked pleased.

He reached out and brushed his right hand along her jawbone. The light in his eyes was alarmingly warm and familiar, as though this were a day for contentedness and pleasure. Sabra wanted to make sure it wasn't, but her voice seemed stuck in her throat, and all she could do was turn her head away.

"I know this isn't what you hoped for," he said softly, "but in time--"

Sabra's voice returned miraculously at these words. "You should know right now that I loathe you. I despise everything you've ever done, and I hope for the sake of the people you rule and who surround you that the Maker brings you to an early grave."

His eyebrows went all the way up. Oddly enough, he looked truly confused. "Really?"

"I'm not finished. You said once that you would allow me to choose the depth of our affections if I wedded you. Well, I can assure you now that those affections will be non-existent."

Mahzar took her hands and looked down at them for a long moment. "I know you can't see it now, but I *will* be a good husband." He looked up into her eyes and gave her a small smile. "Believe it or not, I have never respected another soul as much as I do you. I may not agree with your interpretation of the law, but that doesn't mean I have come to regard you meanly in any way." He pulled her forward and pressed his forehead against hers.

George had done this very thing. And yet Sabra now found herself wishing she could scratch Mahzar's face off.

"You are a rare soul," he breathed. "And I intend to treat you as a queen as much in my home as you were ever treated here."

In his home. Sabra nearly passed out. Before this moment, she had never allowed herself to even consider the dragon's home as her own. But in just a few moments, it would be hers until the day one of them died.

Maker, she prayed, *if this is the way it's going to be, please don't leave me here for long.*

"Dragon."

Sabra's head shot up and she whirled around the best she was able to, as her hands were still in Mahzar's.

And there, in full battle armor, was George.

His eyes were red and glassy, and his left shoulder was slightly lower than his right. Black, blue, and red patches covered his visible skin. But he was standing.

He was alive.

Can Sabra and George find their happily ever after? Can they defeat the dragon and all the cowards who follow him? Find out in *The Sentinel's Song: A Retelling of St. George and the Dragon*.

Dear Reader,
Thank you for following Peter and Wendy to their happy ending! If you like free stories (including more about Peter and Wendy) visit BrittanyFichterFiction.com. By joining the Brit's Bookish Mages newsletter, you'll get bonus stories, sneak peeks at new books, book coupons, and more!

Also, if you enjoyed this book, please consider leaving a review on your online retailer or Goodreads.com.

About the Author

Brittany lives with her Prince Charming, their little fairy, and their little prince in a ~~sparkling~~ (decently clean) castle in whatever kingdom the Air Force has most recently placed them. When she's not writing, Brittany can be found chasing her kids around with her DSLR and belting it in the church worship team.

Facebook: Facebook.com/BFichterFiction
Subscribe: BrittanyFichterFiction.com
Email: BrittanyFichterFiction@gmail.com
Instagram: @BrittanyFichterFiction

BREAKING NEVERLAND: A RETELLING OF PETER PAN, PART II

Copyright © 2020 Brittany Fichter

Publisher's Note: This is a work of fiction. Names, characters, places, and incidents are a product of the author's imagination. Locales and public names are sometimes used for atmospheric purposes. Any resemblance to actual people, living or dead, or to businesses, companies, events, institutions, or locales is completely coincidental.

Breaking Neverland / Brittany Fichter. -- 1st ed.

Edited by Meredith Tennant